For

JANE AARON

Today the glacial lake of Llyn y Fan Fach, nestled high up under the Black Mountain peaks which form the western, Carmarthenshire section of the Brecon Beacons, is an isolated spot frequented only by the occasional hill walker. But during the first half of the nineteenth century local people flocked – in their thousands, according to one commentator – to the lake side on each first Sunday in August, in the hope of a close encounter with the Tylwyth Teg (the Fair Tribe, i.e. the fairies). For Llyn y Fan Fach is the site of the best known Welsh Fairy Bride folk tale; according to legend, it was from the near-by farm of Blaensawdde, which still stands south east of Llanddeusant village, that a young man climbed the Beacons to woo and finally to win the lady of the lake. When north-east winds blew on the lake in early August and frothed its surface into high waves, the credulous believed that his fairy bride might still be glimpsed or heard, calling up her cattle from the depths of the lake.

The story of 'The Lady of Llyn y Fan Fach' remains a general favourite amongst Welsh folk tales, but those new to it will find as an appendix to this book a transcription of the first English-language version, published in 1861. Collated, translated and inscribed by William Rees of Ton, Llandovery, from the Welsh-language oral narratives of the villagers of Myddfai, a mile or so to the north of Llanddeusant, this version of the tale was initially presented as an explanation of the phenomenon of the 'Physicians of Myddfai'. A historical family, dating from the thirteenth century, the

Myddfai Physicians were from generation to generation said to possess extraordinary healing skills and knowledge of the medicinal powers of herbs, supposedly passed down from the original mother of the family, the fairy bride of Llyn y Fan Fach. Fairy brides whose native homes were under water were, however, by no means unique to the Myddfai area. Half a dozen lakes in north Wales, and at least two others in south Wales as well as Llyn y Fan Fach, have also supposedly been the source of supernatural brides, and water-born creatures mate with men in Irish, Scottish, German and Scandinavian folk tales as well as Welsh ones. In an article on 'The Fairy Bride Legend in Wales' published in the journal *Folklore* (1992), Juliette Wood associates the popularity of such tales not so much with their occasional function as family origin legends as with their abiding role as a focus for reflection upon the nature of marriage, which always involves the bringing together of two initially separate worlds and points of view. The disparity between the world of the human wooer and that of his watery bride represents, albeit in extreme form, tensions which exist in all marriages when an outsider is brought into a family group and necessary adjustments and compromises have to be made.

Given her characteristic preoccupation as a writer of fiction with the theme of the ill-matched marriage, it is not then surprising that Hilda Vaughan should have been attracted to the tale of 'The Lady of Llyn y Fan Fach' as the possible source of a novel plot. Many of the ten novels which Vaughan published between 1925 and 1954 feature unhappily yoked couples, and her novella *A Thing of Nought* (1935, reprinted by Honno in *A View across the Valley: Short Stories by Women from Wales*, 1999), which is generally considered to be her best work, is also primarily concerned with the clash of spiritual and emotional values between husband and wife. Born in 1892, in Builth Wells, Breconshire, to a successful

IRON AND GOLD

IRON AND GOLD

by

HILDA VAUGHAN

with an introduction by

JANE AARON

HONNO CLASSICS

To Anne
&
To Thomas

in gratitude for the hospitality of
Hatherop Castle and Dean Farm

Published by Honno
'Alisa Craig', Heol y Cawl, Dinas Powys
South Glamorgan, Wales, CF6 4AH

First Impression 1948
This edition © Honno Ltd 2002

© Roger H. V. C. Morgan for the estate of Hilda Vaughan
© Introduction Jane Aaron 2002

British Library Cataloguing in Publication Data

ISBN 1 870206 50 9

Published with the financial support of the Arts Council of Wales.

Cover: 'Lady of the Van Lake' (c.1915) by Margaret Lindsay Williams.
Any information regarding the copyright would be
gratefully received by the publishers.
Republished by kind permission of the National Library of Wales.

Cover design by Chris Lee Design

Typeset and printed in Wales by Dinefwr Press, Llandybïe

Contents

country solicitor and his wife, and married in 1923 to the novelist Charles Morgan who encouraged her to develop her own writing career, Vaughan's concern with unhappy marriages cannot easily be straightforwardly related to auto-biographical factors. One particular chapter of her personal history may be of relevance, though. During the First World War, from 1916-18, Vaughan served as the Organising Secretary of the Women's Land Army in Breconshire and Radnorshire. Her role involved placing young women who volunteered for farm work in posts as labourers on the isolated farmsteads of the Welsh borders and the Beacons, and supervising their progress. It is easy to imagine that the sudden arrival to stay of unknown young women, in lieu of conscripted sons or local male labourers, might bring to the surface latent marital tensions in the neighbourhood, and involve the Organizing Secretary in the counseling or replacing of members of her 'Army'. Be that as it may, it certainly is the case that Vaughan's fictional dysfunctional couples are generally located in the rural outposts of Breconshire, Radnorshire and Carmarthenshire. The geographical isolation of their setting, and the narrow and inflexible values of the small town or village communities which provide their chief point of reference, often exacerbate the marital discord.

Written in the United States, to which she and her two children were sent by Charles Morgan for their safety during the Second World War, and first published there in 1942 under the title *The Fair Woman*, the novel *Iron and Gold*, published in Britain under that title in 1948, may then be considered one of the most characteristic, as well as the Welshest, of Hilda Vaughan's works. And yet it is the only one of her novels not based upon a plot of her own devising, but instead patterned closely, with, as we shall see, but a few significant variations in terms of narrative detail, on the 'Lady of Llyn y Fan Fach' legend, very likely known to

Vaughan from childhood. The rewriting by women of well-known folk tales from a female or feminist perspective has in recent years become a familiar literary device. The American poet Anne Sexton's *Transformations* (1972) consisted of witty, often bitter, rewritings of the brothers Grimm's fairy tales. In Sexton's verse, the plight of such legendary heroines as the Sleeping Beauty or Rapunzel becomes representative of her own sense of entrapment and malaise as a woman who came of age during the 1950s, a decade seen by later feminists as retrograde in terms of women's development. Angela Carter's more up-beat versions of such tales as 'Red Riding Hood' or 'Beauty and the Beast' in her short story collection *The Bloody Chamber* (1979) provided the old stories with unexpectedly assertive, 1960s-style, heroines, capable of breaking free from the traditional conventions and moralities which proscribed their reactions in the originals, and of enjoying liberated celebrations of sexuality.

But what Hilda Vaughan does in *Iron and Gold* is not so much to rewrite the legend, as to bring to the surface themes and preoccupations which may be said to be latent within it. She does so by providing the sequence of events which boldly follow one another in the story 'The Lady of Llyn y Fan Fach' with a psychologically credible frame of cause, action and consequence. This frame serves to expose the story as a reflection on the value of a marriage of opposites as the potential source not only of material fertility but also of imaginative creativity and joy. It tells too of the difficulty of preserving such a union over time, as the opposite, the outsider, becomes familiar. Indeed, caught within the exigencies of daily life, partners in the union may positively desire the other to become less strange, more conformable to his or her own habits, and thus more controllable and restful. The sense of incipient doom, within both the tale and the novel which follows its folklore source so closely, then becomes expressive of the virtual impossibility of preserving throughout life a disposition free from the desire to live by rote, and open to seeing what is strange as beautiful. Given that in this story it is the female partner who is required to conform to the male's world, rather than vice versa, Vaughan's sympathies are strongly with the woman's point of view, as much so as Sexton's and Carter's in their rewriting of fairy tales. But, as Juliette Wood's analysis of the Welsh legend would suggest, in the case of 'The Lady of Llyn y Fan Fach' the gender perspective within this tale itself is from the outset unusually sympathetic to women.

When comparing Welsh fairy brides to those of other countries, Wood points out that unlike their counterparts, the Welsh brides have no bird or animal form; they are not seals as in Scotland and Scandinavia, mermaids as in Ireland and Scandinavia, or swans as in some Germanic legends. This difference affects the circumstances of their eventual leave-taking of the human world. While all watery brides quit their spouses in due course, the bird or animal brides generally do so for reasons connected with their shape-changing: they find their lost animal skins, for example, or are discovered in their original form and hence have to give up the human disguise. But in all the Welsh fairy bride legends, not only in 'The Lady of Llyn y Fan Fach', the bride leaves her husband because he breaks the conditions against domestic violence that she initially imposed. In the south Wales variations of the legend the condition is that she will leave him if he hits her three times; in north Wales that he must not hit her with iron. The fact that the Welsh fairy bride imposes these conditions makes her at once more assertive than her counterparts in other cultures and more human, in that the violence she attempts to forestall has been, and of course still is, a serious problem within marriage as a human institution. She may, indeed, be perceived as a universally relevant and potentially supportive role model for women: were all prospective brides to have the self-respect to warn, 'No violence, or I'm off,' and then the strength to act accordingly if necessary, much suffering might be averted. From the first, then, the fairy tale provided Vaughan with a myth, rooted in her native locality and culture, which was unusually responsive to the vulnerabilities of women within that institution she was herself most interested in exploring in her fiction, namely marriage.

With regard to the variations in detail between the legend and Vaughan's rewriting of it, it is not always easy to pinpoint the innovations and omissions she deliberately made, as discrepancies exist between the original's many variants, and there is no evidence to indicate which version she was herself familiar with. Although the condition that the bride imposes in *Iron and Gold*, that she should not be struck three times in anger with iron, would appear to constitute a deliberate combination of south and north Wales variants of the legend, it may be that that, simply, is the tale Vaughan was told. Similarly, the omission in *Iron and Gold* of the scene in the 1861 version in which the fairy's father appears, and forces the suitor to pick out his chosen bride from three identical sisters, may have been deliberate or may not from the start have been included in the story as Vaughan knew it. Again, the introduction of the husband's infidelity, in the 'Winter' section of *Iron and Gold*, may also not be entirely original; in his account of the Llyn y Fan Fach legend in *Celtic Folklore: Welsh and Manx* (1901), John Rhys describes one variant which suggests that the cause of the final quarrel between the couple was a female rival, and that the fairy called her cattle back to the lake in order to ensure that no other woman should milk her cows. Vaughan may well have read John Rhys's detailed account of the many variations of the legend, and have made her own choice from the possibilities it offered.

Some of the scenes introduced into *Iron and Gold* would appear to be entirely her own, though. It is not, for example, bread, however baked, which wins the fairy bride of *Iron and Gold*, unlike her legendary prototype; on the contrary, she laughs at her suitor, Owain, for attempting to woo her with this symbol of promised sustenance and support, while pitying women forced by material circumstances to accept such an offer. Rather, she succumbs and promises herself to him only after his suicide bid, when, in despair of getting her to join him in his world, he plunges into the lake's waters in an attempt to enter her element. That is, she is won by his vulnerability and capacity to suffer rather than by his strength. He, however, as soon as she has stopped his death-quest and joined him on dry land, very quickly recovers his self-assurance and starts priding himself upon her capture. It is in response to these alarming indications of Owain's self-centredness, and to his apparent assumption in their first conversation that male dominance is attractive to women and a given in marriage, that she imposes her conditions.

At the same time the fairy accepts that having entered her suitor's sphere, she must conform to the requirements of her new role, and learn what it is to be a human wife. The character who aids her most in acquiring an appropriately wifely disguise is Owain's mother, who has a far more extensive role to play in Vaughan's version of the story than in the original legend. The mother greets with delight this opportunity to fashion another in her own image, hitherto denied to her as she has no daughter. She dresses the fairy up like a doll in appropriately demure gear, and proceeds to 'tame' her by means of an intensive course in housewifery, and a barrage of instructions as to how to play the wife's part. 'I've made you grow like to myself,' she finally tells her daughter-in-law triumphantly:

'Same as myself, *fach*. No different, see? That be a mortal's wish for her own daughter . . . When I'm gone, you'll be taking my place quite natural. And if only you was to bear him a daughter, she'd be taking your place after. And her daughter and granddaughter, on and on. My grannie. My mother. Myself. Doing the same work for our men, always. That's how it has been. How 'twill ever be. A chain o' women. All alike. Every link. That life may hold unbroken.'

The manner in which women traditionally embraced their chains, and colluded in the reproduction of female subordination, is tellingly delineated in Vaughan's novel, which at the same time shows the fairy bride pitying her mother-in-law's enforced self-repression and the scarcity of joy in her life. It is also shows the difficulty of keeping a marriage alive and developing when the bride is required to become no opposite but a familiar replica of the mother figure. For Owain as he ages becomes inhibited in his intimate relation with her, and tries to sustain his vitality by seeking as a sexual partner a new outsider, the gipsy rival who becomes his mistress. And yet he himself, nearly as strongly as his mother, had desired his bride to conform and adopt the maternal image.

But though on the surface she may appear malleable, the fairy in fact never abandons the set of values and perspectives that she brought with her from her lake world; indeed, it is her refusal to do so which leads, in each case, to the three blows which destroy the marriage. Strongly pro-life and anti-egotism in all its forms, she refuses to take part in any talk or activity which involves competitiveness, malice, or cruelty towards others, animal or human. This attitude limits her capacity to merge with the mortals about her, but the fairy seems impervious to any expectation that she will join in the spirit of communal gatherings. Although this aspect of her character is implicit in the legend, it is brought out more clearly in Vaughan's handling of the tale. The bride makes no attempt, for example, to compromise in her dealings with her neighbours and her husband's brothers, and remains in their eyes always a stranger and an alien. Owain, on the other hand, is peculiarly susceptible to the influence of those around him; 'the heart of another' easily sets 'his own beating to a new rhythm,' and he cannot bear the conflict within himself which ensues when his wife, whom he would consider part of himself, refuses to take her note from the general feeling. All the blows he gives her are occasioned by his tension when she publicly manifests her otherness. He first hits her when she is inappropriately sorrowful during their son's christening festivities. The 'terrible words' spoken by the clergyman about original sin are to her a crime against life; it 'do wrong the mercy o' God, whom man has created jealous, even in man's own image' that a child, a 'blossom, ready to open natural as a flower-bud to the sun, be taught to credit such dark imaginings.' The second blow occurs when at his mother's funeral she insists on joyously celebrating the event as the happy release of an imprisoned being rather than putting on any show of mourning. Lastly, partly out of guilt at his own infidelity, he hits her for letting her sadness show at their son's wedding, though by then, with her husband publicly flaunting his relation with the gipsy, the fairy has good reason to think of marriage as a cause of sorrow. And yet it was of course because she represented a different world from that of his natal community, and awoke in him rhythms quite other to theirs, that Owain was initially attracted to the lady of the lake.

The emphasis placed on rhythm, song and poetry throughout *Iron and Gold* is again not entirely without precedence in the original legend. One of the most memorable features of the folk tale is the fact that the fairy speaks in verse, when initially responding to the proffered of bread and when finally

calling her cattle dowry back to the lake. Many of the innovations Vaughan introduces into her account serve to suggest
that for her the nature of poetry is as central a concern of
the fable as the nature of marriage: in her novel, the fairy's
suitor is from the outset a poet, or at least desires to be one;
the songs he sings under his bride's influence intersperse the
prose account throughout; and the prologue and epilogue
which frame the story present a 'Bard' as its narrator. Indeed,
the two themes are intertwined, the marriage on which the
fairy bride and her suitor embark being seen as a potential
source of imaginative as well as material fertility. Vaughan
would appear to agree with Virginia Woolf's suggestion in
A Room of One's Own, that for the creative to ensue there
needs to take place, within the creating mind, a marriage of
opposites, a marriage in which the masculine and feminine
principles unite. In *Iron and Gold* she gives to the masculine
element that capacity to empathize largely with the point
of view of others which Keats saw as essential to creativity;
Owain appreciates the rhythms of a 'Iago' as well as an
'Imogen,' and is eager to reproduce them and to communicate
them to others. But he is too indiscriminately responsive to
others for his own good as a poet; he is made uncertain of
himself by fears of his community's disapproval, and accords
with his neighbours' values to such an extent that for a while
he gives up poetry entirely for the more generally shared
aspiration of money-making. The fairy on the other hand
has very little interest in communicating with others. She
sings her songs to no-one except her husband; in fact most
of the songs given in the text are voiced by the husband
composing under her influence rather than directly sung by
her. She has the power to hold on to her individual way of
seeing, but very little sense of the need to communicate it.
He, however, has an abundance of that gregarious desire;
clearly both their faculties are needed if composition is to
ensue.

At first, the fairy sees no difficulty in bringing about this union. She gives Owain her element – gold – and tells him to combine it with his – iron – to make one ring. Theirs will be a both/and marriage – both iron and gold, both the masculine and the feminine – rather than any divisive either/or, masculine versus feminine, arrangement. But his community and culture do not provide the young man, labouring away with crude tools at the blacksmith's forge, with the instruments to forge such a union. Iron in this text represents the dominance of man over natural life: though the fairy appreciates its usefulness, she also fears it as the main element of the ploughshare which rapes the earth, or the instrument of war which tears the flesh. It is also associated with that industrial development which is presented as darkening the lives of the Bard's south Walian contemporaries at the opening of the book. The Bard's memory 'reached back to a time when the land had been green and whole' but the young men about him are gone to hew coal in the pits, from which they emerge with 'faces, blackened over, and blue scars upon them that could not be washed off'. The story takes place within the framework of an Age of Iron, a masculine world in which the feminine has little place and is undervalued. Not all the best intentions of the suitor can keep them together as equal partners once he has persuaded the fairy to step into his frame. But the epilogue suggests that, while natural rhythms and the human capacity to appreciate them survive, a combination of the feminine and masculine within one responsive and expressive creating mind always remains potentially a possibility.

That the novel *Iron and Gold* should prove discussible in terms of its interest in a marriage of contraries, and a re-evaluation of the feminine and of nature, as sources of poetic creativity, will have the effect, for certain critics, of defining it as part and parcel of the so-called 'neo-Romantic' movement within mid twentieth-century Welsh writing in English.

Vaughan, it may well be said, could not have written as she does had she not been influenced by the ideas of poets such as Blake, Wordsworth and Keats. But in *Iron and Gold* the evident origin of the author's concerns lie fairly and squarely in the old Welsh legend she is rewriting. Her work may well serve as a reminder that the Romantic movement itself owed its origins in part to late eighteenth-century antiquarian interest in reviving the literatures and myths of a pre-Norman Celtic Britain. Indeed, it could be said that it would be no more inappropriate to label the Romantic movement 'neo-Celtic' than it would be to categorize *Iron and Gold* as 'neo-Romantic'. Be that as it may, what Hilda Vaughan is exploring in this novel is a nucleus of concerns which lie at the heart of the Welsh folk tale, and the culture it represents. The plot of 'The Lady of Llyn y Fan Fach' provides her with a structure which she can use to anatomize the nature of marriage and of creativity at greater depth and length than in her earlier books; her novel also highlights the continuing relevance of the legend itself for a contemporary audience, particularly a female one. For both these reasons, it is fitting that *Iron and Gold* should be included in the Honno Classics series.

The Child and the Bard

'Badger The Bard', the children called him, because there were grey streaks and white in his black beard. His eyes, however, were the blackest part of him. There was no more seeing down to their depths than if they had been pools in a turbary. Neither, at times, was there any fathoming the sense of his speech. He wore knee-breeches and blue hand-knit stockings, long after the young men with ruddy cheeks were gone to The Pits to hew coal. They came up out of the earth in grimed clothes of a new cut, with bleached faces, blackened over, and blue scars upon them that could not be washed off. They sang hymns to the organ in the chapel which they built. But he went to church of a Sunday, and on weekdays chanted, in a fading voice, ancient love-songs to the thrum of an ancient harp. His memory reached back to a time when the land had been green and whole. That was simple enough to understand, for he was 'getting on' when the new century began. But legends of an age yet more remote were woven into his talk; and the tales with which he held children in thrall were told as if he himself had taken part in them.

One day, an eager boy asked his mother, 'Mam, did Badger the Bard *hear* Owain o' the Harp? Was he *seeing* the Fair One at the wedding feast?'

'Something he did hear and see, no doubt, when he were a fanciful odd little lumper, same as you.'

'But, Mam, folk do say as the lady o' Llyn-y-van-fach was coming up out o' the water while yet the Welsh was fighting some wicked old Norman kings?'

'Oh-aye. Maybe. If come up she ever did? There's a deal o' such hearsay spoken. There did use to be, whatever, in my Grannie's day. O' this lake and that 'twas rumoured in olden times.'

'He's telling lies then, is he, Mam?'

'I 'ouldn't say that, boy.'

'But, surely to goodness, he wasn't never alive, not in them days?'

'No, no. O' course not.'

'Then 'tisn't true as he saw . . .'

'Can I judge what be the truth to a poet?' she answered with a shrug of comfortable shoulders; and with steady hands went on paring apples.

The child watched the glossy peel snake from beneath her knife and fall in patterns curved as the letters he was learning. He thought of Eve and the Serpent. He thought of the maids who, on All-hallows Eve, tried to guess who their husbands would be. Very much he wished to know if the bard's tales might be believed.

Seeing him frown, his mother said with a smile, 'Mind you, he's not telling fibs o' purpose. Not artful, *bad* ones, see? He isn't knowing hisself, not rightly, poor old fellow, what he do remember, neither waking nor in dreams.'

At that the small feet shuffled and stamped. 'Can't no singer, no storyteller, know for *certain-sure* what was happening to him in his own lifetime? Why not, Mam? Why not?'

She began to laugh low, in the way of grown folk who put him off with a jest. 'Can *any* o' us, I do wonder?'

It angered him so that he cried out, 'There's a dull way to be!'

'Not near so dull as you'd think, *bach*. Life 'ull learn you, now just, how unaccountable queer life be.'

So the boy lost patience and ran away back to the puzzling

harpist, about whose knees the more docile children pushed without question. He, at least, did not mock their wonder, but seemed to share in it as he talked on over their bobbing heads. And this is the fable he told them.

Spring

When Owain returned at sunset and stood in the doorway opening to the west, his mother looked up at his bright crested hair. Behind him the puddled farmyard was awash with gold. The ricks were gilded and lichen glowed along the barn roof. Then she was no longer afraid of the mountains, dark against a molten sky, but said to herself that, surely, joy was come back into her life.

All day, to an echo of her clogs upon the flagstones, she had awaited his homecoming and had remembered the patter of many feet, mirth and laughter, the rattle of company at table, a rough hug at evening, the warm sweat of her master's body. Now her son's face was in shadow. His haunted eyes stared past her to the window. Not a smile! Not a word of greeting! She grew angry and slapped down a bowl of flummery upon the long table where one place only was set.

'Come on in, can't you? Your supper's cooling, you sluggard!'

To make him start and unsling the little Celtic harp from his breast was something. She had broken in upon his dream and the gnaw of her loneliness abated. Still he made no haste to cross the threshold but stretched like a sleeper awakening. He was the tallest of her sons, broadshouldered, slim-loined, a proper man to get her grandchildren after her heart. Time he was wed. Yet she did not wish it, not though she chose the bride, and choose she would with care. Her mouth tightened, tucking the upper lip on which pale bristles were growing. A rounded mouth hers had been, two ripe cherries pressed together. In her impatience she plucked at it to feel

4

such a shrivel of age that rebellion against the law of all flesh broke out in scolding.

'Am I to tend the fire all night, boy? Have you no pity on my tired feet, gone as flat under me as slabs just? Whatever's hindering you to eat, mun?

Owain came in, groping, dazzled by the afterglow. 'I'm not hungry, Mother.'

That made her quiver inside, like water in a cauldron about to boil. 'Name o' goodness,' she cried, 'patient as Job, meek as the martyrs, dumb-humble as a loaded ass, that's what you'd have me be!'

He smiled because, not understanding her passion, he found it less pitiful than foolish. 'Why is it angering you so greatly if I don't swallow all you set before me?'

'Why? *Why*? Who but a simpleton 'ould ask? What has my life been but baking and brewing for men? Don't I gather sticks, and fodder the beasts, and slaughter and clean and cook that you may be fed?' The loose skin wrinkled like a toad's on her thin fingers as they drummed upon the table. After a pause, quieted and sad, she complained, 'The fresh sweet buttermilk it is, I was churning for you today.' She took up the wooden bowl and the spoon with rim sucked sharp and brought them to him. His shoulder hunched itself against her touch; and this, also, wounded her. Too hurt for anger, she began to coax, 'Taste you it, there's my good boy, my baby!'

He tried, without relish, to eat because she stood over him: never letting a man be! And he wished that she would hold her peace when she asked, 'Where have you strayed this long while?'

'Up on the mountain,' he told her, but, seeing her frown, he added, 'Shepherding. What else 'ould you have me do?'

'By the lake, I'll be bound!'

''Twas your cattle I drove there; your sheep I was looking to.'

'Yes, yes,' she conceded; but she rocked from foot to foot in curbed annoyance. 'To be sure, the grass do lie lush along the water's edge.'

He smiled, not looking at her. 'Green as a silken mantle o' the Fair Tribe.'

'Will your wild fancies bring us profit?' she cried, her temper flaming up again. 'Must you lie there, dawn and dusk, singing your windy songs, and not a soul to listen? 'Tis a sharp farmer a widow do need for son, not a lake-crazed bard, a dreamer!'

'You were the first to praise my singing, Mother.'

'So I was when you sang ballads with some sense in them, ones I was learning you myself; and when others praised you, yes. But all alone! Whatever's the use? No clapping. No pay. Selfish, I'm calling it.'

At that, his smile, which had been secret, began openly to mock her. 'The stock do well up yonder. You can see your black kine fatten; and since gain be all you're crying for, whyever should you fret?'

She watched him push away his supper, and, very tired, sank on to the chair which had been the Master's. It was big but he had filled it, with her upon his knee; for she had been plump, as well as brisk and merry, in those days. 'My wedded wanton,' he had called her when she pulled up a red striped petticoat to show her pretty ankles. This had been long ago. Yet she felt the same hunger for joy within her withered bosom as she crossed her arms above it and pressed tight. Leaning forward she stared into her son's face and searched the distant eyes for tenderness. Full of dreams they were, but empty of the affection for which she craved.

'Every time I do look at you, I am caught as a fish on the line. So like to your father you be, that you're giving me a tug. But I'm fighting to be free, because you are unlike, too – you heartless boy! For *he* was loving me.'

'Come, Mother, whatever is it now you want?'

'You asked why I was fretting? I'll be telling you. Then, maybe, you'll know: a little, whatever . . . 'Tis because you are bewitched; clean gone away from me; gone further nor any o' the rest.' Her indignation was spent. Like the drying rind of a cheese, her sallow skin began to pucker and the tears which came into her eyes glistened on their white lashes. 'Seven sons I bore your father,' she said. 'That's not meaning nothing to you but hearsay. A man's knowing fear and pain in battle; but he's in company, even though he should die. The tramping feet! The marching songs! I've heard old soldiers tell o' them and their voices regain a brave strength.' Over her face, emotion ran like a breeze upon a field of corn; but soon it was passed and the creases left by suffering about her shrunk mouth deepened. 'Always I was dreading to be alone. Even as a girl, mind. And yet *my* strife I had to endure, there, in that dark stilly room, where now I lie awake o' nights: alone. Alone,' she repeated, staring past him into the shadows, as he had stared over her head towards the light. 'How can you understand, though? . . . Listen now. Madoc was my first; and never was there a lovelier. The very neighbours said so, the mothers with boys o' their own. "The lovechild" they called him in sport; though he was born in wedlock and not a day too soon. Some declare as you can judge the courting by its fruit. Well indeed, 'twasn't for this poor mountainy farm as I took your father; nor he me for my dowry. No, no,' she smiled, nursing bygone vanity, 'a shift to wear and one to wash was all ever I brought him. And hands to work, mind you. That's how our Madoc was love's apple, rosy-sweet. Was it a sin to be puffed up with his beauty, I asked myself when he was scarce sixteen and the girls a'ready after him like flies about honey, mad to unwing their silly selves for just a sip o' pleasure. Afore he'd whiskers on his cheek, a rich dealer's daughter spied him at a fair. A Saxon.' Scorn flickered over the Welshwoman's face. 'Ugly she was; but able to buy an angel, if ever she'd looked that high. So he was lost to me; for he shouldn't come near his own folk, as were beneath her pride. Nor have I seen my grandchildren. Never once, the pretty ones.' With the back of her hand she smudged away sudden tears.

'But I had other sons at that time,' she began again. 'Howell was my second, lusty as my first but not as uncommon well-favoured. Mischievous wild he was. Dear, how his pranks did make me laugh! He ran away to sea, though. Loving the world so well, he must look on the whole of it, mermaids and cities and all. The Lord do know whether he be living or drowned.

'After him, I bore Rhys and Gwilym; and they were fighters both. 'Twas the hot blood of their sire and my young glory in it I gave them to suck at my breast.' She clutched the hanging folds of her bodice. 'They had to fly the country, along o' the spiteful old English magistrates setting a price on their heads.

'When I was carrying my fifth, I'd gone low-spirited. Maybe that's why 'twas a girl I craved for, a little soft girl with tender ways to comfort me. 'Tisn't comfort, see, but a joyful pain, a woman's drawing from the husband she do love with a jealous heart. "Now a daughter," I was saying to myself . . . But lonely I had to be. For though I made her dainty clothes with ribbons all, and fancied, those long months, how I'd lead her by the hand, a boy it was of whom I was delivered. Well, well! He was weak and I was loving him in a fashion new to me. There was laughter over the cradle o' my first four; but tears fell on this poor wreckling as he slept – a waxen puppet.' For a time she was silent; then said in a bleak voice, 'The second bitter winter cut him dead – my frosted white blossom.'

'And then?' Owain prompted her. Watching a woman's raw heart exposed, he was filled with curiosity.

'Ah, I'd no stomach, I tell you, boy, for the sixth! And when he came, he was ill-shapen; nor did it surprise me. Dan, we christened him. Why I couldn't say. I was never liking that name; but I'd gone tired and was leaving it to a pack o' old sisters-in-law. Folk whispered as he were a changeling. The Fair Tribe 'ull slip one into a Christian cradle, see, if the mother isn't watchful. Sour as a crab-apple he was, to bring spittle into mouth. When our eldest left us, and then the next and the next after; when sorrow entered this house, brought by every child he'd begotten, the Master turned hissy-tempered and beat the sullen boy. Then Dan began to lie and to pilfer and his father beat him the more. Hurtful days they were to me; my own body gone sore with the blows. A mother can suffer that way, see, through the child she is loving least. At last he brought shame upon us, as were honest, upright folk. A highway robber was Dan the ugly. And like enough he's hanging this hour, tarred and in chains, at some crossroads.'

Owain leaned forward from the settle and clutched her hands to stay their twisting. 'Mother,' he said, 'I wasn't knowing half o' the sorrow you've passed through.'

'Passed through,' she repeated, her lips screwed in as if she had bitten a sloe and would laugh at the misadventure. 'Yes, indeed, pain is going by, same as pleasure. But I'm not able to forget neither. Happy is the woman that is never looking back. Lot's wife was given us for a warning.' Yet Owain knew that she kept warm her memories as a broody bird guards its eggs. 'Ah, well,' she said, the bitterness gone from her smile as swiftly as it had come, 'no more sons did your father get on me till I was near over age. Then, one spring day I was feeling you dance in my womb; and for all I'd been crossed in my children, I broke out laughing: laughing again like a girl.'

The young man stared at her. 'You're valiant, Mother.'

''Tis a married woman's way.'

'And my father, was he glad?'

She did not answer but turned her head aside, moving it to left and right. 'Next day he was up cutting green rushes off the mountain. Awaiting his return, I stood at the door in the sunlight. Warm it was and the air sappy; and I smiling for a secret; for there were seven magpies in the meadow yonder. As sharp I saw them as if they'd been limned in soot and snow. To this day I cannot look upon them ill birds without the old English rhyme tolling in my head: "Seven for a secret that's never been told." But *then*, I was promising myself a treat. "'Twill be like early days, having something to tell the Master." Again she was silent while Owain watched her dry mouth quiver and saw that her lips were pale as ash.

'He was cutting rushes up yonder? By the lakeside, Mother?'

'Ah,' she exclaimed in fury, 'there's magic in them wild heights to rob a woman of her man!'

''Twasn't never that day he had the fall from which he missed to come right? Not that day?'

'Oh-aye, that same day it was. And I had no chance to tell my secret, but to deaf ears and cold. We don't none o' us know what's ahead o' us nor o' those we be loving best. If we did, we should keep back nothing for tomorrow's joy, but be spendthrift every clock-tick o' the hour . . . When he was gone, I mended his clothes and cooked his favourite dishes; for there'd been times I'd failed to do so. How many an act o' love is done too late!'

'Poor Mother, *fach*!'

Now that she had aroused it at last, she thrust aside his pity and said in a matter-of-fact tone, 'So that's how 'twas, boy, there went tears, a crockful, as well as that first catch of laughter, to your making. Like as not 'tis why, for all your bright hair and strength to make you merry, you are singing a sad note on times, a peewit's cry in it.'

'Those mountainy songs you are mistrusting, Mother? But some are gay, and all are sweet, look you. If I could bring down from the high places the half o' what I am hearing up there, you, too, should be spellbound.'

'Never!' she protested.

He did not heed her; and thinking of his own troubles, complained, 'But 'tis no more nor a snatch, and gone again with the breeze.' She was not listening to him, he saw; and remembering her story, he forgot the dreams he dreamed by the lake-side and was touched again with compassion. Taking up his harp, he said, 'I'll sing you what shall make you smile, seeing yourself when you were young and mocked your many suitors.'

He played first a gay jig; and though to its opening stave she groaned and pursed her lips, soon her head was bobbing to the lilt. 'That's it! That's it! How clear you do bring it back!'

One summer's day, she recalled, the meadow below Grannie's cottage, the scent of clover and green stubble, clipped tidy as a mat, the hay being newly carried. She was wearing a scarlet shawl, a small one, about her slim shoulders, to honour her big sister's wedding. Proud she was of it, too proud to take it off, until she could abide the heat of jumping up and down no more, but like the married women must sit quiet in the shade. She had a red ribbon in her thicket of dark hair and had felt its gloss, smooth to her fingers, as she tied it this way and that before a twilit mirror when the birds were shouting dawn. But she had forgotten which of the lads had brought it her with gingerbread, a fairing – such a plenty of gifts, sighs and tappings on the window-pane at dusk had caused her laughing triumph, before she met the Master. No sense in her till then; nothing but vanity. It made her laugh again to think how very flighty she had been. Rising, she went to the hearth, and her flattened feet shaped anew the pattern of a country dance, while she held her head on one side and looked archly at her son as if he had been some other man and she still able to torment desire. The peat gave out an orange glow, and when she threw on fresh turfs bright flames leapt upward. Gazing at them until she blinked, she could see herself as she had been, clapping her pretty hands. Their palms were sticky, for she was hot; and hotter yet with anger when a boy kissed her on the lips. The sting of the blow she gave him was with her still and the shout of the chase. Fear seized her as she ran, not fear of what he would do but of finding her heart made captive. He was upon her, holding her down; and she was powerless, in a rage, quick with pleasure, glad of the tussle which her rash teasing had provoked. They laughed over her, the others. They dared! For long she would speak to none of them, but toss her head and stamp, as hill ponies do when haltered.

Owain had changed the tune; and now it beat to the rhythm of trotting hooves, steadily. Her pulse was a stream's that has passed the shallows. Into a swirling pool she was being drawn, and she did not resist; for the Master had looked her in the eyes and she was free no longer. They were riding home from the feast, boys and girls together, who had danced in the churchyard among graves, never thinking that any of their lively company must die. Her unspoken sweetheart had stooped to place his hand beneath her foot; and now, as she rode pillion on his horse, she held tight round his waist and laid her head against him. She feared it might be but a pin-prick which she had given him; and his sword gone deep into her heart! What did she know of his secret mind, who clung so close to him that she felt his chest expand when he shouted to the lad ahead of him in the dusk? That one had a girl behind him also. She heard the huzzy answer with a titter, and it was enough to bring out fever spots of jealousy; for all day long she had burned. Every girl living she hated, even those that had walked with her arm-in-arm and made garlands for her hair. Because she was so stricken a captive, tears of shame crept down her check. She wiped them off on his shoulder: and he never knew. He never knew nor guessed!

The old woman smiled and sighed. A madcap season was April – showers, gleams and rainbows – never one thing for long, nor anything at rest. When at last he came courting her, it was he who must bite his lip for jealousy, and she be fickle and coy, lest he should find her tame or over-bold. The quarrels they had, and her mortal dread of his never returning to throw pebbles at her window in the night! How she had run, barefoot, to open the lattice quick!

There she checked her memories, ashamed before her son, as if she had spoken these foolish things aloud. Having taken a harp in his hands and fixed his eyes upon her, he could read her thoughts as a scholar his Bible. At other times he knew nothing, she told herself, nothing whatever – the dreamy careless boy whom she must tend and scold!

But hear him now, playing the grave proud march of her bridal! Where had he learned that music out of the past, the hymn of those newly wed, who go soberly to church, arm-in-arm, through the harvest fields? In a little while he was crooning the lullaby with which she had hushed her seven nurslings. It set her rocking to and fro, a part of the sleepy cadence, once more the wife who never spoke a sharp word to her husband but was steeped in contentment. 'Like a sop in milk,' she sighed, 'drinking it in; the happiness he brought me, for a while, grown such a part o' myself, that I was changed to other than I had been.'

As the fire began to dwindle, Owain sang a dirge which filled the darkening house with sorrow; and she heard the feet of the bearers, heavy beneath the Master's coffin. She had been tying on her widow's cap, afumble because of her tears; yet she had felt unabated pride in his stature. 'A

weighty corpse,' the neighbours would admit, 'and a funeral
to do the dead credit.' Remembering the mourning, she wept;
but not in sobs as she had done then. Her tears were running
dry. Even grief was forsaking her – that rage of grief which
she strove not to let go, because it was the stream of
departing life, and she knew that, when it was spent, she also
would be frozen and motionless as he had been when the lid
was nailed down over his face.

But Owain, being intent to tell a woman's tale, must last
of all sing, very low, the spinning song of crones who turn
their drowsy wheels in the nook beside the hearth. No wind
blows there, nor small draught stirs. 'Yet it do grow cold,' she
muttered, 'a cramp o' cold stealing up from the foot on the
treadle towards the slowing heart.' She shivered and rose,
telling him tartly to have done. Her life, which she yearned
for, to this day, in hot abundance, was cooling off, so that she
hated this child of hers, with the good years before him, for
knowing so much of her passion, gathered and gone by, and
because he used his knowledge to make a song. He would
sing her youth and her prime to others when she, to whom
they had belonged, was robbed even of remembrance.
Heartless it was, she cried out within her echoing mind; and
aloud she said, 'I'm tired o' your senseless singing. Goodnight
now.'

'Mother *fach* . . .' His hand was stretched towards her.

But she would not kiss him, though all the lonely day she
had waited to touch him for her comfort's sake. 'Time you
slept, or you 'on't be up early to finish the spring ploughing.
The yoke-oxen be eating their idle bellies full, same as you,
mun. The colt did ought to be broken; and the thatch over
my dairy do leak shocking bad. You missed to see to en in the
autumn, with your truant scowling up the mountains. There's
hedges to pleach and a mort else to do; and I've but one pair
o' hands, and you no head on your shoulders!' Grumbling,
she went to the door and slammed it after her.

Yet when her shrivelled body lay within the curtains of the bed which she and her husband had so warmly shared, she began to cry and to bless the lad who could bring back her past. 'All I have left! All I have left! And he is giving it to me again, as I was once giving him life.' She knew then that her gratitude for his gift was greater than her envy of his span on earth.

But soon, from the room next to her own, she heard him singing in a voice wild as the cry of migrant bird passing high overhead in the still of night. The melody stirred in her no memories. It came from the hill-tops, cooled by clear water, and was free from human passion as is the wind among reeds. She sat up trembling, no longer because her blood was thin and the night chill, but in terror. Often, since he had begun to haunt the mountain lake, she had heard him singing thus, an air he never learned among living men. 'Bewitched,' she wailed, and would have gone to rate him for frightening her, but dared not. Pain she could bear without flinching, and peril of the common sort; but this mystery made a coward of her and stole away her child as the grave could scarce have done. Long after he was silent she kept vigil, asking herself in dread whatever had her boy's eyes seen, to which her own were blind? 'Headstrong fool,' she thought, 'he 'ull pay for it, as sure as moth at candle 'ull burn its venturous wings! There be danger in differing from others; and he who is climbing high, and alone, has the further to fall, should he slip.'

The old house whispered as if it, too, were afraid. There was sighing in the chimney and one ivy leaf tapped, like a warning of death, upon her window pane. She strove to sleep but could not, because love made her anxious, and anxiety enraged her, who had small store of patience or philosophy.

*   *   *

Owain rose at dawn, restless from a night of dreams. He took barley bread of his mother's baking, lifted the latch in stealth and shut the door upon her. At sundown, glad to have him home, she would complain that he had not stayed for breakfast. Food and shelter: that was all she thought of! Eager to escape, he crossed the fold where an early cock crowed challenge, and, went to the meadow in which her black cattle grazed.

To folk in the river valley, his birthplace was 'up yonder'; but for him it was 'down here'. Living among the mountains, he was used to look heavenward; and now he felt imprisoned because the heights were hidden when he raised his face to them. Homestead and sparse fields, fenced in against the wild, crouched in the lap of a dingle. An apron of mist spread over them.

The beasts that were lying down seemed to float, humped islands on a pond; those that were standing, to wade in milky water. He left the cows with calves for his mother to tend and drove the bullocks and heifers through paling twilight towards the mountain-top. They knew the way and went in single file, their breath, sweetened with clover, drifting back to him. It would have been pleasant going, had he not been in haste; but they were so tedious, snatching slobbered mouthfuls as they passed, that he feared he might be late in reaching his journey's end; and in the hush of daybreak, he dared not shout to hurry them. 'Go on, go on, you slow dullards,' he urged in a mutter. A voice, free as the cry of a curlew, might ring out overhead, and he not be there to listen.

Already, as he breasted the last rise and saw the lake gleam, it was a looking-glass for clouds tinged on their lower edge with rose. Every time he came to this lonely place, so far above the dwellings of men that none climbed to it but himself, it seemed to him more magical. He was filled with an aching delight, and longed to make a song of praise; but only when the Fair One appeared to him could he sing as he yearned to do. Lacking her, he was a common bard, good enough to please the crowd, but to himself a failure. 'Kindle me with your own wild fire,' he prayed, as the pink clouds turned molten. The cattle squelched through the reeds to drink with supping noises; and, under the brightening sky, the ripples they caused ran outwards in circles ribbed with saffron. Along the margin, millions of tiny flowers, like pearls with gilded centres, began to shine. The spring green of rushes grew livelier. Up flamed the sun. An arrow of gold shot along the water and struck him. He was dazzled and closed his eyes.

Soon, the throb of wings drawing near aroused hope of her coming. Music and verse to greet her pulsed in his mind. 'When I am seeing her next,' he promised himself, 'melody and words 'ull take form as never before; and I shall strive no longer in confusion to bring forth I'm not knowing what.' Yet for a long while he was afraid to look. When he dared do so, she was there, floating, he believed, within his reach at last. Her arms were white as the swans all about her; her dress as the flag leaves that blow now green, now silvered; and the sparkle of early morning lit her pale hair. About her shoulders it stirred, more bright than the pollened calyx of a lily; but where it lay awash, like seaweed that sways upon a tide, its faint green matched the stems of plants under water. Her eyes were neither blue nor green nor grey, for they changed with the lake when sunshine came and went, or ripples darkened its surface. This he saw clearly; but he knew that, when she was gone, he would ask himself if she had ever been.

'Stay with me! Stay with me, *cariad*! Let me look until I be sure o' you,' he besought her. 'Let me tell what you are, that I may have it in words by which to remember till death.'

And because she smiled at him, he found confidence to

sing her beauty, likening it to ungathered wild flowers and to foam, the flight of birds and of wind-driven clouds, a shaft of moonlight, a rainbow curved by leaping fish, the gauze wings of a May-fly that lives for a single day. To everything brief and lovely, not to be grasped, he compared her; and she listened, still smiling, and came closer that she might share the joy he had in paying her homage.

But when he grew bold in desire, and, having nothing of his own to offer, held out his mother's bread, she laughed. Her eyes turned blue as the ribbed water, a breeze being risen with the sun, and she answered him playfully, deriding mortal women who hungered for so hard a crust. The tune she sang was more cool and gay than the splash of little waves along the shore; and her passionless voice had the envied freedom of a lark in air. Mockery from her drove him mad. He sprang into the lake and would have swum out to seize her, but she cried, "'Tis not easy to catch me,' and vanished as she had always done before. Only the startled swans were left where she had been, to hiss at him and sail out of his reach. Chilled by the plunge, ashamed of his own insolence, he waded back to land and flung himself down to brood on his disappointment. Again and again it had happened thus. His impatience, his lack of humility, had driven her far from him; and until her return, he knew that, like a parched land or a woman deserted and barren, he would bring forth nothing.

All day the sun on his limbs was warm, the breeze upon his forehead cooling. Sharp with height, to whet a man's hunger, the air held scents of moistened sedge, of moss and flowering wild thyme; and the springy, sheep-nibbled turf might have lulled a king to sleep. But Owain could neither eat nor rest, since in trying to seize, he had put to flight his rare visitant. 'Never shall I capture nor keep hold o' her,' he groaned; and wandering about disconsolate, he struck with his crook the tender bracken shoots, curved like a crozier. He wanted to kill and lay waste, as men do who are self-thwarted; and with an angry shout he called home the cattle at evening.

*   *   *

'Mother,' he said, when she met him on the threshold, ready to stab with reproaches, 'you'll be having your way. I can sing no more the songs I learned on the mountain, not even such snatches as I did make sure of once. The sweet free airs are gone from me. For I am over-hasty.'

He went into the darkening kitchen, flung aside his small harp and covered his eyes. When she forced him to look at her, she saw that they brimmed with tears. So she pulled him down on the settle, pressed his head against her heart and crooned over him. 'There, there, there!' Was he not her child and ailing?

'My honeyseed, you shall sing at fairs and weddings, a merry song, as you were always doing; and the neighbours 'ull be praising you again, see? Who's wanting the music o' the hill-tops as none but a few can make shape of?'

'*I* am wanting it,' he said. 'Having heard its rare beauty, I am craving for no less a thing.'

She lifted his face from her breast and peered into it, puzzled. 'Why are you craving for that which has taught you sorrow?'

'You did ought to know, Mother *fach*, loving life as you do.'

'But life is like hot heady mead to drink, boy; *young* life, whatever; and age has its flavour, even in the dregs. Who can be drunk on spring water? Who can court the wind, as though it had lips for kissing?'

'A bard can, Mother. To him, mortal women are but patterns o' the one sought and never found.'

'There's joy at fairs and weddings,' she protested.

'A hot sweaty joy: oh-aye. I have tasted and relished it, too. The girls' shrill laughter; handling their soft flesh; the lads scrambling past one another to get their arms round the prettiest; fumy drink to make a man feel a giant; bawdy jests to put a brave face on what he's afeard of in secret; and singing loud in chorus.'

'Well? You are young. Aren't you wanting your pleasure, *bach*?'

'On times,' he answered, 'yes. Then, in their midst, I'm all at once a stranger, remembering cooler music, a haunting o' sights more rare.'

'A danger to give ear to,' his mother cried. 'A danger to see! Safety is in herd and flock, as cattle and sheep do know.'

'Maybe,' he sighed. 'But I 'ould risk all, rather nor stay deaf and blind to what is fairest.'

At that she grasped his hands, and commanded him: 'Hide this from me no more, mun. Say just what 'tis has turned your eyes so strange? There's hours I 'ouldn't know you for my own.'

It was not easy to tell her of music she had never heard, and beauty transcending flesh. So he talked aloud to himself as a bard in his solitude must do and as she listened, her mouth agape the drooping lids of age creased up, exposing her eyes. But he did not heed her neither when she spoke nor when she sat with bowed head and wrung her hands.

'My dread come true! Bewitched, you are! Bewitched! Whyever was I bearing a son to be carried away by the Fair Tribe? 'T'ould have been better for me had you wed a Saxon and scorned your mother, like my first-born. Or gone away to sea to venture the world over. Or fought the cursed gentry's law until its power drove you from home. Yes, yes, or died, even, in the cradle. Ah, then, your Christian grave, 'ould have been close to mine, some day! Better to have been a robber and wicked, same as my ugly Dan: for these be natural things. But *you* have given ear to unearthly music and are beguiled. Never again 'ull your life be as that o' other men.'

He had no retort, but asked her many times, 'What's to be done? What's to be done, now that 'tis so, and I must seek what I must?'

She pondered and at last rose, weary but resolute. ''Tis the lot of a mother to give her child whatever he do crave. Bound I am to help you.'

'God bless you, Mother *fach*!'

But at the door she turned to snap at him, ''Tis against my will, mind. And you be a swamping great fool.'

He waited, wondering, till she came back with a crock full of barley flour. Setting it on the table, she fetched a pitcher of water and balm to make the dough rise and salt to season the bread. With a grunt, she rolled up the sleeves of her gown above her bony elbows, and mixing all together, began angrily to knead. Owain sat watching her.

'You are good to me, Mother,' he said.

Her lips smiled, relenting, but not her eyes. 'Well, well, I suckled you. 'Tis only habit.' After she had pummelled hard, she heaped sods of peat upon the fire and set the crock beside it, covered with a cloth. 'By dawn,' she pronounced, ''twill be risen light and soft as a puff-ball. Take you enough for a loaf in this clean kerchief, see? Maybe bread that's not baked 'ull tempt your Fair One. They be captured only by taking a mort o' trouble. That's what an ancient old bard was telling me when I were a small little girl. Pity on him! He'd been in a plight same as yours, by what I could make out. It was leaving him crazed ever after. But, *ddwch*, how he could sing! . . . Now go you and sleep a while.'

But Owain could not sleep. When her restless turning in bed had ceased and snoring came from her room, he stole downstairs again to sit alone, hearing the tick-tack, tick-tack of the grandfather clock, the creak of the cooling house, the squeak and scurry of mice, until the glow from the hearth faded, and the window became a pale square in the darkness. Then he scooped so much of the warm dough as his two hands would hold, laid it on the bleached linen, and, carrying the kerchief by its four corners, went out into the twilight.

*   *   *

The air was chill and the mountain stooping over him frowned like a giant; but as he climbed upward, the horizon began to gleam with hues soft as a wood-pigeon's throat; and when he reached the lake, it shone.

''Tis lovely as herself, in token o' promise,' he thought. 'Surely she must come.' But as if to teach him that no vision is foreseen, that love and beauty visit with surprise, the hope of dawn faded into an overcast day and no golden arrow pierced him with delight. He could only guess the sun's rising by an increased pallor of sky. The water turned leaden and not a swan floated upon it. Like a harbour from which the white-sailed boats are gone, it lay desolate. Waiting through the hours beside its soundless brink was weary work. At noon, the veiled glare overhead so tired his eyes that he closed them and felt a gust fan his lids. The wind was rising. Soon, cross waves lashed at the reeds, bent all one way; a frill of foam whitened along the pebbles, and squalls of rain pockmarked the lake's grey surface.

Above splash and rustle, he heard, when he least expected it, the beat of wings. The sun glinted between torn rags of cloud, and a host of swans alighted close to him. She was there, with green cloak flying among the tossed rushes.

To the stormy margin he ran and held out his mother's bait of uncooked bread; but she laughed at it, flinging up her white arms and dashing cold spray in his face. Now loud, now faint, her song, swirling past him, pitied mortal women who must accept whatever men chose to offer. By no such hunger as theirs was she enslaved. Again he plunged into the water, mad to catch her. Again she fled from him; and crying, 'Unbaked is your bread. I will not have you,' dived like a fish, leaving a silver-bubbled wake. In a moment the waves had effaced even this sign of her flight, so that he stared at the dreary scene, asking himself in bewilderment, 'Whatever am I seeking? Is it none other than a dream o' my own conceiving?' The angry swans sailed hissing away. ''Tis my arrogance has punished me with her loss,' he lamented, upbraiding himself for having believed that she would be easy to win. 'Not thus is captured the heart's desire, oh fool! But with the heart's blood must any great prize be paid for.'

Rain fell in a grey curtain and he was wrapped in its blinding cold. At dusk, shivering and discouraged, he drove the cattle home.

*   *   *

Like an angry dog, a gust rushed in at the door with him. Peat ash swirled about the clammy stone floor and drops spat down the chimney. His mother was on her feet, alert to welcome him. 'Well, boy?' She saw the answer in bleak eyes and lower lip sucked in, and hurried to strip off his soused coat. Sullen, he left it in her hands and flung himself down on the settle. She followed him and knelt to tug at his buckled shoes and peel the wet stockings from his shins. From habit she looked to see if they must be darned.

'Hot leek broth is in waiting,' she told him.

'Leave me be, can't you?'

'Put on this nice warm waistcoat.'

'If she will not come to me for my fine voice and songs,

praised as they were at many a randy, what use did you fancy your sodden bread 'ould be?'

Often she had scolded him for nothing; but now she was patient with her sick child. 'Come you! We must try again.'

''Tis useless, I'm telling you.'

'No, no. The ancient old bard did say as her like were to be caught, at length, by the taking o' great pains.' And when she had forced him into dry clothes, she fetched a load of faggots and split logs. Her body bent aslant as she heaved them into the furnace. 'I've been chopping ashwood, see, in case o' need. 'Tis baking the sweetest bread, look you. Take courage now.'

But he heard without hope the crackle of kindling and watched her come again with her pitcher and crock. This time she brought wheaten flour and moistened it with milk. The sallowed skin of her arms was powdered white and she kneaded the dough with the strength of a younger woman. Before it was set to rise, she had renewed his spirit.

'Oh, Mother, are you indeed believing . . .?'

'Hush now! You shall have your wish, if you be willing to pay for it.'

They leant together, warm at the hearth, and hoped and waited. The clock struck midnight.

'The fire inside must be burnt low now and the oven be well heated,' she said. 'The hour for baking has come.'

Then he prayed under his breath, 'Break this bread o' my mother's with me, my love; and thereafter let me eat, all my life-long in your company, or I shall perish o' hunger!'

He clasped his hands so tight that the joints whitened and cracked. In the red glimmer, his eyes shone bloodshot, following each movement of the old woman's. Her face was flushed, her fingers flame-rimmed, as she raked the wood embers out of the brick oven, careful not to leave a trace of cinder to smear her wheaten loaf. Sprinkling fresh flour within, she gently closed the door.

'There! Not a puff of air to hinder it from rising, light as foam. Go you on off to bed, boy. I'll be keeping watch.'

'No, Mother, no! Not a wink could I be sleeping till 'tis safe baked and in my hand for offering.' And for an hour he kept urging her, 'Don't you let the crust turn hard, mind.'

'Oh, sing your mountainy songs and leave me to my baking!'

They were angry with each other before the clock struck one. But at last she lifted out the bread with crust gold as sunshine upon stubble. Its warm smell filled him with kindness, so that he jumped up and put his arm about her. He did not stay, however, to speak his gratitude.

'Quick with your best clean kerchief! I'll carry en hot up the hillside.'

'April's fool,' she retorted, and gave him her finest linen.

*　　　*　　　*

In the small hours he reached the lake, whose tranquil lap made soothing answer to the heart-beats by which he was shaken; for he had run uphill. Foolish and hasty he felt, ashamed as a child in its tempest, who is reproved by a gentle voice, 'Be still, little one. Now listen.' The rushes, weighted with raindrops, cold to his ankles, did not stir. The wind was fallen, having swept all cloud from the sky. In the east it began to gleam, a shield of polished pewter, causing the stars to fade. They slid along the water's surface, thin streaks of silver that quivered with every breath. The stars of fortune were trembling, thought Owain, because a man threatened to grasp what he lacked virtue to hold. His beloved, though she had often lit his horizon, as the rainbow does, with promise, inspiring in him many unfinished songs, kept aloof now in dread of betrayal; and must not the blame be his? She would have trusted him had he been worthy.

'Come to me. Stay with me,' he implored, 'and I will prove myself your faithful servant. I will be humble and diligent, from this hour forth, to do your bidding.' And kneeling down upon the wet earth, he raised his gift to her. 'Take you my little offering. Given with a single heart, poor as it be, it may become of value at your touch.'

Lake and sky were empty and he was aware as never before of his own smallness in a vast space. Then with wonder a song entered his mind; and he sang it, not knowing whence the words came, to a melody tender as the rustle of young willow leaves along a river's margin.

> 'Swan in dark pool mirrored,
> Come to me once more.
> Sway, ripple of green water,
> Sedge-whispering inshore.
> Lake again discover,
> White as feathered spray,
> Wings whose flight awakens
> Cradle-hush of day.
>
> Pinions wild to fetter,
> Fearless sink to rest.
> What prison shall confine thee?
> Wide harbour is my breast;
> Where, if thou lie enchanted,
> Peace shall mirror thee,
> Safe as ship at anchor,
> Wind and water free.'

But though he invoked her often and held out his arms until they ached, he received no answer.

The east turned pink; then molten. Up came the brazen sun and long-legged shadows stretched to westward of grazing sheep. At noon they grew short, stealthy in their movement, as he slept like a dog that has been hunting, his limbs sprawled where he had fallen. Towards evening, he awoke and stared at the shade cast by his mother's loaf, thinking how it resembled that of a toy hayrick. What vain plaything was it which she had made for his brief consolation? By the barn door at this hour she would be feeding her poultry, and with eyes narrowed against the glory of sunset, look for his homecoming and frown because he tarried. 'Over-fond and fretful. Poor old woman!' Not for long, however, did he waste pity upon her, but mourned his own diminished hope. 'My love will never share this common bread,' he told himself; and neither the honeyed light, spread over the hills, nor the scents of spring could comfort him. The sun was enlarged to twice its midday size, a huge ball of orange balanced upon earth's darkening rim. It sank; and its last level rays set the whole lake on fire. When the glow without heat was departed and mouse-grey dusk crept round him, Owain was cold and forlorn. Yet he did not crave for the hearth which had warmed him from childhood, but remembered with relief that today he had not driven the cattle to pasture on the mountain. Having come without the loitering beasts, he need not plod downhill at nightfall to endure his mother's scolding or feel the probe of her blind love; he would be free to await moonrise in this high solitude.

The stars were white at first and tiny as pin-pricks in heaven; then brighter and bolder than they had been at dawn. In a sky of blue so dark that it was kin to black, they winked as swung lamps do. Their reflections lay aquiver upon the water, recalling to his mind a looking-glass in a silent room where candles light the dead. Gazing at them, he longed to shed desire and hope among their tapers: and he fell in love with death. When the horizon silvered and a full moon stared into his face, he went down to the unstirred rushes and parted them with his hands. This time he did not plunge in headlong but waded step by step into the icy water that crept up to his heart. Her element, it should embrace him also. For if she would not come to him, he must go to her.

'Come back,' he heard her voice call. 'Come back and sing on earth.'

In the shudder of death he was stayed, but could not credit her commanding him to life. He made no answer, therefore, staring ahead over the glassy darkness level with his eyes.

Then she summoned him again. 'Since you have offered me yourself, I will stay with you until you drive me away.'

Not daring to believe it true, he turned and saw her stretching her arms towards him. So he flung himself on to the water and found that he could swim as fast as an otter. As he neared the shore, weeds dragged at his legs. He kicked himself free with lusty strokes that left a wash behind him and the juicy snap of stems. Through the shallows he splashed, running, and shook himself like a dog; and he felt the hot blood tingle in his veins beneath the chill of goose-fleshed skin. He could have laughed and shouted aloud; but lest he should scare her away, he came softly to the bank where she awaited him; and not venturing, yet, to touch, he knelt before her. Nevertheless, triumph was in his heart; and it was she who was afraid now, looking at him as if his confidence were a threat to them both.

'My love,' he demanded, 'what brought you to me at last? Was it the songs I was striving to make for you?'

She shook her head. 'No. For I myself had given to each its tune.'

'True,' he said, humbled again. 'Words and airs were your own. Was it then the wheaten loaf, neither hard baked nor doughy, but the best as my home could be offering?'

'No. Not that either. Not you but your mother made it; and out of her love for you – never because she desired my company.'

'What then? My yearning for you? Answer me, "Yes". 'Twas that? 'Twas the power o' passion to breed its like?' He was proud of being a man.

But she told him, 'You suffered. You knew that you must die seeking me. Without pain I am not won. Neither am I held by the careless, I warn you.'

He was vexed; but what did her reason matter if she were gained? 'Having earned you so near-by death, I'll be holding you fast, never fear.'

Her smile came and went. 'More steadfast, more patient, too, than a virtuous woman, must my bard be; not fickle, as folk suppose who hear him sing a hundred different songs and never guess that one abiding loyalty . . .'

He would not listen; but taking up the loaf, he urged her, 'Share you it with me. I've not been breaking my fast all day, for I was having no relish to eat alone. In halving this, we'll pledge ourselves to join our two lives together, each single pulse of them.' And he was very hungry.

Still she must test him further. Drawing back a step, she looked gravely into his face. 'You loved what you saw and heard afar off – a glimpse of beauty, a bar of music, unfinished. By such things a poet is kindled. But will a man desire them, and them only, all his days?'

He swore many oaths that he would do so. 'Only marry me, and I'll be keeping faith with you till death.'

'Yet if you have me to wife, you must see me day by day. Then, unless you are constant, I shall cease to be either rare or strange. For it will be your sight shall keep or kill my beauty. Moreover, should you tame me to your daily use, though I may serve you well and bring you worldly profit, you must watch me grow old as a man's servant does. To her, a just master is grateful; but in her he takes no delight. For in age the faithful servant is no longer fair, not in the manner that you see me now, when kneeling at my feet.'

'I vow . . .' cried Owain, straining up at her.

But with her cool fingers she closed his lips. 'Do not vow rashly; but remember this: as you desire me, so shall I become. Safe at your hearth, you will not find her whom you sought upon the hill-tops.'

He answered that he loved and would love her equally in all guises. If he took her in his arms and kissed her many times, he asked himself, would not his passion thaw her dread of change? He rose, came close and felt her trembling. He, also, trembled, but with desire, not in misgiving. Before he could embrace her, she had started back.

'That metal which is yours for toil and battle! I am afraid to touch it, being so hard and chill.'

He glanced down at the iron-buckled belt about his waist, from which hung a shepherd's knife. ''Twill do you no hurt,' he said, smiling, not displeased that in matters of common sense he should prove more wise than she. 'No hurt at all, no more nor that clasp o' gold as you be wearing.'

'Not unless you should strike me with it.'

'*Strike* you!' he exclaimed, astonished. 'Strike *you*!' He laughed at her as she had been wont to laugh at him when she was free and far away.

'It will be in your power to do so,' she told him.

'In my power, maybe. But never . . .'

'Give me your iron to feel,' she said; and when he had unfastened the belt, she bit her lip and put her finger-tips to it and drew a deep breath. 'Yes. It is serviceable, if you use it well – the tempered metal of a man's labour, that is his tool. With this you plough and dig and prune and make tight the strings of your harp?'

'Surely,' he answered. 'I could not be setting your airs to mortal music without this stuff which you be foolish to fear. And indeed I do promise faithful to be using it only in your honour. I'll be staking my life on that pledge . . . And now shall I lay my hand upon your gold?'

'Take it. It is yours to keep while you will. But mind to what purpose you put it. My gold will dwindle away if misused; and no brightness be left, remember.'

He was clumsy with joy as he fumbled at her girdle. ''Tis fair,' he murmured, 'and wonderful soft, being without alloy.'

'If you would wed me,' she said, when her clasp lay in his palm beside his own buckle, 'you must make me a ring of both metals joined together. Bring it here and I will come to you. And when you have put it on my finger, I will not leave you, but will break bread with you. And you shall drink water from the cup of my hands. And we shall not be parted.' She gazed at him. 'Unless by your betrayal.'

'That is the same as to say "*never*",' he boasted.

'Rashly spoken; yet truly, since you believe it.' She gathered a rush and bound it around her wedding finger; then gave him the little green circlet. 'You must make my ring so big, neither more nor less, to go on but never again to take off, dear partner.'

All this while he had not touched her; only the silk of her girdle, cold as water-weed. Now she slipped past him and was gone to the lake before he could cry out at his loss. The swans were ghost white in the moon's silvering. She floated out among them, faint as her own reflection upon the dark mirror framed in a ring of hills.

Yet as her singing came ashore to him, Owain heard with surprise and delight a song as simple as that of any maid who entreats her lover not to trifle with affection. The rhymes were artless, the tune, to match them, such as his mother, when a girl in love, might have found ready to her need; for it was one ancient as woman's labour at spinning-wheel and cradle, and oft-renewed as hope.

> 'Softly close your fingers
> Over my fairy gold.

Pure metal will not harden,
Nor in your clasp grow cold.
Be gentle, then, my captor;
Cherish the gift you hold.

Firmly grasp your weapon.
On its hilt be sworn
A vow as true as tempered steel
In passion's furnace born.
Let not that blade turn traitor
To stab my breast forlorn.

Gold is fair, but steel is strong
To forge the bridal ring.
Then steel and gold together . . .
Only those lovers sing
Love's triumph song, who to Love's shrine
Both soul and body bring.'

The former wild magic of her voice was gone. He rejoiced to
find in it now a note of supplication, human as his own. A
tender sweetheart he had willed his wayward vision to
become; and behold, she was changed to that which he had
longed for! So deeply was he touched that he kissed her clasp
and laid it against him, vowing that he would teach her all
mortal woman's joy but never her sorrow.

*   *   *

Down in the valley, hours later, the blacksmith was awakened
by bellows' sigh and hammer's clink. He broke out into a
damp of fear and pulled the coverlet over the wiry tufts that
sprouted from his ears. But being a man of violence, when
the sounds had long robbed him of sleep, he started up and

cursed himself into courage. Seizing a cudgel, he tumbled downstairs in his greasy nightshirt.

'I'm not afeard o' you, meddlesome goblins,' he roared, flinging open the door of the forge. There, red in the fire's glow, with his shadow wheeling black across ceiling and walls, was the known shape of a man. '*Dwall* take you,' he gasped in relief. ''Tis only the widow's son from up yonder! Are you mad, boy, breaking in here at midnight and tampering with my gear?'

Owain glanced up at him, frowning with effort. ''Twas having to be done on the instant; and I wasn't venturing to rouse you, see?'

'You be moonstruck crazy, not to wait till honest folks are astir – making me fancy as the Fair Tribe had broke in! But that's uncommon queer, I thought in my bed, for they dursn't touch no iron. The horseshoe over the lintel be enough to keep 'em away.' He came to the anvil and laid his grimed hand upon it, as some men touch wood for safety. 'What be you doing with my metal?' he growled.

'Not yours nor any man's, but my own it is. The buckle off my belt, as I've beaten white-hot into a ring. A tidy piece o' work,' Owain added, proud to feel the sweat he had expended on this token cooling upon his ribs. 'Look, mun, I'm not ashamed to show en.'

The blacksmith scowled, envious that one not of the trade could do so well. His jutting eyebrows came down like thatch neglected and grey. 'You're not uncrafty with your hands indeed – not for a madman, whatever. But tell me, why, name o' goodness . . .?'

Owain did not heed his questions. 'The gold,' he kept repeating, 'the lovely gold! 'Tis over soft and rare for me to handle. Iron I've been learning, since I were a small little lumper, to shape decent enough. Spade, ploughshare or axe – I can be making the stubborn old iron serve my turn. But *this*, that do gleam like sunshine, is proving as ticklish to hold.' He leaned against the anvil, all of a sudden despondent, and gazed at the gift which had promised pleasure, but proved to demand pains. 'Did you ever stretch forth your hand,' he asked, 'when you were no higher nor the knees o' the tall folk about you, and try to catch holt o' the flicker o' light on a wall? None but a blind mole 'ould deny the truth o' that light. 'Twas plain to see. Warmth it was having, too. Yet though 'twas so living, closed fingers could not keep it. Wind and water and sunshine: these be three fair things and real. All men are knowing and desiring them. But no man is their master.'

'There's fanciful you are! If I were to repeat your sayings in market, who'd offer you an honest price for your stock?'

But Owain was careless of his elder's sneer. The ring he had to make was his sole concern. 'I was carving a groove to hold the sun-brightness. There, see? Right around my iron ring. But can I snare the rainbow? Ah, if that could be captured, 't'ould cease to be a symbol o' promise!' Looking at the precious metal in his palm, he sighed. 'I have wasted much of it a'ready. What if I let slip the rest between my arkard fingers?'

'There's not another lad living as I 'ouldn't clout over the head for the turn you've been giving me tonight,' swore the smith. 'But I'd be sorry to still a tongue as tuneful as yours, boy. A lively song be warm in my vitals. Like mead it is or a fight, or night-courting when I was younger. I'll be helping you, you blackguard! Come on, man, give me your trinket!'

'No, no;' and Owain's fist closed tight upon his treasure. 'None shall ever touch this but myself and her.'

'Oho! For your sweetheart, is it? But whoever heard o' gold and iron blent? Make you it o' one or t'other, boy.'

'My iron and her gold must mix, I tell you.'

'Then make two rings, you swamping great fool, and let

them lie together on her finger. Side by side; that be good enough for a start,' he chuckled. 'Courtship must come afore marriage; and if she's respectable . . .?'

'I must do what she bade me,' Owain cut short his jestings.

'Go on! You must do as best you can.'

This, after struggle and failure, was what Owain had to make shift with. He was not satisfied; but saying to himself that she would never refuse an offering which was the finest within his power to make, he went out into the dawn to his betrothal.

The blacksmith watched him go; and malice was in his grin. Good! Very good! For long he had been stung by the praise which neighbours gave to a mere stripling's songs. Now he would have a tale to tell of this night's folly would make them listen to himself; and eager, too! 'When time do cheat a man o' his songbird's voice,' he said to himself, 'then, if he's sharp, he's learning to whet his tongue, cutting-edged as a scythe. Music is pleasing to young ears. But gossip's meat and drink to the middle-aged. Look out for yourself, you golden-crested lark! *I'll* tell on you! *I'll* make you a laughing-stock!'

*   *   *

Along the lane as Owain climbed upward, hedges and trees, their shapes distinct against a brightening sky, took on the colours of day; but on the mountain-top a veil of mist waited to enfold him. Lake-cold, unstirring, silent, he felt its purity before he breathed it in; and when he had entered it, he found himself wrapped in a calm transparency which did not blind or hinder, but served to keep his mind steadied upon the track ahead of him. No longer a weathercock to winds veering over a many-patterned scene, he went straight forward, hearing the constant throb of his own heart, feeling a vast pulse and the breath of a life more ample than his own. Often, haunted by a tune he failed to capture or in vain quest of words for a song, he had listened to the stillness of the heights. Today he was a part of it, his blood an ebb and flow with ocean tides, and in his lungs the whole expanse of heaven.

'How pitiful small am I,' he thought, 'when peeping out from myself upon the world, considering what I can pilfer, the very same as a greedy-eyed mouse at the door o' his hole! Yet how big whenever I do feel this "I" no more, but am like a blade o' grass warmed by the sun, blown by the four free winds, his little roots borne through space on the mighty motion of earth!'

Thus, in unity with all creation, he found his way without seeking it to the place where she was waiting. The lake washed with a whisper at her feet. She was pale in the mist, and her hair hung motionless as the waterweeds clinging to her cloak. When she gave him her hands, however, he was not astonished to find them warm and comforting: a woman's. Forgetting his fret in the night because he had made her two rings instead of one composed of both metals, he put on her wedding finger the iron and the gold.

She looked down at them, then up at him and said, 'Yes: if it must be so. We have met and touched and shall lie close. I will stay with you, while you cherish me. And even death, maybe, will not part us. For, should you drive me from you, having known me once, you will not desire to live in so barren a loneliness . . . But on this earth, we shall never be wholly one.'

He cried out against that, his will striving for reasons to convince her that she was wrong; though the more he found eloquent words, the further they forced her from him; until, in her aloof silence, close to his side, she seemed to have departed on a far voyage. The moment of ghostly union had flown; as he seized her in his arms, he felt his man's body, and crushed against it her soft limbs. Her lips were hot and moist, yielding and eager in reply to his kisses, as he wished them to be. Yet there was division in his thought, '*Her* lips; and *mine* upon them.'

When he let her go, she sighed and murmured, smiling, 'We have this much; and much it is, my heart.' He caught her to him again but she slipped out of his grasp. 'Listen, before I come with you to be your wife. Today you are burning with love and I am happy; but if you should strike me three times with your iron, that will not blend with my gold, then you will drive me from you; and death, which might have come kindly to call us away together, will take me first, leaving you desolate.'

'But you,' he exclaimed, 'be immortal! And because we are to be wedded, you have set me free from common dread o' the grave. How, then, could this come to pass?'

'That I should grow old and feeble, and you be widowed at last? Why, because whatsoever a man's secret heart imagines, the same shall his eyes behold.'

'May I tear the soul out of my body with my own hands,' Owain swore, 'if ever I strike my beloved one with iron.'

She gave him a look of compassion. 'Though here we cannot be wholly one,' she sighed, 'from henceforth, neither of us may suffer without the other.' Then from a nest which she had built among the rushes she fetched his mother's loaf; and in silence, looking into each other's eyes, they broke it between them and ate.

''Tis moist with the dew o' your mountains,' he said.

'It is pleasant, wholesome food,' she answered. 'I am glad that I should taste it.'

After that, she knelt among the sedges and filled her hands, as if they had been a stoup, with water and brought it to him to drink. He saw the gold ring and the iron which he had made for her, glistening wet. 'And I fancied, but yesterday, to drown in your element,' he cried, laughing for relief. 'Now it is only my drink with which you are serving me.'

'Yes. Even as your bread, a daily thing, shared between us.' When she, also, had drunk, she turned to the lake which she had left, saying, 'Look. I will bring you gifts.'

'Nothing am I desiring. Only to have you with me.'

A caress was in her smile. 'Yet you must take what I offer. It is part of the marriage bond,' and she began to call over the hidden pool, as folk call cattle home.

Out of the mist white kine appeared and waded through dim reeds ashore. A stately bull came first, snorting two jets of steam from his nostrils. He pawed the ground as though to him earth were foreign and mistrusted; and suddenly he uttered a bellow that was answered in a muted tone, flat and hollow as the cuckoo's note, echoed from unseen rocks. Owain coveted the splendid beast, of finer breed than he had seen in field or fair.

'That gift o' yours I 'ould like to ring and to show to the dealers. But can I be mastering him?'

'Why, yes. For everything of mine, that you do not fear, is yours to enjoy;' and she laid her hand among the crisp curls upon the bull's massive head. 'Fierce horns will not gore a brave master. He was mine and is now yours.'

After him in line came fifteen cows. They passed Owain with a stare of liquid eyes and four calves trotted behind them, gambolling, with tails arched like the handles of jugs. Last of all tottered a fifth, so young that legs outweighed frail body and ears flapped from a drooping head. It bleated as the newborn do, until a cow with milk oozing from a full udder, paused to moo over it and to lick its wrinkled hide.

'They are the very same as mortal kine, these gifts o' yours,' said Owain, 'but that they are more comely.'

'Gifts fit for a mortal man,' she replied, glad to see the pleasure he had in them. 'Lead me home, my heart. While we go linked, my dowry will follow us.'

So he took her by the hand and was filled with pride in her beauty and in all that she had brought him: and because he felt strong in his joy and merciful, when they had gone a little way, he had pity on the suckling calf, lifted it up, set it on his shoulder and carried it, still holding his betrothed by the hand.

'That is gently done,' she told him.

He was pleased with her praise and decided, 'This one I 'ont never kill.'

'Kill? Why should you kill any?'

Time enough later, he told himself, to teach her how a farmer must live by slaughter. This morning he would not dwell upon any fact but life; for it was good and abundant. Stretching before him, like a road without turning or shadow, it promised to lead on into the mellow sunset of his age. But of that he would not think: not yet awhile. True, he had no misgivings about growing old, if indeed he failed to share her perennial youth? The harvest of his years would bring him only ripeness. There was nothing to flinch from in the prospect of time or change, with a wife whom he would love ever more dearly, woven, warp to his woof, into the fabric of his thoughts and ways. Their companionable twilight was far off, however; so let them rejoice in this daybreak while it was theirs to share.

The mist was lightening. A round plate, without heat or brilliance, the sun stared blank at them; and as they descended further, pale sunshine filtered through a thin gauze which melted away faster with every step. Of a sudden the air was warm upon their faces and the grass about their wet feet glittered green. Far below them they could see the dingle where they would live together. Among its chequer of hedges the small thatched house and buildings huddled. They looked, thought Owain, as if he had never before seen them for what they were, no braver than a litter of brown and white mice. 'My homestead,' he told her, 'and those be my mother's fields.' They appeared to him neither large nor many enough. 'I'll be needing to enclose more land and to build new byres for the cattle,' he said; and was so busy planning, that for a moment he forgot his sweetheart. When he remembered that it was she who had made him rich, he turned to her again. 'What is it, my love?' he cried.

She was looking back in wistful longing at the heights from which he had brought her down. Then with a pang of self-reproach he understood that her mortal joy was a fragile thing, delicate as the petals of a windflower. By him who held it now and from henceforth, it might be crushed with a single rough touch or frost-nipped by neglect; while of her immortal nature, what would he ever know? In secret he feared; and to hide this even from himself, he uttered aloud a valiant promise. 'I will never from this hour cease to remember and cherish you.'

Her fingers, which had loosened within his clasp, curled fast about his hand and she smiled, but not without effort. 'I trust you. Take me home and keep me there in safety.'

*   *   *

Hand in hand they came to the fold. Opening the gate, he led her in and her tamed kine followed them. When they were entered, he made fast the latch and drew her towards the door of his house. She hung back and asked, 'Must I live in there?'

'Under my roof it is warm and safe. And how could I sleep in comfort with stars for ceiling?' he said with a laugh of happiness.

'As you will,' she agreed, and again her fingers locked with his own.

His mother rushed out with strained face, the tendons in her neck atwitch, and cried, '*Ddwch*! I was dreading as you were lost to me, you madman!' But seeing a girl with loose hair and green robe at his side and a herd of cattle behind him, pure white as flowering cotton-reed, she was stone-still and blinked her eyes and had not another word to say.

'Now, Mother, you'll never be able to scold me no more. I've brought you back my bride, see? And her fine dowry too.'

The widow stared and stared. At length she muttered, 'We'll be rich, then, as when I had the Master alive and a batch o' strong sons growing up to labour.' And she smiled, showing the teeth that she had left and the spaces in her gums, and turned to the maid, curtseying to her seven times, very low, as if she had been the new moon.

'There's no occasion for you to do that, Mother,' her son said in a lordly tone. 'She has eaten with me the bread you baked and is wearing these rings o' mine, look, upon her bridal finger. She has become one o' us now, see?'

'To be sure,' said his mother, much relieved; and at once lost her awe of the stranger. 'Still, your bride do be bringing you riches. I was only thanking her for that, as is decent. An heiress can't never be treated same as a pauper, for sure. Come you in, my dear. You're kindly welcome. I must be finding you clothes fit for my son's wife to wear – shoes for your naked feet and pins to do up your elf-locks, nice and tidy; petticoats, shawl and apron, too. You are not enough covered, you poor strange thing!'

'Must she be dressed like other women?' Owain asked with regret.

'T'ould be a scandal if she went about so wild – the pretty one! She'll do you credit in church, when I've had the dressing of her, whatever.' She counted the cattle, marked how many of them were with calf, kissed the girl on both cheeks and bustled her into the kitchen. For years Owain had not seen her so cheerful or brisk.

'What's your name, my dear?' she demanded.

Standing dazed upon the threshold, the bride groped for her lover's hand. 'It is dark in a house,' she whispered. 'And close. The smells are hot and heavy.'

'What's your name?' she was asked again.

'He may call me whatever he pleases.'

'There's queer,' Owain confided to his mother. 'I've been catching glimpses of her often – why, it do seem since first I craved to be a famous bard! And I've heard snatches of her songs, as well you're knowing. But never, in this long while, have I learned her name.'

'Nor will you ever know any one but that which you yourself shall give me,' said the low voice at his ear.

The old woman uttered the clucking note of a hen. 'Mercy on us! Must we be having her christened then, as well as married? No, no. The neighbours must not guess where she was coming from. Envious they'd be and saying as 'twasn't right.' She sat down and pondered while the lovers stood before her, Owain waiting to obey, so little did he care for anything but his joy in ownership. 'Yes,' she said, after she had reflected, biting her thumb and grimacing as though she had the toothache. 'This is how we'll be contriving. We are equal to any now, owning such fine profitable beasts. My son shall go into England – today, mind – to his eldest brother's.' And although this was said to both of her listeners, it was at Owain that she nodded over the head of her daughter-in-law to be.

'Go away!' exclaimed the maid, and held tight to his hand.

'But, Mother . . .' he began.

'Yes, yes. Go; and sleep, too. 'Tisn't right for you two to

lie under the same roof, not until after you're wed. Three weeks you must be gone, while I'm settling with the dull old parson about the banns and all, and making ready for a swelling-out feast and letting folks know as you've a wealthy bride come here from foreign parts. An orphan. That's the way of it. An orphan! There's a deal I shall be having to learn her, too – how to behave crafty in company and what lies she must be telling.' There was mischief and importance in her brightened eyes at the thought of deception. 'Meantime, I'll hire to serve us the simple mute, Thomas, that none 'ould have at the hiring fair last autumn. Lucky that! Toiling like a gelded ox he'll be and not able to report nothing o' what he may see nor hear.' She cackled with laughter, and went on scheming merrily. 'Ah, I'll prove too sharp for the whole prying pack o' neighbours! Never fear! You, boy, shall bring my handsome Madoc home-along for your randy wedding. And my grandchildren, also, mind you, as the proud Saxon's hindered me from blessing. 'Twill humble her pride nicely to see the champion dowry this pretty innocent's bartered away for a song – she having wed my Madoc for nothing only his looks. Making the best o' their wares my boys have been indeed; and you, the Benjamin, doing better even nor my eldest, with his rich ugly wife.'

Like a shallow brook in spate she babbled on, while Owain listened with a smile of male tolerance, and his betrothed stood by. After everything was settled by the mother to her liking, she gave her son food and made a change of clothes into a bundle. Then having told him where to go and upon what day to return, she flapped him with her apron from the house. 'Get on with you! Off to go, quick!'

In the fold he lingered among the patient white kine that lowed for water. They gazed at him with eyes soft as velvet, their flanks heaving pitifully in the noontide heat, and the flies a torment which they must now endure.

'Will they cross, are you thinking, Mother, with our common black cattle?'

'That they will,' she chuckled, rubbing her hands together as she did to clean them after making pastry. 'Nature's nature, high and low, you simpleton! A great lusty brindled herd we'll be having soon – butter and cheese and butcher's meat; and young ones o' your own, too. And I shall be their Grannie. And under my own roof they'll bide, the lot o' them. Pretty they'll be as her, see, and strong and doing well as you, boy. For doing wonderful well you were, indeed now, with your fanciful singing – you artful dreamer! There's business, after all, to be made by verses, and money to be catched from courting one o' the Fair Tribe.'

Such words shamed him; and reluctant to leave his beloved, who would give him riches above common folks' understanding, he looked long and tenderly at her where she stood pensive in the doorway. She was so virginal a figure in her green-silvered robe which had lost its girdle, and still so free, with hair falling about her slight shoulders, that for all his pride in possession, he grew sad to think he should never again see her so sweetly untrammelled, nor so young, shy and strange. It had been painful to her to enter into his house and his gratitude was her sole reward. 'Little enough,' he sighed. But the moment of compunction was brief. He would make her live to be proud of her bard. He would live to be proud of himself.

As he set forth at his mother's bidding, he tried to sing one of his sweetheart's songs, with the south wind soft in its melody; but his thoughts strayed to his unknown brother, whom it was his mission to make envious, and there were fettered. Trudging downhill, thereafter, he heard nothing but the beat of his own footfalls; and by nightfall these had grown heavy.

Summer

Through a glory of morning late in May, the bridegroom rode to claim his own. Not a cloud in the sky laid shadow upon earth. The valleys were live green and buttercup gold. In folds among the hills lay snowdrifts of hawthorn blossom, almond-scented, sleepy-sweet.

Last evening, returning with his kinsmen, he had begged leave to see his betrothed; but she was kept prisoner while they barred the door. 'No, no,' his mother had cackled, thrusting out her head, on a neck lean as a plucked fowl's, from a window in the thatch. 'Come you tomorrow with your troop o' young men, as is fitting. Not before. Easy fed is soon filled. Hunger's twin to vengeance. 'Twill grow with waiting'; and she had slammed to the lattice. Little, thought he, could she fathom the depth of a love that would outlast life yet never lose today's fresh ardour. For in his happy arrogance he was sure that none had ever been so true a lover as he.

Having lain but slept little at a neighbouring farm, he galloped into the fold with a clatter of jovial companions. House and buildings had been new lime-washed, whitened as mushrooms sprung overnight. The cobblestones were swept, the place was astir with men dismounting and horses whinnying from the stables. He hurried in to find the kitchen strewn with rushes and garlanded in flowers. Every brass candlestick and copper skillet which the widow owned or could borrow was ranged along dresser and mantelshelf. She had spread the table with bleached linen and her best lustre-ware; while herself was a-simmer with importance, greeting guests and giving orders. Her voice rose shrill above the chatter of women in scarlet cloaks, crowding the room with colour. Bright glances and arch smiles greeted Owain; but he had eyes for none, because his bride was nowhere to be seen.

'Mother, where have you hidden her?'

She gave him a hug and a kiss, so that he felt her thin body's trembling and the dry, hot flutter of her lips. The oily smell of fleeces was still upon the yarn of her gown. Her apron crackled and her shoes creaked; for all were new. 'So hasty for your pleasure!' she mocked him. 'Stand back then at the foot o' the stairs and I'll be fetching her to you.'

Though so much needless commotion and delay made him impatient, he could not but smile at the pride she took in his wedding. 'She's a champion good mother after all,' was his comment. But never a thought more did he give to her when she came down, leading his beloved by the hand.

The maid was clothed like another in Sunday best. Blue ribbons laced a frilled white cap that all but hid the sleeked parting of her hair. She looked demure in tight bodice and bunched skirts, a shawl covering the shapeliness of her bosom. There were stockings of lambs' wool and buckled black leathern slippers upon her feet, whose naked beauty he remembered with a pang, asking himself in misgiving why he had allowed this change from the wild and rare to the commonplace. Scarce would he have known her, had it not been for the oval of her face. Despite what his mother had done to make her resemble an ordinary bride, her eyes of water-green were lovely as ever. Gazing into them, he felt his passion cool to worship; and he had nothing to say.

'Aren't you going to kiss her, you laggard?' But he hung his head; and behind his back girls tittered and men guffawed. 'I've called her Martha,' his mother whispered. 'And told the neighbours so. 'Tis a useful name and respectable, taken as 'tis from Scripture. Not too fanciful neither.'

'No, no! I'll be calling her Glythin, which is meaning a dewdrop. Martha's no name for a beauty.'

'More likely for a wife, you soft simpleton!' They argued in angry murmurs, until she conceded, 'We'll be calling her the both then, since you're so dubbid obstinate. Martha Glythin . . . Say it after me, my dear.'

'Martha Glythin,' repeated the bride in a low voice.

'Glythin Martha,' Owain corrected her.

She smiled and whispered, 'Yes, *bach*. Let it be Glythin first. It is for my master to christen me.'

And when he looked up, he saw that her white neck and her face had turned rosy. He had never before seen her flush like a shy girl aware of man; and it so delighted him that he took courage and kissed her heartily. At that the guests laughed and clapped their hands.

'Now off to go,' commanded his mother. 'And no making believe to run away with the bride, mind. For I'm gone stiff in the joints and do dread a fall from horseback.'

So they rode leisurely down the dingle towards the church in the valley. Owain and Glythin went first, side by side, in charmed silence. Warming for noon, the air was sleepy with scents of cowslip and bluebell, nor robbed as yet of last month's showery freshness. Here, high above sea-level, spring and summer met, like two fair sisters lingering to embrace. The sparkle of streams running along their path flashed in the eyes of the wedding pair all the way.

'Look. The blessing o' your mountain water is going with you,' Owain said.

'It has flowed down to render your land more fertile.'

They smiled, swift and secret, and looked away ahead, while after them jogged the others, singing loud snatches of song. Only the Saxon wife of Madoc rode with her fat blond children in a gambo, pursing her lips at every jolt and brushing straw from her silken lap to make it plain that she found herself in low company and would not condescend to the least enjoyment.

The pointed windows of the church were small, and ivy grew over their diamond panes, tinting green the light which filtered through. The air was cold and motionless as water at the bottom of a well, and even those youths and hoydens who had joked the loudest were awed as they tiptoed in, feeling the stagnation of prayers, once alive but long since formalized as the carving upon the chill, massive stones of the corbels. Heavy breathing and the creak of pews at his back made Owain aware that eyes watched him. 'Envious they are o' my good fortune,' he told himself; and was so mightily satisfied to know his future secure, that he forgot the giver, rejoicing only in her profitable gifts. When he glanced at her to relish her beauty, she was turned pale as a corpse. Surely, he thought in dismay, the greenish light was to blame – naught else? But he was anxious for her well-being and much relieved, as he watched her lovingly, to see the colour steal back into her cheeks. Then the solemn service began and he knew nothing any more of neighbours and kinsmen, forgetting his mother, also, his own plans for the morrow, and all his past with its many fickle fancies. Alone with Glythin, as in a magic circle, he stood facing God's minister and repeated vows of lifelong fidelity. Her arm touched his, his muscles tautened; a quiver ran through his limbs and a pulse drummed in his throat. He swallowed, dry-mouthed, finding it hard to say aloud what he believed with his whole heart.

'Wilt thou love her, comfort her, honour, and keep her in sickness and in health; and, forsaking all other, keep thee only unto her, so long as ye both shall live?'

'I will,' he swore, and blessed the brave finality of a promise he did not doubt he should hold sacred.

Then she, also, made her vow; and in gratitude that stung his eyes with tears he thought, ''Tis true!' Humble and proud he proclaimed, 'With this ring I thee wed, with my body I thee worship . . .' But he saw in consternation that she was already wearing his two rings upon her finger. For not down here, in time-worn words, but on the heights and in speech that sprang from their hearts to their lips, their troth had been plighted. She heard him falter, and looked up at him with a smile that seemed to ask, did the symbol matter, since their love was known by them to be hallowed. Eternity is symbolized in a circle, because it has neither beginning nor end; and they who have understood this, have no longer any need for a ring. But Owain, glad that the parson's sight was dim, wondered whether any among the onlookers had noticed. Therefore, the spell was broken and he was no more wrapped wholly in the love of his bride.

There was, however, much satisfaction in company, he granted, when he led his wife down the aisle upon his arm. Let the boys crane forward and stare over the high box pews! He was not abashed now that he had become a husband. Moreover, the girls were admiring him. He could see that from the corner of his eye and he relished it; though, from henceforth, the longing which his good looks, famous voice and turn for verse aroused in them would cause him no temptations, so he believed. His was a prize, hard won, for which he was willing to forgo the easy pleasures of less aspiring youth. With this conviction, he felt his chest swell big in the pride of ownership and the new neckerchief tightened over his Adam's apple. In the porch, folk jostled to wring his hand and wish him joy. He beamed upon them, every one. They were his friends, his well-wishers. More good and kindly men and women never trod a happier earth. But why was his mother crying? That seemed a foolish way in which to greet his triumph; for did not his married life lie

spread in front of him, plain to read as a map? He saw the
whole acreage of enclosure, in which wealth was made sure
and beauty held a constant captive. Why then should the
silly old woman turn her back on him and drop tears upon
Glythin, as though a dear-loved bride were to be pitied?

'For shame, Mother,' he whispered, jogging her elbow.

'Shame on yourself,' she answered angrily. 'Men! A lot o'
gluttons they are! *Ach a fy*!'

But she was chattering and cheerful again, bright-eyed as
a robin, when they entered her house, where women who
lacked church-going best had been put to baste joints and
keep kettles on the boil. A great to-do she made getting
everyone into place in order of rank and telling Madoc how
to carve, until his wife remarked that in her country they ate
fresh meat every Sunday of their lives. After that, the Welsh
ceased being civil to the Englishwoman and her broad face
grew more than ever like a scrubbed turnip. She began to
watch the bride and to nudge her husband, who looked ill-
at-ease. Owain guessed what she was hinting at – that
mystery encompassed Glythin; and he scowled. His mother
also saw and gave him a warning shake of the head; and
though she joked and gossiped, her quick glances became
wary, from which he knew that she had scented danger. ''Tis
arkard having something to hide,' he admitted to himself,
finding that it marred his wedding jollity.

At first the guests were busy quenching their thirst, the
men with gulps of ale, the women in sips of tea. Madoc
heaped slices of meat on to their plates. The boiled potatoes
were islanded in puddles of gravy. Red juice oozed from legs
of mutton and pork, and the hot kitchen smelled fleshy.
Smacking his lips, the blacksmith declared that his mouth
watered. So did theirs, exclaimed others, who waited their
turn to be served; and they rubbed their stomachs and
grinned. But the bride would touch nothing more than a
bowl of curds and whey.

'That's all she fancied last night,' announced Madoc's wife, 'though she was offered prime fried ham, of the best. Is the girl ailing, then?' There was malice in her tone and she put her hands to the loop of gold chain where once she had had a waist, casting with her eyes a lewd question towards the married women. Everyone agreed to think it queer; and the blacksmith, because he was even more jealous of Owain's voice than the ugly Saxon of Glythin's beauty, abetted the slanderous hint with jocose winking, becks and nods. As feasting made his friends more bold, Owain began to perceive their common curiosity and to be less confident of their goodwill. First one and then another asked him why he had been so sly over his courtship, where his wife's home might be and of what breed were her cattle? To these and many more questions he knew not what to reply and glanced in confusion at Glythin. But she, saying not a word to help him out, shrank into herself like a startled child that is prodded and pinched by its elders. It was to his mother he must turn for help and she commanded his gratitude by proving a match for the busybodies. Her answers were so wily that they learned nothing, yet were ashamed to press the matter further. By the time so much food had been eaten that the young were dancing to shake it down and the elderly blinked round the hearth, conversing for civility's sake and yearning to unbrace and sleep, the blacksmith had drunk many a pint and started to joke about rings of iron and gold. The allusion raised a laugh and Owain thought in consternation, 'There now! The crafty gossip's spun a fine tale out o' my midnight visit to his forge, making me look a fool afore folk as did use to prize me highly!' They had danced themselves out of breath and formed a circle round Glythin, staring as cattle do at a stranger in their field. Inquisitive eyes peered at the hands clasped in her lap. With her right she covered her left, on which were the two rings, his tokens; and she looked to him in her distress, so that he was sorry for her – shy creature, untrained to the prying of mortals! But he was sorrier still for himself, his pride having been wounded.

'Sit you down, all o' you,' his mother cried. 'Twilight's setting in. Time for a song.' She signalled encouragement to him and he wondered what he would have done without her worldly wisdom.

'Let the bridegroom give us his best,' the blacksmith bawled. 'He did ought to be in full song today, whatever, same as the birds afore the cares o' nesting have dulled their plumage. Come on, mun, come on now! Raise you the roof with your loveliest tune and a jollock chorus fit for a merry-making.'

With a look of challenge he thrust Owain's harp into his hands; but Owain was timid, never having ventured Glythin's songs in company; nor, in her presence, those that won him neighbourly applause. While he thrummed the strings with fingers turned stiff and inept, he gazed into her eyes. They were cool as the pale green gem that is named after water and the ocean; and the songs in which men celebrate love and hunting, battle and carousal, were washed clean from his memory. Instead, he recalled those questions concerning the soul that had haunted him in solitude. 'This body o' mine,' he thought, 'what is it but a husk? When it is fallen asunder, from the grain within, fresh corn will sprout in wider fields, maybe? Is this the truth of it – the Reaper Death, each harvest, shall lay the ripe wheat low and the chaff shall be winnowed away on the threshing floor o' the grave? But that from which the green blade do spring, I know not how nor why, shall never perish? For is it not immortal, like God Himself, from whom it do come and to whom 'twill return for refreshment?' It was to solemn music, with the sigh in it of wind across lonely spaces, that he sang these words:

Swift and unseen as gale of spring
To quicken sap and earth,
Whence came you, vital spirit,
Breath of my life at birth?

In what far home again received,
When my last sigh is drawn
And night to me is starless,
Shall you behold – what dawn?

I, in the leaves that fall and rot,
In pale grass trod away,
Shall feed the soil that bred me,
To rise no more with May.

But other leaves, not I, shall stir
And grass the earth re-cover,
When you that blow in seed-time,
Lightly my grave pass over.'

Having ceased, he was aware of being cold, as though the window had been opened. He glanced towards it, and, surprised to find it shut, stared at those who had listened, surprised, also, to see them there. They were mute, their faces gone blank, and none clapped him. All kept their seats, inert as the stuffed sacks down at the mill which as a child he used to make-believe were stout pallid men and women. These folk had been his friends and his admirers. Now they were all turned hostile as his brother's wife and were foreigners every one.

The weighted silence was broken by the blacksmith, who, being the boldest, was the first to clear his throat and spit into the hearth. 'Well indeed, there's an uncommon old ditty! What's on you, boy? Have you been seeing your own corpse candle, mun?'

It was in Owain's heart to answer, did not each infant
follow that light of warning into this brief life, even at his
birth? But the guests, whom his song had made uneasy, were
chattering fast and loud around him; so he held his peace
and exchanged with Glythin a comprehending smile.

"Tis a funeral you did ought to make such dull old verses
for.'

'Was that the most frolicsome as you could be giving us
on your wedding day? For shame, you doleful bride-groom!'

'He's lost his pluck, see? Broken-in by wedlock a'ready, he
is, poor fellow!'

There was a spurt of laughter and he felt the blood hot in
his face. Gazing into his beloved's eyes, he had dismissed
other hearers; and thus had made a laughing-stock of
himself. For a man has no armour against mockery, but that
of being himself a leader of the laugh; and many, therefore,
who are not themselves fools, learn to provoke foolish mirth
in their own defence.

'Ah, they're glum, are the old married men,' said the blacksmith, triumphant in derision. 'Here's to the jolly bachelors!
Owain o' the sweet voice be not the bard he was!'

'Enough o' that now,' Owain heard his mother command,
in a tone crisp as the crackle of a frosted leaf. 'My boy was
only showing how easy he could cast you down with a grave
song, afore lifting you up with a merry one, see? *I'm*
knowing his artful tricks. Take no heed o' them, neighbours.'
He could feel her standing over him, taut as a cat that is
ready to fly forth and scratch out eyes in battle for its kitten,
or else to drag it by the scruff into safety. A rollicking ballad
of her own youth she ordered him to play, while her fingers
bit into the flesh of his thigh beneath the table; and when
with a shrug he shook himself free of her pinching, her
cracked voice led the chorus.

Before long, good temper was restored and everyone but

Madoc's wife was shouting so lustily that none heard the door open. A dark man stood looking in with a grimace so sinister that at sight of him the widow uttered a shriek. There fell a silence, startling after the cheerful din, and faces were frozen, stiff-set in dismay.

'What's on you, Mother?' cried Owain, at her side in an instant.

''Tis Dan come home, as I made sure was hanging . . .' But at that she shut her mouth fast as a sprung trap.

'You thought wrong, Mother *fach*. Some good Christians do make the mistake o' supposing as what they hope for is true;' and strolling in, Dan leered at one woman after another. He was neither tall nor well-favoured as Owain and Madoc, but he was of great strength and his movements were agile as a rat's. At his belt hung a cudgel and an ill-threatening knife. The guests stared at them and more uneasily still at the bulge in his right-hand pocket which betrayed a pistol. He was dressed in a long riding coat with capes, once a gentleman's but now much weather-stained. 'Have these honest folks scoured your board and drained your barrels? You've a crumb and a suck left, surely to goodness, for your own son? Ah, but there's dull I am, forgetting as you fancied me safe and swinging,' he grinned. 'Well, well, kinsmen may come unbidden, same as ghosts. 'Tis lucky there's been such a mort o' chatter over Owain's strange bride, from none knows where, even I should hear o' this sudden swift wedding o' his.'

'Fetch him whatever's left in the larder. Make haste all,' his mother urged the women who had cleared the table. With haggard face she stood watching as he shook first Madoc then Owain by the hand and slapped them on the back, acting a jovial part.

'You've done well for yourselves, brothers. Rich wives and comely too.'

Madoc's plain matron bridled and, not displeased, suffered him to kiss her on the baggy cheek. Next, he went over to the bride, who was risen and stood quivering like a reed in the wind. He put his blunt-fingered hands on her shoulders and, having looked her up and down to strip the clothes from modesty, kissed her full on the parted lips. Alarm broke out upon the watchful faces as she uttered a small shrill cry. It was as if a wild bird were trapped and fluttering with terror in their midst.

'Leave her alone you,' growled Owain in a fury against his brother for making so bold and against the onlookers for staring amazed at Glythin. He was vexed with her too, because she had not tittered or pouted, accepting a kiss as brides most commonly do.

Dan glanced at him with contempt; but at Glythin he looked evilly. 'You do well to fear me, pretty one; for I'm an arkard enemy,' and turning to Madoc's wife, he added in a tone so smooth that oil seemed to slide from his tongue, 'But a useful friend, Ma'am.' Then he drew his father's chair to the table, sat down quite at home and began to eat. His mother, close-lipped, served him with ale while he plied the Saxon with compliments, the insolence of which she was too vain to perceive.

Though it was the custom at a marriage feast to sing late into the night, the guests soon made excuse and left in a close-pressed bunch; and seeing his mother let them go without a word of hospitable protest, Owain was both affronted and relieved. Madoc now roused his children, who were fallen asleep on the settle, a clot of pink limbs and tousled yellow heads. They rubbed their eyes and whimpered, 'Mammy, why can't we stay?' Made gracious by Dan's flattery, she objected to her husband that they had intended to stop for a day or two; but Madoc, with pushes and frowns, shepherded his flock away. 'No, no. Better not, after all. Too many we are for Mother's small little house. We'll be making a stage o' the journey afore daylight;' and in a few minutes their cart rumbled out of the fold.

Owain knew that he ought to have sped them from the gate, but he dared not leave Glythin alone with Dan, her conduct had been so queer in response to effrontery that asked for no more than a laugh and a shrug. There lolled the villain in the ingle-nook, his mouth twisted in a derisive smile. He was covertly watching her; while she, with bent head, would not once glance his way. He stayed. Night fell. The widow kept adding peat to the fire; and by its light she and Owain exchanged anxious glances, waiting and striving to talk in a natural manner. At last Dan rose and filled his deep pockets with bread and cheese and meat, scornfully thanking them for their kind welcome.

'I'll be calling in again afore long.' His voice reached them as they stood by the threshold, to peer after him into the darkness. 'I'm liking to learn how the newly-wed are faring; and you two be no common couple, indeed.' They heard him laugh, not pleasantly. 'That's a wonderful pretty ring as your bride is wearing, brother – the gold one o' the two, she seemed wishful to hide away, shy as a wren. Many's the coin and trinket I've handled. But never gold *that* colour.'

His horse plunged on the cobbles, striking sparks with its iron shoes. By the sound, they judged it to be a powerful animal. 'That one has galloped a thousand miles from the law,' Owain whispered, and his mother nodded. When the thud of hooves had died away, they hastened to enter their house and to make fast the bar. Having slid it into place across the door from jamb to jamb, they regarded each other with frowns of shared misgiving.

'Ah,' said she, 'this do come o' your not being content with the lot o' others. There's outstanding you had to be, is it? But wasn't I warning you it 'ould bring us into trouble?'

Glythin heard and looked at Owain with eyes so strangely green, though the light from his hearth was hot upon her face, that he seemed to hear the lapping of lake water and to feel a coldness numb his limbs. 'You are not regretting your choice already, my heart?' she asked him, and rose as if she would be gone.

'No, no, no,' he assured himself, taking her hand and leading her towards the stairs. ''Twas only dull folks' cattle-staring and bad ones' malice did draw a veil o' mist, as 'twere, betwixt my eyes and you. Now they are gone, I can see you for what you were to me on the hilltops, and for what you will ever be. And I 'ould not change my rare good fortune, neither for safety nor for comfort. Not for wealth nor honour,' he added, 'though I should prove mistaken who fancied to gain all things through you.' As he spoke these words, her beauty seemed to increase, so that all rewards were his and he added from the heart, 'If you do bring me trouble as well as joy . . .' He paused, not having foreseen that this must prove so. 'Well, never mind,' said he, ''tis worth it a hundred-fold.' But though this was true, he began from the same hour to hope that he might not pay an unlooked-for price for being more favoured than other men.

*   *   *

Henceforth, the widow slept in the room that had been her children's and Owain lay in the big bed where generations of his line had been begotten. Its posts were rough-hewn of oak that had grown upon the land tilled by his forefathers, and its solid comfort gave him ease. When all the secrets of Glythin's white body were known to him and she had answered his passion, first with a bride's yielding and later in an ardent wife's response, he was proud and happy. There began for them, also, by day, a life of labour shared and of gay laughter over trifling things. But she was happier in the open than under a roof. On the slope of the mountain she would sigh and turn back.

'Mother will be needing me in the dairy, my heart. I must leave you. Ah, but 'tis dark in there and golden-bright in the sunshine here with you!'

'Then stay with me, this once, all day,' he urged. 'Take off the shoes she's making you wear and run free over the grass.'

But she was becoming a dutiful housewife, because he wished her to be so, and declared that she must learn to skim cream with a steady hand and to rinse butter so that not a streak of water marred its firmness. Knowing that at this season a woman ought to milk the cows and the restless ewes, curd cheese, stir jam and gather herbs for drying against winter, he let her go. 'Some other time, then, we'll be singing your songs together on the hilltops.' They would keep, he told himself, and meanwhile there was money to be made. But when corn to weed or haymaking kept him near home, he was glad; for then he could enter to rest at noon and have her run to greet him at the door. He would kiss her fingers, stained with purple fruit-juice, and say that they were gloved like any queen's. His mother grumbled at such a pair of children and looked envious; yet she smiled, despite the lonely echo in her heart, 'Why was I doomed to lose *my* joy? Why *mine*?' She grew fond of her daughter-in-law, while complaining much of her odd ways. What was the use of a farmer's wife, she asked, who would not put knife to chicken's throat nor even feather and draw a bird; who ran out of sight with hands to ears whenever a pig was slaughtered and refused to taste black puddings? 'No sense in it!' The girl had learned to bake and brew, to braid her hair tidy and go to church in stockings like a Christian. Why then could she not stomach the shedding of blood? A fine lady you might fancy her one moment – the graces she gave

herself when there was killing to do! Yet the next, she'd be
helping that lump of a bastard boy with a heavy load. 'There's
odd! No proper pride on her, as if she wasn't caring to rise
in life with us!'

The mute, Thomas, was Glythin's slave, following her with
eyes of worship. It angered Owain that she should smile so
kindly on one of no rank, whose lot it was to serve; so he sent
the lad up to the lake-side with the cattle and went there no
more himself. Nor did he sing any longer those songs,
unfettered as the wild swan's flight, of which his mother had
been afraid. But every evening, at his own safe fireside, he
took his father's harp and chanted to Glythin the love-songs
common to his race. Busy at her spinning, she listened with
joy if they were blithe or tender, but when they were sad, a
plaint for trust betrayed, her hands would drop into her
aproned lap and the wheel slow down and cease its soothing
hum. 'There's foolish,' the old woman scoffed at her, 'giving
over your work for some make-believe trashy song, and your
eyes gone swimmy with tears now! Time to weep when
you've sorrow o' your own.' But Owain took it for a tribute
to his singing and was gratified. He stood up, stretching
himself in lazy strength, and pulled his wife to her feet. There
he held her close to him. 'Good-night, Mother.'

'Good-night, both,' the widow muttered, and would not
look at them, for she was envious.

There was none other in the world for Owain when the
door of their room was closed and he watched Glythin let
down her long hair. Pale gold it shone by their candle flame;
or, if he blew this out, silver by moon or star light. When her
shoes and stockings were off and her naked feet, like flower
petals, showed from beneath her white gown, he remembered
that he had wooed one of the Fair Tribe. Then, half eager to
forget it, he took his loving, obedient wife in his arms and
carried her to bed.

Sunday was a day less blessed than others; for at his mother's bidding he must pass through the graveyard with Glythin in her prim best at his side. The neighbours glanced at her askance; and he was sure, as he hurried her into his pew, that behind his back they nudged one another and winked. 'Daring to make mock o' the finest singer amongst 'em,' he thought, suspiciously watching the musicians in the gallery from the chinks between his clasped fingers. After the droning sermon, when the congregation sauntered out to lounge on tombstones and gossip before trudging home, he loitered in the porch, waiting in vain for them to be gone. But though they no longer hailed him friendly nor urged him to favour their merry-makings, they would not let him go his way unmolested. He was wedded to a stranger; and those who mistrusted what they could not comprehend, jeered at him for his marriage.

'My heart,' Glythin whispered in his ear, 'they can do us no harm, so long as we are faithful to each other. Of what are you afraid then?'

'Of every man's opinion,' he might have answered with truth; because, having fed on applause, he hungered for that sugared food, now denied him. Ashamed to own it, he boasted to her that he cared not a straw what anyone thought of him. ''Tis tiresome, though, when I'm singing so grand, to be no longer sought after and to have my house shunned by such deaf fools and blind.' To feel himself different from others by reason of his greater vision had flattered him. It was not so pleasant to be suspected of madness.

'Mother,' he announced, ill-tempered over dinner, 'I 'on't go to church no more.'

'You'll do as I bid you and go regular, you jackass, to show folks as you be respectable.'

Thereafter, the old woman sought occasion to rate Glythin for her childishness and folly. She had put trashy weeds in the best lustre jug; it was wicked to sing a lovesong on the Sabbath; could she not hit the cat when it jumped on the table, instead of giving it milk? 'This water-sprite o' yours be enough to make a bishop curse and swear,' she would complain, including her son in her anger, and often driving him on a Sunday afternoon to stride out of their home in dudgeon. With his elbows on a gate and a stalk between his teeth, he sulked, asking himself how it was that his mother tarnished the beauty of his wife for him, so that what was most rare in her made him ill-at-ease and he increasingly desired her to grow more commonplace? At such times, he recalled none of the songs she had inspired, but dwelt instead on his bachelor companions, rioting home from a fair, the merrier for drink and bragging of the girls whom they had fondled. These were no proper thoughts for a married man. With an effort he held them in check and strolled about his fields to look with satisfaction at the sleek kine. The cows had calved. Next year he would sell bullocks to dealers in the lowlands. His mother and Glythin must make cheese and butter in plenty for market, that money might be stored under the hearthstone while he enclosed yearly more land and hired fresh labour.

At supper-time one Sunday in August, when he had been thus occupied, he entered the kitchen. His eyes, greedy with plans for growing rich, looked only into his bowl. 'Flummery again, Mother? But come you! Soon we'll be eating like gentry, more nor our bellies can hold.'

'Glythin's gone out. I was hoping as she was with you this long while?'

He was taken aback. 'There's careless I am! I did clean forget to ask her was she wishful to come with me.'

They avoided each other's glance, for, having quarrelled over dinner, both felt guilty, though neither would own as much.

'My little one, my little one, come home,' he began to sing in his heart to a small sad tune; and in the late twilight she stole in. Her hair, crowned with wild forget-me-nots, hung loose over her shoulders. She carried her shoes in one hand and from the other there dangled green trails of water-weed. Owain heard the patter of drops upon the flagstones. Like tears of reproach they were; and when the old woman opened her mouth to scold, he was quick to make a gesture of clapping his hand over it.

'No, no, Mother! Not a word!'

She swallowed her indignation, thinking, 'The fool! Lifting his flighty wife's blue-cold fingers, all wet, to his lips! Is he a love-sick lumper then? The Master never treated *me* so soft; not after we were wed.'

'You left us, *cariad*,' Owain said, 'because my thoughts had made you lonely? Dull I was indeed, to let you slip, who are the light o' mine eyes; and without you blindness!'

A smile trembled over her face; and suddenly laughing as though excess of joy had driven her mad, she tore the wreath from her head and flung it about his neck. Flushed with happiness, she rubbed her cheek against his sleeve and ran to kiss his mother. 'Ah, forgive me! I feared . . . For you and he had shut me out with your quarrel.' Her mother-in-law gasped and stared after her as she darted upstairs.

When she came down again, treading sedately from step to step, she looked a meet wife for a farmer, with smooth plaits coiled at the nape of her neck and clean apron, in readiness for washing-up, tied over her dark, Sunday gown. 'There, you see, Owain *bach*! I shall appear even as you desire me.' Smiling and demure, seated opposite her husband, she ladled fresh flummery into his bowl before she filled her own.

*   *   *

That night as she lay warm beside him, Owain asked himself whether this comfort were all that he craved of her. 'Glythin?' he whispered.

She sat up at once: 'You are awake then?'

'Yes, yes. Now I am. Come wide awake, as if . . . as if, I know not . . . Draw you back the curtains, fach. I can see you but dimmed in this small little cramped-in tent.' At once she arose and was at the window so quick that he fancied she might fly out of it. 'Stay you for me,' he cried. 'Wait, *cariad*, I will follow.'

'No need to go from here,' she told him, opening the lattice. 'Look up. There are the hills. How steadfast-calm they abide! And the stars over above them have never put out their tapers; nor ever shall, though night by night we slumber and dream no more, hooded in darkness.'

As he sat upon the edge of their bed and heard her speak thus, there slid over his limbs a chill, sharp with elation; and like a brave man going into battle, he shivered yet was eager. For he was in love again with her cool voice, her white face and the deep shadows under her brows that made her dark eyes of great magnitude, and a point as brilliant as moonshine upon crystals of snow to shine in either of them. Yet he had no wish to touch her; but only to listen, look and worship.

'How my heart is beating,' he said, 'knowing you, once more, for what you are! Give me my harp, quick! You have put into my mind strange thoughts, as when I courted you up yonder.'

She was gone from the room and was back again, it seemed, in one movement. He heard the light running of her naked feet and her gown's flutter, and felt the strings taut beneath the balls of his fingers. Then in a flash he knew the words he must sing and to what melody, both having sounded within him. So he closed his eyes, and, flinging up his head, sang aloud:

'Waking at dawn to labour,
My dreams I put away.
With homely fire rekindled,
My hunger greets the day;
Yet through all tasks and pleasure,
At dusk, in noonday's heat,
Far from my hope and seeing,
I hear the wild wings beat.

But when my limbs are sleeping,
I watch my spirit's flight,
Beyond my narrow window,
Pierce the high roof of night.
Once, at the final issue,
A gleam of angels shone;
Then, at the edge of being,
I shook, and I was gone.'

*   *   *

Throughout the decline of summer, he did not again neglect her. If neighbours at church or market stared him into ill-humour or he and his mother had exchanged high words, he pressed Glythin's hand into the crook of his arm, saying, 'Come you, sweetheart. We'll be strolling up the mountain, you and I.'

She fell into step with him at once, singing the homely songs she had learned from his lips, those that were merriest. Along the steep ridges the turf had burned ripe peach colour and was so slippery that they laughed, holding each other up, like two unsteady skaters. Under a roof she was subdued, less talkative than other women, watchful to serve her husband; but on the open hills where her eyes shone and her hair was blown about, she became gay as a linnet. Sometimes she danced ahead of him, holding up the skirts that trammelled her, until he swore it was a pity to tame so nimble a fawn. Down the stony water-courses, only a trickle moistened the velvet moss, and she would lay her cheek to it, so that if he kissed her face, it tasted cool and wet. Giant bracken fanned over their heads and in its fronded shade she splashed into a shallow pool, sending speckled trout darting for cover beneath the agate stones. 'Catch you this if you can,' she cried, having learned his trick of speech, and flung a shower of glittering drops at him. But though she loved to sport with water, she would never go within sight of the lake; for she knew that he no longer wished to be reminded of it. 'I must forget the place I left to become your wife. Yours is the home I chose, since you could not live in mine; and 'tis perilous to our earthly joy, as you would have it be, if I remember another.'

Curious about her former life, though afraid to dwell on it, at times he asked her questions; but she heard the drag of misgiving in his voice, and smiling, shook her head. 'I have forgotten much, my heart, by living down there with you.'

'Tell me something, whatever?'

'There's useless 't'ould be. While you are afeard to know, there's little I can tell.'

'But look you now, up here, today, far from others, and from Mother most of all, I am fearing no knowledge – none as you can give.'

'Is that true?' She stared past him, her gaze so distant that he regretted his curiosity. Then she hummed a foreign air, that awoke the ghost of dreams, and began beneath her breath to sing.

> 'Still at heart and silent,
> In light unshadowed, calm,
> Deep beneath toss of tempest,
> Safe beyond whirlpool's harm,

Peace waits the soul's escaping
Thought's trivial, fretted death,
Where Time and Space dissolving
Fail in a single breath.'

'That is telling me nothing as I can understand,' he complained.

'The shallow waves pass over,' she sang, smiled at him
again and shook her head. 'I can talk to you, now, only in
words; and they do tell but little, being cups too small to hold
what I 'ould put in 'em . . . 'Tis a kiss you be craving?'

'Yes,' he laughed. 'There's clever to guess, you are!'

'Then take you it.'

*   *   *

The harvest had been garnered and the grain was go to the
mill. Around the fold stood ricks, those of hay a faded green
and those of straw bright golden. Beyond, spread the stubble
fields like a blond beard that is turning white. Owain, leaning
upon his orchard wall, looked down into the valley but could
not see where the river wound for it was veiled in a quiver
of haze, while violet ranges seemed to float upon the pale
horizon. He glanced up at the near mountain, warm and
friendly, ochre and apricot, to watch a load of bracken, red
as a fox's pelt, lumber towards him with groan of drag
beneath wheel. Slackened with labour and well-being, he
flung himself down at the foot of a ladder whose topmost
rungs were hidden among boughs. Sunlight slanted through
dark leaves, making him blink as he stared upwards and
searched for the gloss of apples, rosy or soaplike yellow.
Scarce one remained ungathered. At his feet they were piled
in a coloured pyramid whose odour gave him the pleasant
sharp foretaste of cider. The droning of insects made him

sleepy; yet he would not let himself doze, for he enjoyed watching Glythin in his mother's blue cotton pinafore stoop to pick up windfalls.

For days they had been storing fruit together and he had felt her closer to him, more hot and human even than is shared passion. Secure in happiness, lulled by the peace of companionship, feeling her to be part of his own health and toil and contentment, he had not seen her with outward and observing eye, so near had she been to him. Now, as he watched her busy hands, he noticed for the first time how sunburnt they were grown. Freckles like flower pollen powdered her rounded arms, which were less slender than they had been in spring, her beauty having mellowed with the landscape. Late in September there was a comfort in it, which early in May had been lacking; and as he smiled at his partner, all the wholesome store of earth came to mind, things simple and needful, which formed a song, placid as the purr of her wheel when she sat spinning. He called her to him, bade her sit quiet at his side and sang to her.

> 'Each scented herb in garden,
> Ripe fruit of orchard tree,
> Gold quince, blond pear, red cherry,
> My wealth, I'll share with thee.
>
> Brown crusted loaf from oven,
> Honeycomb, woodbine sweet,
> Curds from a cave-dark dairy,
> Set at thy milk-white feet.
>
> A daisy-chain for necklace,
> A song, a cowslip ball,
> Gifts none but love could value,
> Take, for they are my all.'

When he had done, she nodded and held out her hands to him. 'Fill them, my master.'

'What with, you poor man's mate?' Today he was humble and wished himself rich for her sake only.

'Your own,' she answered. And when he had put his hand into hers, she laid her head on his shoulder and said, 'Next summer I'll be bearing you a child.'

'Next summer?'

'Yes. You'll be seeing.'

He began to laugh, teasing her gravity. 'That's more nor nine months hence. How can you be telling, foolish, if you are not yet quick?'

'Because then I shall be ripe to give birth to your son.' And when he went on playfully to mock her, she asked him, 'I'm no longer the wild thing I was, am I?'

'You are all I could wish for in a wife.'

'Fit, in that case, for mothering your children. And so it shall be.'

He laughed at her no more, but said, 'You're a rare strange creature. Don't you be making me uneasy again now, by predicting over-much.'

But he forgot his moment of disquiet as they went back to the barn, carrying between them a basket laden with apples.

*   *   *

When the days grew short and gales screamed down the dingle, Owain sat snug at night in his chimney corner and plaited a whisket. Thomas, the serving-boy, could shape nothing deftly with his splayed fingers, and was allowed near the hearth only that he might peel hazel wands and pass them to his master. Nobody spoke to the mute, for he had never an answer; but Glythin smiled encouragement to him from time to time, while her mother-in-law grumbled.

'There's not near the warmth in this damp old peat as used to be. You missed to dry en long enough in stack, Owain.'

'The fuel's good enough, Mother. 'Tis your ancient blood's gone cold,' he answered, too intent upon his basket-making to notice that he vexed her.

'True, your turfs are not to blame,' said Glythin in a soothing voice; 'but Mother's right, none the less. Chill it is. I can feel the tempest driving in upon us, as if 't'ould break down our home.'

'Now, who's at the door?' Owain enquired, when above the wind's howl they heard a loud knock – neighbours, he hoped, come back at last to beg for one of his songs.

Glythin went to open; and there stood two unknown men with tossed beards. One was tall and had been fair as Owain, as could be seen from his bleached, tufty hair and fierce blue eyes, though his skin was weathered brown as a gipsy's. The other, a head shorter, looked like a kinsman, too, he also being lean, iron-muscled and bold of glance. Both were in rags and each carried the stick and bundle of a tramp.

'Well, Mother,' shouted the first to thrust his way in, 'still in the same old homestead? A cosy place we were driven from by Saxon squire and keeper!'

'*Dwall* take and roast their souls,' cried his fellow, 'but God bless you, Mother *fach*!'

She started and trembled as first one, then the other, seized her in his arms. Astonishment and joy made her face young again and she began to laugh and to cry, 'Rhys! Gwilym! You bad wicked lads! You good-for-nothing scamps! There's glad I am to see you! Making sure I was as the king's men had killed the both o' you. How were you escaping the villains? Wherever have you been this cruel long while?' She did not wait for an answer but forgetting to be stiff, ran hither and thither fetching food and clothing and talking all the time. 'Dry stockings for your poor flattened feet. The soles o' your shoes worn to paper, a shame to see! The tastiest morsel from the larder, Glythin, quick girl! Ah, but you boys aren't knowing who she is – your brother's wife, indeed; and this be he, Owain, my youngest, not born when you were driven away by those black-hearted tyrants. Not as you didn't deserve it, never heeding your mother's cautions! Are you come back to take your revenge? We'll be planning a rare crafty one, is it? Go you on, Owain, fetch them drink, mun! Don't you stand gauping there, same as a stuffed scarecrow! There's lapped in comfort all your born days you've been, and gone too idle, I shouldn't wonder, to lift food to your mouth or to father a child now.' She was angry with him because, year in year out, she had poured upon him alone the love and care she had yearned to spread over her seven sons. 'Make haste, you swamping great sluggard, and draw ale for your betters! Plenty of it, mind,' she commanded, and, thrusting a jug into his hands, pushed him, as if he were a disgraced child, towards the door. 'Now sit you down at table, my dears, my little ones, and tell me all.'

It was a tale of many adventures which they related far into the night, of flight across the sea in fear of transportation, and how, in hatred of the English gentry, they had served in the French army. The patient mute gaped at them, uncomprehending, as they described murderous battles and the drunken sack of cities. Glythin turned pale; but when they boasted of loot, their mother's lidded eyes opened wide and rekindled.

'You came home laden then? Where have you stowed your riches?'

They glanced at each other, unabashed, and laughed. 'In the lap o' women not to be named afore you, Mother *fach*, nor the boy's wife here; and in treating our comrades like men. A soldier isn't hoarding what he do gain, same as a timid farmer, look you. We were spending free – blood, strength and coin. *That* be the way to live.'

'Improvident,' muttered Owain, smarting under their

patronage. 'The parson 'ould denounce the both o' you for evil-doers.'

'The *parson*!' They roared with laughter, making him wince in confusion at what he had said.

'There's something uncommon gallant in living open-handed,' he admitted later, when he had listened for hours to their swaggering talk and had studied their handsome faces. Was it envy, admiration or disapproval which they chiefly provoked in him? He scarce knew what he felt, except a desire to sing at the top of his voice; for always when the heart of another set his own beating to a new rhythm, he must find vent in song. These men did not look sly as Dan the robber did. They spoke without rancour of foes whom they had killed. With captives they had shared their food; and not even an Englishman did they hate if he were a stout fighter. They had a noble love of freedom, Owain conceded, and would never betray it for gain, but were ready to die avenging their country's wrongs. Before the evening was over, he had begun to wonder whether his life were not tame, maybe even unmanly? In a mood of dissatisfaction, he snatched up his harp and burst into the fiery songs to which the Welsh had marched in bygone ages. Then he sang the passionate dirges that women of his race had wailed over their slain; and tears trickled down the creases in his mother's cheeks. In the soldiers' eyes, too, they shone; for Rhys and Gwilym were no more ashamed of grief than of unbridled mirth, or lust or rage. Only cowardice they despised, and caution and thrift.

While Owain sang on, heartened by their applause, Glythin, troubled and aloof, sat gazing at him. She had never before heard him sing in praise of hatred and vengeance; and at midnight, when they were gone to bed and he laid his hand upon her breast, she trembled and hid her face in the pillow.

'What ails you, *cariad*?' he asked. 'Was I stirring all hearts over-much?' He smiled to himself in the darkness. 'There's grand I was singing, indeed!'

'But not *our* songs,' was all that she would say. 'Your brothers have changed you.'

'Go on!' And he silenced her with a kiss less gentle than a lover's.

*   *   *

The vagrants stayed at the farm winter-long, though often they would be gone for days at a time, returning with game they had poached and tales of brawls in taverns. Their laughter and swearing was loud in the fold whenever they helped to fodder the cattle; and with them, nightly, their mother was fierce in talk of Saxon tyranny. They petted her till she grew lively in their company, declaring that the martial songs they caused Owain to sing revived the brave blood of her youth. And because this made him jealous, Owain sang more than ever; but now it was nothing save to their warlike taste. To Glythin they were courteous, praising her beauty as if it were too pure for any man to desire. If either of them gave her a kiss, as Dan had done, it was no more than a brother's, and she shrank back so little that it went unobserved.

In the new year she was with child and Owain became as proud as if he had made a new song, but he wished that she had not foretold the future, for he desired to forget in what way she differed from the wives of other men.

Once again the old woman was in a fume of importance, rustling in coffers and shaking out the garments which her children had worn. 'Owain. Glythin. Come you on here. Look at the fine fancy stitches I was putting in them small little tucks. Ah, my young eyes was good, then! None could best me with a needle.' Despite the mother's wish to make all new for a first-born, she would have her grandchild wear what she herself had made. 'Now then, girl, leave you it all to me,' was the phrase most often upon her lips. The smell of bees-wax and turpentine tanged the kitchen as she polished the cradle with its worn rockers. She talked of how she had been brought to bed of *them* and of their infancy, until the men were wearied of both topics and winked at one another behind her back. 'If the neighbours 'ont call in passing, on account o' your wife being strange,' she told Owain, 'they'll come willing enough when I bid them to a grand christening – the greedy carrion crows!' And every day she planned a more lavish bill of fare. Since the white kine were bringing in money, she hired a servant-girl and enjoyed rating her from morning till night.

Glythin had little to say in the house where she performed with tranquil obedience whatever tasks were set her, seeming in such matters to have no will of her own. But when spring breezes blew the mist from the hill-tops, and grass, sparkling with moisture, began to sprout afresh, she went out for many hours and wandered from field to field, singing in a low voice to herself. At such times her face had a charmed beauty which Owain was loth to disturb. She would stand to watch him ploughing and, when he turned the oxen at the end of a furrow, would smile and put into his hand a posy that he did not know what to do with. As he thrust it into his shirt against his sweating chest, she went her way, leaving him sorry to find how soon her wild flowers faded.

Primroses came first in sheltered hollows where young oak leaves fluttered yellow-green: after them, violets, without scent, on every bank, and daisies, sprinkling the pastures white. Later, the woods sloping down to the valley were sweet with bluebells that spread like pools of water reflecting a cloudless sky. The windflowers trembled among them and brazen glossy kingcups flaunted from marsh and ditch. Then came forget-me-nots and fragrant cowslips, purple campion, ragged-robin and etched orchis, ladylike mauve cuckoo-pint, bold dandelions and all the pied blossoms and feathered grasses of fields put up for hay. Along the hedges dog-roses blushed pink and the air began to taste of honeysuckle.

Through this scented splendour Glythin followed the stream down the dingle until she could hear the deeper note of the river far below, a steady strong lullaby. Among the water-side ferns she would seat herself and rest so still for such a while that birds came fluttering close to her, unafraid, and butterflies lit on the bunch of flowers in her lap. The tiny tickle of insects running over her wrists did not make her move; and sometimes a green or a mottled-brown spider spun a thread of gossamer across her eyes. She did not leap into any pool or frolic with water as she had done before she carried Owain's child; but moving more slowly as the months went by, took a lover's care of the life that burdened her swelling body.

* * *

One evening in June, when her time was near, she could no longer sit at her spinning for discomfort and rose to pace about the kitchen, holding to table and dresser for support.

'Whatever's making you so caged-beast restless?' Owain asked, as he looked up from the halter he was mending, to find her gone from her place. If he was not singing battle songs, he was always at work now in the house; for he was disturbed by his brothers' presence and, like her, could not repose. Therefore it was with a prick of impatience that he repeated, 'What's making you back-and-fore like a chained wild vixen?'

'Waiting,' she murmured, looking past him through the open door. 'How mortal women do have to wait and wait –

for life when they are young; and then for death; and at all times for the love without which they know themselves to be but naught!'

As she spoke, she glanced in compassion at his mother, dozing by the fire, her mouth dropped open. Like a slug's track, spittle glistened down the wrinkled chin; and Owain, following the turn of his wife's eyes, said, 'Well, she has had her day. My father loved her once.'

'And now she's ahunger to be first in *your* life.'

'You are that, *cariad*.'

'I know; and I do pity her.' Thinking to comfort Glythin he grasped her arm as she went by.

'No, no,' she told him, gently freeing herself. 'This, which you desired of me, is a thing we cannot share. But with your mother I can share it, now that I, too, am knowing what she has known; for you willed me to be a woman like any other . . . Here come your brothers; and they be closer company for you than I, this while.'

Rhys and Gwilym strode in and their mother awoke to enquire with a gossip's relish what news they brought from the valley. 'Who's to be wedded, bedded or buried? Be there any new quarrels or bastards on the parish,' she chuckled, 'biddings or prospects o' merrymaking? Aged as I am, I could do with a randy, boys. Food is still making the mouth water, though the feet have ceased dancing to music.'

But they were both in fury, having heard that one whom Rhys had beaten in fair fight was stirring up the magistrates against them. 'The crafty coward,' swore Gwilym. 'We'll not shift from here till we've stopped his traitor's tongue from wagging. After that, Mother, maybe we'll have to slip off over the hills to sea.'

'But surely to goodness,' she cried, 'the old English gentry can't prove nothing against you? Not now, boys? 'Twas years ago, and you two harmless innocent lads when you killed one o' their keepers by mischance; and a good job, too!'

"Tis said, this time, as we're in league with our brother Dan – a common thief they be looking for to hang, and we honest soldiers that have run many a man through the body but 'ould scorn to pick a pocket!'

'The wicked lie! And you two living here as respectable as churchwardens, doing nothing only a small little bit o' poaching; and in *that* you've not been found out!'

Owain and his mother lashed themselves into rage at such injustice and began to threaten a pitiless revenge.

'I'll come with you, boys,' he shouted, snatching down his father's cudgel from among the flitches of bacon on the cratch slung from the ceiling. They should no longer taunt him for being a timid husbandman. He would prove himself as valiant and reckless as they were, and thus gain their respect.

But his mother clutched at his sleeve. 'Not so hasty, mun. Leave you vengeance to me, *bach*. A worse one 'twill be, look you.' The creased lids came down yet lower over her eyes, till they were slits of night. 'Tallow I'll be taking as I'm moulding candles of; and when 'tis warmed soft, you shall tell me the shape o' this villain. Then I'll form an image o' him . . .'

'Holt, Mother,' exclaimed Rhys, 'I'll have naught to do with killing a Christian by magic, not though he were my foxiest enemy, see? 'Tisn't right. I am having my principles. No, no! We'll knock out his brains, like decent men, with a stick.'

She went on muttering, however, and rocked from foot to foot as if her brittle body were working up strength for a cat's spring on a mouse. 'Before a raging hot fire I'll set en to dwindle away; not all at once, mind you. The man as do wrong my sons shan't die easy nor swift. Strike him senseless with a stick, is it? Too merciful you are indeed now. Day by day I'll put en on the hob for a spell; and I'll watch en shrink and shrivel, and all the while say curses I learned off o' my

Grannie. When I loved your father the tender way I did, 'twasn't for nothing I was storing every word o' murderous hate, lest man or woman should dare hurt the one I cherished. No, indeed! You'll see! You'll see! The Judas 'ull weaken in his flesh as the tallow do sink; and when 'tis clean dripped away, his hell-black soul shall leave his wasted body. I'll make his own wife and bedfellow turn from him in a cold sweat.' She laughed and bared her teeth, so that they saw the gaps between them and her pale gums as she reefed her upper lip in a snarl. So changed was she by hatred, her sons stared at her amazed. 'I'll show you,' she nodded, holding her little body erect and quivering, 'as a woman's vengeance, nursed day and night in her deep heart, can work more mischief nor ever a strong man's blows.'

And Owain, though he was not sure if this were true, felt his heart beat in unison with hers; for he, also, desired, by one means or another, to be of importance, so that none should say, 'Whether he loves or hates, is pleased or angry, makes no odds to the world.' But Rhys and Gwilym held obstinately to their soldiers' code; and while the four took counsel together, debating whether witchcraft or plain murder were best, Glythin stood with her back to the wall, watching her husband's face. Her cheeks were white as milk.

'On a dark night,' said Owain, 'if we were to bury the corpse . . .'

She shuddered and stole out alone into the summer's twilight. No one saw her go, except the simpleton, Thomas. The servant-girl had been sent upon an errand and he was waiting in a corner for his supper, his patient face vacant, his eyes, like a cow's, void of wonder, staring at the savage talkers. After the gentle mistress whom he worshipped had gone, he arose and lumbered out to see her weighted figure toiling up the dingle. Timid as a dog that has been left behind and fears rebuke, he followed at a distance, stopping whenever she paused to gather strength. In his dim way he understood that she was troubled, love making the poor fool wise. It was night and the enclosed air grown hot within the house, when he lumbered in again.

Owain was shouting above his brothers' wrangle, "Tis folly, I'm telling you, to set on a man near the toll gate . . .' He broke off and swore at the mute for tugging at his coat. 'What's on you, mun, pushing in where you're not wanted? Get by, fool! Loose me go!' Thomas held tight and Owain in a rage at his insolence struck him across the mouth. He reeled backwards and tears flooded his mild eyes. Still he clung to the hem of his master's garment and tried to drag him towards the door. 'Are you mad, boy? Chained up, is it, you want to be?' But it was plain that he was not pestering for his supper, since with his disengaged hand he kept pointing out of the doorway. 'Can something be amiss then? *Dwall* take the idiot lumper for keeping no tongue in his head!'

Seeing his odd behaviour, the widow, in fear for her property, forgot to hate and ceased to plot revenge. 'The cattle stolen maybe? Follow him, Owain,' she exclaimed. 'Quick, boy. 'Tis something serious, see?'

There was no need for her warning. Owain was already seized by terror. 'Glythin! Where is she? Who's been seeing her this long while? She'd passed clean from my mind while you was all talking this trash.' He called her name, making it ring through the house; but there was no answer and Thomas strove to force him into the fold. 'He's knowing where she is, look you. Good boy! Good boy! Make haste! She's likely in travail. Lead me to her. Be sharp about it. Come on, all o' you. Come on at onst and help now.'

He rushed out into the darkness, urging Thomas to go faster than his clumsy legs would carry him and calling to his brothers to fetch a lantern. Their shouts sounded far below him as he ran uphill, '*Hell-o-o-o*, there! *Hell-o-o-o*! Where are you?' long drawn-out as the hooting of owls.

'*Heear*. Up *heear*. Bring you the light.'

He saw it twinkle, starlike, out of the gloom, the night being heavily overcast, so that the mountain and sky were scarce to be divided, both black as the pit of his dread. Ahead of him something white began to loom, a ghost, he thought in panic, and then remembered that high up among the hills, the hawthorn trees bloomed late. It was to one of them that Thomas led him. He smelled the almond sweetness of its bridal canopy, while its thorns stabbed his groping hands and cruelly scratched his wrists. The one whom he loved, but had forgotten in his hatred, was hiding from him here. He heard her groan, and kneeling down beside her, he broke into a sob. 'Why were you leaving me, *cariad*? Whyever were you fleeing from me to bear our child alone upon the mountain, far from my house?'

'The white flowering trees,' she answered faintly. 'They are not ugly with anger.'

'Come you on home with me, *fach*,' he implored. 'Only come home in trust, and my roof shall be sheltering you. There shall nothing hurt nor distress you there, from this day forth, my love.'

He lifted her up and carried her with aching tenderness downhill; and though she seemed more heavy than an image of lead, who had once been light as a leaf, and the labour was a torment, he would not allow the others to touch her. The burden that he had brought upon himself should not be lessened. He, alone, must know its weight as she clung to him and stifled her groans against his shoulder.

His mother met them with a shaking candle in her hand, for once as silent as she was afraid. When her son's wife was laid upon the bed in which she, also, long ago, had given birth, she hissed an order, 'Leave you her to me, boy', and the stranger maidservant, with important face, thrust him out of his own room, as much as to say that all of her sex were priestesses in whose terrible rites of pain a man was unworthy to take part. But he would go no farther off than the head of the stairs, where he crouched, shuddering at every sound of his beloved's anguish. Had she not told him truly at their betrothal that from henceforth neither of them might suffer without the other?

In the grey of dawn, a day and a night later, Glythin was delivered of a son. And after the women had done running to and fro, swishing water, tearing linen and calling out to the father that it was a fine boy, they let her have the new-washed child, bidding her take heart from the bleating cry of life at its outset. She was too weak to lift even so small a load; but she contrived to curl her arm in protection around the child; and when his blind mouth began to seek her breast, the milk flowed warm at need. So touched was she to learn this response of flesh to flesh in natural loving-kindness, so glad and weary, that she wept.

'Not now,' her mother-in-law scolded, standing over her, haggard with watching through the hours of struggle, but over-proud as yet to feel fatigue, ''tis safely done with, girl. What be you crying for?'

Not for a while could she answer, but lay still, feeling milk, blood and tears steep from her tired torn body. Then she murmured, 'This it is to be a woman, even as my love ordained I should become. As a woman, now I am whole, having felt to the full.' After that she slept.

* * *

He had been afraid that she might die. In peril he prized her more than he had done in safety. So, while she lay abed, he would not be drawn into the fury of his brothers against their foes; but, having laboured as he must, spent quiet hours in contemplation of his blessings. The child of love's union growing day by day in a still room, caused the angry voices without to seem of no more account than the distant buzz of wasps. Let others whet their quarrels on the grindstone of talk. For him, to look into Glythin's face was to be purged of malice and trouble.

She was paler than she had been as a maid, and no longer wayward as April. Suffering had refined the June strength given her by wedded happiness; and as health stole back, the harvest of joy and pain made her mortal beauty ripen towards its August.

'You are in all ways now the woman I longed for,' he said. And if, by summer's gain, he had lost any part of spring's secret, he was too well satisfied to perceive it.

'My brothers be gone,' he told her one day, relieved for her sake that it was so. 'You'll be hearing no more talk o' bloodshed and battle; and I'll be singing only songs to your taste. The traitor as informed against them was found half dead by his door. None can prove who was to blame; but Rhys and Gwilym taking no risk o' the gallows, are fled out o' the country.'

'So that's why Mother sent the servant-girl to tend me?'

'Yes, indeed, *fach*. I forbade her to come near, vexing you with lamentations.'

'Poor mortal! So old and yet so burning! She do love her flesh and blood and do cruelly hate those that cross them.'

'She will love our son something tremendous. You'll see.'

'Yes, she will love him. Because he is her grandchild.'

Owain was elated when he carried his wife down to the kitchen and saw her rock the cradle his mother had polished in expectation. But having lost her two runaways, the old woman declared she lacked heart for the christening of which she had chattered with so much relish. Yet she disliked her daughter-in-law's wish to have the child baptized in quiet. 'Same as a pauper bastard! No, no. That 'ould never do for my son's eldest; and a boy, look you.'

So the junketing was delayed week after week, sheepshearing, hay and corn harvest serving for pretext, until the parson spoke his mind. 'You are risking an unredeemed infant's death, denying an innocent his hope of heaven.'

Then the grandmother, flying out on him like an old hen whose chick is attacked by a carrion crow, forgot to fret for her absent sons. 'There's a spiteful nasty thing to say, mun! Did you ever see a more harmless babe? Nor one less like to die, shame on you! Isn't he coming o' the lusty stock I reared? The Master's hatch and mine weren't cankered with no decline, like many as I could name, see? And if he *should* be taken, who's to dare tell me as the Lord 'ould burn him in hell, for nothing only to pleasure some sour old English-speaking clergy?'

'Hush, Mother, hush,' Glythin whispered, laughter in her eyes; and the parson clapped his shovel hat upon his wig and stalked out of the house, striving to achieve dignity.

'Well, well,' said the widow, when by spitting she had cleared her mouth from the taste of wrath, 'we'll be having the neighbours to a Christian feast then. But only them as can be trusted, mind; for my poor wronged boys be hidden – I, alone, am knowing where. I'll be sending word to them by Owain; and they shall come home-along for an hour, whatever, to relish the champion fare I must be wasting on others. Greedy old rooks, they are, pecking up the food that's belonging to my brood!'

She scoured and cooked and chattered in a temper, never appeased until the maidservant wept and Owain banged the table and shouted at her, 'Stay your scolding now, for mercy's sake!' But Glythin carried her child out to the sunlit stubble fields where a covey of partridges hid, and into the shady pastures, whose hedgerow trees were thick in August leafage, to show him the white kine. They breathed at him in pleasant fashion and let her pass unharmed close to their savage horns.

She seemed so tranquil and glad with her child in her arms, that Owain marvelled to find her grave to the verge of sorrow when all were merry at the christening supper. Why should she, who could be sparkling-bright as a May morning when alone, fall silent as frost in a crowd? Gossip, jesting and rivalry put most women on their mettle. It drove her to retreat within herself; and he wished his wife to shine before the world, that she might do him credit. 'There's lovely she is,' he told himself, 'more nor any female present; and her beauty be of a sort that's uncommon rare, too. Yet I, that am married to her and have the rights of a husband, am not envied as is my due. Whyever not, I do wonder?' And of a sudden, in his vexation because the crowd were hostile to her whom they did not understand, his own love was tainted with hostility.

'What's making you so glum?' he whispered in her ear as he thrust between table and wall to replenish tankards.

'The terrible words spoken in church about original sin,' she murmured, and looked down in pity at the infant nestled in her lap. 'Must this little blossom, ready to open natural as a flower-bud to the sun, be taught to credit such dark imaginings? They do wrong the mercy o' God, whom man has created jealous, even in man's own image.'

This was no time to reason with her about what his church taught and folk were wise to accept but not to dwell upon. Displeased that she should disturb him with her fancies, he passed her by to converse with others on cheerful humdrum topics. If her presence made him ill-at-ease in company, he must put her out of mind. Resolutely, he joked with this dullard and that on the sly scandal from taverns and the sharp bargains struck at market; and soon he had forgotten her, himself laughing with the rest at the expense of those who had been cheated of love or wealth, or made by some other mortification to look diminished. The cruelty that lurks within common humour reared up, snake-cold, behind his outward goodfellowship.

When Rhys and Gwilym entered, ragged and unshorn, there was a stir and the guests changed their tune, seeking favour with their host by vowing in assumed indignation that a wrong had been done to honest men. The outlaws ate like wolves and Owain served them plentifully with liquor; but this did not make them of good cheer. It kindled their rage, so that the deeper they drank, the fiercer grew their threats against the oppressors of the Welsh. First one man and then another was stung by the whip of their words to recall a tale of injustice; and all agreed that gentry and clergy were Saxon at heart, even such as bore the names of a nobler race.

The room by now was become oven-hot from a cooking fire and hazed with fumes of fried bacon and pipe smoke. Since afternoon, thunder had rumbled overhead along the echoing mountains, and clouds, stiff-piled as curded cream, towered in a hard blue sky. Night came on, aswelter. The little window was shut. Against its panes, with the first clap of the storm, big raindrops thudded. The door burst open; and there, harsh-lit in a flash of lightning, stood Dan. In his left hand he grasped the reins at which his horse was tugging. Owain saw the powerful black animal plunge and rear. The whites of its eyes were crescent moons rolled from side to side and its stretched nostrils quivered, red within, like embers in the hollow of a coal.

'Make haste from here,' cried Dan. 'No time, you fools, to loiter! There's a warrant out against the both o' you. Up, quick, and off to go!' Rhys and Gwilym sprang to their feet. Chairs crashed on the stone floor and the startled guests stared in dread at the weapon levelled upon them. They crowded together behind Owain. But Dan mocked them when his mother alone ran forward to offer him drink. 'No need to fear me, you meek sheep, driven to slaughter by your betters. 'Tis for armed men and valiant, I'm keeping my powder and shot; and I was willing to risk capture by coming here to warn my kinsmen. I 'ouldn't do so much, not for the small little cash in *your* poor pockets.'

'Good lad,' cried his mother, delighted that at last she could savour kissing him with pride; and tears of gratitude shone in her brightened eyes.

But he, in return, snatched her tankard of ale, drained it, flinging back his head, and with the hairy wrist of his pistol hand wiped the froth from his mouth. His lips were so long and narrow they put Owain in mind of a knife wound. He admired and disliked his brother, and in glum envy of his swagger, watched him, agile as a hunted rat, twist about and spring on to his restive horse. With curb and blow he mastered it, the cruelty and the courage of the man made plain by his use of spurs; and in a minute he was gone into the pit of night before another dazzle of lightning left the cowed onlookers blinking.

When Rhys and Gwilym were run out after him and their mother had burst into sobs and imprecations, the neighbours herded round Owain. Lest they should be thought cowards, they professed to be more furious than ever against the ill-usage of his brethren. It was an hour before the storm abated and they staggered away half drunk, praising his hospitality. The blacksmith was the last to go; and he was ripe for mischief, because no one had pressed him to sing nor sniggered at his jests. He swayed from one door post to the other, leering back into the room where the widow sat bowed, drying her eyes on a crumpled apron. The servant-girl was piling dirty dishes into a tub held by the mute Thomas, while Owain scowled, impatient for noise and disorder to be over. His head ached. He was sulky. This had not been such a christening as he had warrant to hope for, with less favoured men paying court to him and girls begging to hear his far-famed songs. Always, it seemed, since his marriage, he was doomed to be slighted in company.

'Pity indeed,' said the blacksmith, 'as you did fail to make one single ring out o' your stubborn iron and her queer uncommon gold.' His red face, where it burned through greying whiskers, was puckered with insolence.

'What's that you are saying, mun? What ring? You're drunk, no doubt.'

'Sober enough to see, whatever. But who be so mole-and-worm-blind as a fond young husband? That stranger wife o' yours is taking no part in your troubles. Gone she is from here at the first hint o' warning.'

'Gone?' exclaimed Owain, made aware by this gibe that she was not in the room.

'Oh-aye. Stole out of the house, she did, a while ago; taking your infant child with her, too, out into this dousing old tempest.'

Was she mad? Owain asked himself, to do such a thing? Would she desert him whenever there was fear or discord in his home to turn his mind from herself? That she would prove exacting she had not sought to hide from him when he had courted her; but having been stung by a mischief-maker's taunt, he blamed and almost hated her for conditions he had been eager, once, to accept. With a curse on his lips and in his heart accusation, he ran to the stable and saddled his pony. The rain fell thick and straight as though God were pouring tepid water on to the earth, meaning to drown all creation but frogs and fishes; and a rank steam was rising from the midden when he mounted. There was an ill taste in his mouth. He slammed-to the gate behind him and in drenching darkness rode up the mountain. Nothing could he see for the smart in his eyes, but he knew which way to take, having climbed it often to seek her in eagerness and

hope. *Dwall*! Whyever had he brought this fair but perilous
creature into his daily life? No bard, he told himself, should
marry her to whom he sang. Marriage was ordained for
comfort. He ought to have made her love-songs but wedded
a girl of common clay.

At length, in a blink, he saw her figure, a shadow, ahead
of him; and kicking his labouring pony into a gallop, he
shouted after her. 'Can't you bide beneath a roof on such a
night? Aren't you an 'oman o' reason?'

At the sound of his harsh voice, she fled from him. But
he overtook her and in careless haste, as he vaulted down,
struck her shoulder with his stirrup iron. With a low moan
she stood still. He heard the rain falling, falling, as if one
wept in grief too steady for passion, a grief that nothing
evermore could assuage. Drowned deep beyond fear, hope
or chance of consolation, her body did not even shudder
against his own, but leant upon it motionless and heavy as
a corpse.

'That is once,' she said. And in the dank gloom he saw the
pallor of her hand close to his eyes with forefinger upraised.

At that, terror gripped him and he felt the trap-bite of
contrition, at pain of which a man cries out against himself,
'Why was I doing this? Now it can never be undone.' He
strained her to him, exclaiming, 'Oh, my beloved! My beloved!
What hurt have I caused you? Say as 'tis not so great?'

'You have struck me in anger and with iron,' she told
him sorrowfully. 'Now the first part of the curse has come
to pass.'

In the desperate clutch of his arms he strove to make sure
of possession, knowing that men in like agony have held
their dear dead and have begged in vain for response. 'No,
no! For pity's sake, tell me as 'tis not true! 'Twas accident
only. I never was intending . . . I do swear it. I do love you
dearly. 'Tis torment to *think* only o' such loss as that 'ould

be. I will never cease to cherish you, as God be my witness; never, from this wicked cruel hour.'

'Save when you do forget,' she murmured. And laying her head on his breast, she wept for a long while in small strangled sobs as if her heart must break.

When he set her on his pony and led her home with their sleeping child in her shawl, he felt his own hot tears mingle with the cold rain on his face.

Autumn

Because he had forgotten her warning and had broken faith with her once, there slid through Owain's Eden the Serpent of fear. He was afraid of fear, which breeds upon itself; so his will was set to prove it, if not gone, then hidden. When his mother complained that her grandchild's eyes were water-green and their gaze elfin, he laughed, though ill-at-ease, and bade her touch the dimpled limbs. Were they not sturdy, no different from another well-grown child's? Did not the rogue crow when tossed and suck his thumb as babies will, falling asleep, flushed and full fed? If Glythin, bending over the cradle, sang to a foreign stave words that were not familiar, he at once took up his father's harp and thrummed a lullaby. 'Listen now. This is the tune Mother learned off o' her Grannie. I'll be teaching it you.' Obedient in all things, she sang it after him, and the placid spinning songs he taught her and the one she must chant to make the cows give down their milk. She repeated the rhymes of the seasons, from May Day's revelry to the harvest hymn of thanksgiving and the catches the young folk chorused by candlelight on All-hallows Eve. 'That is well,' said Owain, putting his arm around her. 'At last we are having each one o' our songs in common. I'm giving you the first verse and you're answering me with the second. Like a pair o' wood-turtles, we can be keeping it up day-long and never change note nor fail to know what's coming.'

With a gesture that was eager, yet timid of rebuff, she caught at his hand as if minded to cry out, 'Is it enough, this life without a poet's adventure, which you have chosen of late?' But her hands dropped to her sides and the question to which she feared his answer was never asked. As the months passed, it ceased even to lurk in her glance, unless some restlessness within himself evoked it.

'My wife is shaping wonderful well,' he told his mother.

'More tidy nor what I had hoped for, whatever, seeing how wild she were. But if she's coming on, 'tis my doing, indeed now, not yours, boy.'

'I'm not the idle dreamer I was, Mother, fair play to me.'

'Well, well, you're growing a bit more sense with age like,' she conceded. 'But you could do with a cropful yet, mind.'

He laughed at her and, going about his work, dismissed the subject.

After the manner of women in whom the love of husband flows outward, like firelight from the hearth, to warm their children also, Glythin grew pensive when the time came for her first-born to be weaned; and this seemed natural to Owain. Hearing her wistful singing from within the house one evening as he dug the garden, he guessed that his mother and the maid were gone to the dairy to churn, the kitchen window being open, sure sign that Glythin sat alone, close to the sill.

'What's that?' he called, leaning to rest his folded arms on the handle of his tool. Receiving no reply, he peered into the twilit room, in which profound stillness seemed to be enclosed, as if it were something solid. 'Sing it again, *fach*,' he commanded. ''Twas recalling . . .? I am forgetting what.'

Out of the shadows, her eyes looked up at him, a mirror to the clear sky which shone pale with the last of the afterglow to westward, blue overhead and in the east duck-egg green. He could not tell what mood lay behind her gaze. Was it one of repose and completion or of regret? For a moment he was anxious. 'Sad, is it, you are?'

She shook her head and bent over their child who slept

against her bosom, wrapped in the shawl that was wound about her body. Then she made as if to nibble the crest of yellow down above the drowsy forehead. The caress was playful and fond as that of a mare nuzzling her foal and Owain was reassured by one so universal; but when she looked up again and far away beyond him, out to the darkening hills, he was aware of disquieting memories.

'Well? Sing it to me, can't you?'

So, in a low voice, rocking the infant, she sang:

> 'While the limbs of lover
> Lie close and warm at rest:
> While the lips of nursling
> Are soft upon my breast,
> The voyage is suspended,
> Forgotten is the quest.'

'That is how it should be,' Owain broke in, lest she should utter more to disquiet him. 'Come you, 'tis time as you cooked my supper, girl. Moody you're growing, sitting there by yourself; and cold, too, beside an open window. Shut you it, quick, or Mother'll be taking on when she do come back to find the house blown through with air.' He smiled at her, however, and leaning in, patted her arm before she obeyed him. 'There's white as the May blossom you are in the dusk! None fairer. But 'tis pity as you don't keep the kitchen as warm as what Mother is doing. Warmth at his hearth, that's what a man is desiring, onst he is wed and settled.'

This was his main wish in life, that she should stay more fair than other women but be in kind as they were, the compliant wives, content and busy, tamed to their husbands' pleasure, untroublesome companions, smiling at board, a ladle in the hand that deftly served, in bed most loving when desired, in public modest, cause for pride but never spur to jealousy, at all times tender and good-humoured.

Since he would have her so, Glythin became a housewife, gentle and active, humouring his mother, steady in her tactful ordering of his home, so that he heard the clock tick hour after hour as the old woman dozed beside the fire. There were no quarrels in the kitchen, as heretofore; for the Master's word was law and the maid, like humble Thomas, readily served the kind young Mistress, a smile of ungrudged obedience answering that of civil command. If the widow awoke to rail at her son, Glythin was there to signal him into patience or else to turn attention to the grandchild. 'Look, Mother, Nant is bringing you a flower. See how sure on his feet he is. 'Twas you held his hand when he ventured his first step. Aren't you proud o' your pupil?' She called him, 'Nant, my little brook,' though he had been given names from Scripture at the font. And once in a while, when her day's work was done, Owain, going the round of his growing herd, found her leading the boy through the fields.

'What be you showing him there among the ditchside docks and nettles?'

'Herbs to make simples for a dozen ails.'

'Go on! He's over young to tell one from t'other. Best bring him in. Your feet are wet with dew, look.'

Or he would hear her voice float down from the moun- tainside and would frown because she sang that which he had not taught her. But rarely did she thus shake his growing sense of security. Only once, when they had been together for hours, toiling in a thundery heat to carry the last loads of hay, she let go her rake and with a rebel look flung up her arms. They were so strong and sunburnt that he recalled their slim whiteness with regret. Then, quick as thought, in a virgin gesture, she ran her fingers through her hair and tossed it loose about her.

'You be tired,' he said in composed affection, laying his hand upon her shoulder, as a man pats a restive horse. 'Come you. We've been doing well; and better nor ever we shall be sleeping tonight.'

But unheeding, she looked past him, away to the threatening clouds, and said, as if speaking to herself, which made him lonely, 'Cool drops will patter on the poor maimed stubble and it will whisper low. Soon, they will come showering in plentiful refreshment. A steam will arise from the parched earth and it will be softened, grateful, like a woman loved, ready again for bearing. Green growth! Green, sweetly green, and young and wet!' Her voice rose so eager in its youthful outbreak that Owain stared at her in dumb amazement. 'Rivulets flowing where now we stand on dusty barren soil. Swift, singing, free, alive! Ah, how dead is this hedge-bound field, how dry this sorry cut grass, these shrivelled ghosts o' flowers that cattle will chew! Tonight I shall run out into the rain and lift up my face for heaven to bathe, and feel the glad wet land rejoice beneath my naked feet. And I shall live again.' Then, looking at him with challenge in her quickened face, she asked in a voice louder than he had heard her use for many months. 'Will you come with me? *Will* you?'

'Whatever's on you?' he exclaimed, gripping the smooth wooden shaft of his rake. 'Were you not happy, then, at my side all day?'

'I am happy, now, because the rain is coming.'

'Not because you are with *me*, girl?' He was hurt and asked in a tone of reproach, 'Am I not kind to you?'

Her gaze came down from the clouds and the smile she gave him was loving; but a little mockery lurked within the curves of her lips. 'Kind? Yes, indeed. Kind as mortal man could be.'

'Still, you are not content?' he grumbled.

'Ah, how you do love that word! Content! Content!' she derided him.

'You be brimful o' whims today. What is it more you're wanting?'

'Nothing, my heart. Unless,' she faltered, 'there is ought you miss?'

'No. I am happy. You do make me so.' And intent to stop her nonsense, he smiled with resolution that tightened his mouth. 'There! Could a husband speak fairer?'

She gave him smile for smile; but her eyes were lowered upon the haycock between them, and the fountain of bright life in her dwindled until it was quenched in a sigh. 'You have tamed me, and therefore yourself, my bard, into this easy contentment. Is it all of happiness?'

'On earth,' he said, 'it is what a sane man is desiring.'

'Even when he was once a poet?' she asked with lift of her brows.

He was displeased with her. They had been married four summers; and spring's mountain courtship was safer forgotten. 'No,' he said again, more strongly than before, resolute to put from him the echoes of that music which had been her gift and his quest. 'There is naught as I miss, girl. Come you, have done! Let us get the hay carried. Your nasty old rain 'ull be spoiling it if we linger here, talking so childish.'

In silence they resumed work together, steadily raking and pitching.

*   *   *

Next day, in another of his sheltered meadows, he led the line of mowers. The storm had come overnight and was gone, leaving the landscape new-painted in vivid colours, the distance varnished and the foreground glittering. Quaker grass and the feathery pink flower of sorrel quivered about his knees and ox-eyed daisies swayed in a light wind. At each swish of his scythe, they fell around his feet; and he mowed on over them, his body swinging forward in slow, even rhythm. Though his muscles ached, it was agreeable to test their power, lulling to repeat the same motions again and again, without halt: *stretch and slacken, stretch and slacken.* The sweat trickled warm down his armpits and cooled upon his ribs whenever he paused to wipe his forehead. This also, he enjoyed; and breathing in the sweetness of washed air. 'Pity,' he thought, 'haymaking do come but once a year.' After that, he thrust regret from him and was as a wholesome beast, aware only of strength and hunger. He did not want to rest when the men following him complained of thirst, but stood sharpening his blade while they drank in turn from a pitcher and leant panting against the trunk of a hedgerow tree. The rasp of his whetstone on steel, like a corncrake's rough note, gave him pleasure. Not in every mood did he wish to listen to the liquid melody of the blackcap's song, but favoured a note which, as he said, 'had a bite in en.' His own voice was loud and hearty as he shouted, 'Come on, boys! Come you on,' and he livened them with an ancient ballad that lilted to the stoop and sweep of their limbs. Generations, whose blood throbbed through his veins, had toiled with these same movements to this rugged tune and had repeated these words until they were defaced as a coin by long usage, their meaning quite forgot. Knowing no more than a bird does what it was that he sang, he heard his chant rise and fall and gave it no heed.

At midday, he looked up to see Glythin in the glare of sunlight coming towards him. She held her apron by its two corners, the sack between weighted with food; and he remembered from of old the faded blue cotton and the shape of the loaves within, the great rounded stones from the river; for his mother had come to the hayfield when first he toddled after the mowers. She had been the first to give him food when he hungered. Therefore it was of her and of himself as a little boy that he thought, not of the gold of Glythin's hair nor of her smooth brow as she stepped over the swathes, drawing near with a placid smile. 'Time to rest,' she said. He nodded and in contentment without flaw watched his son trotting beside her, holding to her skirt. 'Next year he'll be searching for the nests o' field-mice. I was doing likewise in my time,' he said to himself. 'Mine is a comely child; and the mother will bear me more.' Many more, he hoped, who would grow up strong to labour. He wanted his mother to live to a ripe old age, that she might rejoice again in a house full of noisy children. Clatter and stir were her music and he would provide them to her heart's content. Stretching himself at every joint, as animals do when they arise after sleep, he smiled at the bright horizon – a wide smile that came slow and lingered long. Nothing better did he ask for than this life of earthly health, safety and fulfilment.

So in companionable silence he munched the bread, the cheese and the raw onion which his wife gave him and drank deep from the earthen vessel tipped in her hands. 'Go you back to the house,' he commanded her, after he had dozed for an hour, lying slack beneath the honeysuckled hedge, with his head pillowed in her lap. 'I must be getting on with my work; and you with yours, girl.'

She rose at once and went her way, Nant stumbling after her over the ridges of mown grass which were already paling in the sun and no longer smoked sweetly with moisture. The child, with hot dimpled hands, tried to catch a butterfly, blue as a petal fluttered down from the sky. 'Look, Mam, look!' he cried. 'Pretty. Nant want it.' But she drew him back, caressing his tousled head. 'Let the light-winged creature go. If you're grasping it, 'twill no longer be free to fly; and you, too, will be the loser.' By the gate, she paused to look over her shoulder at the flattened lines of grass; and Owain wondered why her mouth drooped suddenly into wistful-

ness. She was an unaccountable creature who, having become
as he willed her to be, would yet, once in a while, remind him
that he had loved other aspects of her nature. As he looked
at her, remembering these with a renewal of homage he had
long set aside, it seemed as though her maidenhood were
restored. Her face lit up, its character as changed on the
instant as that of a lamp when the flame within is kindled;
and in her former voice, pure as the air of the mountain-tops,
she began to sing.

> 'You shone, fair moons, sun-hearted,
> Across the early day,
> In starry hosts unnumbered,
> Bright as the Milky Way.
>
> At noon, Time's scythe had laid you
> All level with mown grass.
> Your trampled beauty, withered,
> I mourned and would not pass.
>
> And yet that morning vision,
> Because I love, I hold;
> Deep in the night, sun-hearted,
> A starry white and gold.'

*   *   *

Season by season, the years of content went by. His wife
bore Owain two more sons, whom she loved no less dearly
than the first. He was proud of their beauty if others praised
it in tribute to himself; yet did not feel wholly pleased when
the blacksmith declared, 'Their mother's rare gold be in them
children's hair and the still o' lake water, green, in their queer
eyes'; for sometimes he perceived their shining innocence

to be a reproach. Entering his home at even, he heard them sing in treble voices, clear and challenging as the high tones of the missel-thrush, which is less tame than any garden bird. Something young stirred in his vitals then, which the labours and gains of his prime had lulled into a slumber void of dreams; and, that this should not cause him recollection of what it suited him to dismiss, he took up his neglected harp and sang them the lively ballads he had learned at fairs when a boy; or on Sunday nights taught them doleful hymns.

''Tis well,' his mother said, with a brisk nod. 'You are become the image o' the Master as I was wanting you to be, boy; a dutiful son, a kind and careful but sober-strict father; a prospering farmer too, heeding your business. No more flighty nonsense about you, I be thankful to say.'

But Glythin would ask him once in a long while, 'Have you never no longing, my heart, to make me a new song?'

For answer, he chuckled at her, as he refilled his pipe.

'Go on! Those were for our days o' courting. I've a mort o' things to think of now, other nor being a bard – wife and children to lay up for; my ancient old mother to keep. Useless, she's growing, yet must be fed. And the more labour I'm hiring – which onst I reckoned 'ould spare me work – the worse 'ull be the waste, unless I'm watching constant.'

So he would sit at their hearth only for such rest as was needful; and when doing so he told her about his troubles and profits. These were the subjects of his talk: the new shepherd had let his sheep get the fluke; a dealer would have cheated him over his bullocks, but that he had proved too sharp; a tidy price her butter and cheese had fetched. He rewarded her industry with a word of approval; but, since she shrank from haggling with other women, it fell to him to market her wares; and that, also, took time and care. Therefore, he argued, she must not ask him to weave into verse the idle fancies of a lad. A busy farmer past thirty had matters more grave to mind. He talked of them nightly as she followed him upstairs; and within the sheltering curtains of their bed, he spoke in a voice that drowsed away into a snore of what he must do on the morrow.

In spring there was the lambing; and often, tired as a midwife of vigil, he had to be up at night, lantern in hand, going the round of his ewes or watching, in the cavernous dark byre, a cow that lowed in travail. The young mares gave birth with effort, so that once in a way he came to breakfast despondent, having lost a foal. Then his hedges were to be pleached, his ploughing finished and his garden set.

Summer long he sweated in the labours of shearing and harvest, and in the cool twilight rode whistling among the hills. For even in soft weather the foolish sheep would graze the nearest hollows and must be chased by his dogs on to the sparse high pastures, lest winter should find them fodderless.

With autumn, after the strain of threshing, he dressed himself warm and spruce and took his grain to the mill, his fleeces to the wool merchant's and his hides to the tanner. This was the season of most arduous chaffering, when drovers eyed his sleek kine at cattle-fairs, and Glythin, every market day, loaded his cart with kegs of salted butter and cheeses pale as the full moon.

Winter brought long evenings at the fireside, time for mending his gear, but seldom an hour for idling. When frost broke, there was ploughing once again: if snow fell, there were sheep to dig out of drifts; and with the first mild days, he hurried forth to sow.

Month after month, as he worked, he sang lustily the worn songs traditional to each labour; and when he was singing, he was satisfied. Nevertheless, if neighbours treated him with aloof respect because he was grown rich, he regretted the time when they and he had made merry together; and he longed, though he would not admit it, for their once familiar applause. On account of Glythin's strangeness, they shunned his house and company; and despite the happiness and riches she had brought him, he wished he had not had to pay for her gifts by a measure of isolation. 'There's ungrateful I am,' he admonished himself more than once; but he was often restless because the more he possessed of this world's goods, the keener grew his appetite for some new treat. The rough clothes he had once worn in content must be bettered and the plain food he used to eat with relish became distasteful.

'Well, well,' he argued, 'what harm can there be in my wishing to enjoy my wealth?'

* * *

The busiest weeks of the year were over, his barns brim full, no battle left to wage but against rats. As he drove his gay painted wagon home, having bargained to a finish with the miller, he thrust his right hand into the pocket of a coat like a gentleman's, and chinked the hard-edged guineas. Gold! Solid and weighty! 'That be the stuff I've come to like,' he said to himself with a grin; and in excellent spirits, he clicked his tongue at his fine team of horses. He recollected, however, the last time he had played with his wife's wedding ring during one of those hours of dalliance which were now grown scarce, and how he had been startled to notice that her metal was worn thin. 'A mistake I was making in my youth, when I sought to fashion a lasting pledge out o' summat curious and soft,' he had told her. 'My common iron be proving the more durable.' And now he thought, 'Some day I'll give her a new trinket made from one o' these serviceable coins, with a bit o' alloy in en. Summat bigger and more showy-like, it shall be, nor her wedding ring; for I've plenty o' guineas to spare. Some day; when I be yet richer:

when I be less mortal busy.' Meanwhile, under his hearth-stone, he would bury the guineas tonight when the labourers were gone to their loft; and Glythin, holding the candle for him, should be the sole witness of his wealth. He regretted that she took small interest in it, the prattle of their children, bright with innocent fancies, seeming to give her greater pleasure. How often he had heard her laugh in childish gaiety that he lacked the time to share: how often seen her attention wander when he was counting his coins! Yet he could blame her for nothing, save that she was a creature not quite at home in this world, nor able to weigh its riches by the scales of middle-aged folk. Today, being pleased with himself, he forgave her for sometimes pricking his complacence by conjuring up the ghost of a lost man. That stranger in his house, who was not strange to her, he did not choose to meet. Let him lie in his grave of the years. He had been poor, the companion of wild hopes and visionary sorrow. Unhar-nessing his team, he planned to buy her a silk gown. But would she value finery as other women did who were prone to that vanity which a man enjoys both to witness and deride? He was afraid she might say, looking straight at him with her candid eyes, 'I had rather you made me a song.' So he put the plan from him and went to admire his stock.

The pigsties he had built were full of fleshy sucklings. He prodded them with the butt of his whip and watched them skelter, squeaking, behind the bloated sow. At her grunt he laughed, tasting in it already the flavour of fat bacon. Fresh pork and tasty hams he was proud of being able to provide for all his household. Only his wife would not eat of them; and she it was, alone, who shunned him when his arms were smeared with blood from the slaughter. Recalling how, with face averted, she brought him a pail of water and turned swiftly away, he was vexed with her. In this she was foolish, as his mother had right to complain. To be sure, that old mother of his was a wonderful wise woman! And of a sudden he grew anxious; for, in the press of the day, he had forgotten that she ailed. When Glythin came towards him across the fold, a matron of his own age, no longer a slight girl, but mellow in her beauty as the first bland day of autumn, he called out to her, 'How is she?'

They kissed; and she answered, 'Gone feebler. Asking for you, she is.'

He was alarmed, for the first time picturing his home without the crooked figure, so little and lean and now so useless, which had been his life's background, steadfast as the hills. Why, it would be as if gales ceased to blow or earth to yield corn and thistles! 'You don't never think as she's failing?' he exclaimed, his fingers denting the firm flesh of Glythin's arm. 'No, no. Not for many a year,' he reassured himself. Pain that was not close at hand need have no foretaste. A wise man lived in each day's toil and gain.

'She is craving to have her children come back to her, whatever,' said Glythin.

'That's a bad sign, indeed.' He strode into the house and up three stairs at a time to the small room which had been his, where the sick crone now lay abed, propped upon many pillows. Her rusty breathing grated through the silence. He was afraid of this new sound and of the change in her appearance. The nibbling away of the years had, from his childhood, wrinkled her face and shrunk her limbs in a process too stealthy for observation. But in a few hours, the last strokes of old age had been dealt. Lean, brown, scant-haired, with fever-sharp eyes, she looked more pitiful than an ancient rat; and he had never loved her so well. With a deep dumb emotion, not flowering from any beauty or sweetness in herself, but rooted in his own flesh, he yearned over her as a man wishful to keep his own limb, even though it be shrivelled. Clumsy with concern, he fondled her hot dry hand.

'What can I be doing for you, Mother? 'T'ould ease me to *do* summat.'

'Bring me home all my sons.'

'I'll be trying, whatever.'

'Every one o' them, mind – the whole seven as I was bearing.'

One of them lay rotted in the churchyard; and one was believed to be drowned at sea; while who knew what was become of the mercenaries, Rhys and Gwilym, and the hunted robber, Dan? Tears sprang to Owain's eyes. 'Well, well,' he contrived to mutter, stiffening the muscles of his quivering lips, ' I'll be sending for the lot, to pleasure you.' He could not endure to be with her and turned towards the door, saying, 'At once, I'll be sending.' To be employed in making enquiries would excuse him from painful attendance at her bedside. As he went out, Glythin came in with quiet footfall, carrying a basin of broth. How could she keep so calm, he wondered; was it through lack of affection? 'Stay you with her. Don't you be leaving her,' he commanded in a harsh whisper.

'To be sure, my heart, I'll stay. She is dozing quiet when I sit close to her, sewing.'

'Queer it is you can have the stomach to sew,' he muttered, and went out.

He had not understood that his mother was so ill. Now, the dread of her dying made his temper short as the weeks dragged by and the messengers whom he sent to scour the country brought news only of the settled Madoc. His rich brother, with acres over the English border, would not come until his grain was threshed. 'I'd like to take a flail to his own back,' Owain exclaimed; and he scolded his children for playing and scowled at Thomas who daily waited at the stairs' foot with autumn flowers wilting in his clutch, until Glythin should come down and he might thrust them at her in mute homage.

At last Madoc arrived and with a creak of new boots tiptoed up to the sick-room. Owain followed him and they stood at the bedside where Glythin sat stitching. When they spoke to the dying woman, she did not look towards them but went on whispering in rapid gasps to her known companion, the sound of her voice dry as a wind among scorched bents of grass.

'Always, 'twas my wish he should wed you, see? Come close, my dear. Come closer. I do like to see it fine. The pretty yellow hair. Silk-soft it is, and your hands are having kind palms to them. The first time I was seeing you in green. Counting the gifts you brought him, I was. I knew there'd be more to come. Children o' his body. You were a giver and good. Whatever he asked you for . . . And I was making him ask with sense, see? Rich he's grown by laying aside his former idle dreams. But he didn't ought to forget what you was giving him. "He'll prosper," I said, "so long as he's faithful to that one." Ah, I've been as your mother, *fach*! Was you knowing that? 'Twas *I* baked the bread made you mortal. For mortal you had to be. Same as myself, *fach*. No different, see? That be a mortal's wish for her own daughter. The very same. Learning to love and hate; to suffer and serve and endure, after the manner common to us females.' Her gasping voice failed and in a whisper, strained by fear, she resumed, 'On times, still, you are strange, as if you had come among us to kindle memory o' what my son's more prudent to forget. But he is steadied down. Yes, indeed, I've been contriving well, I tell you. I've caused him to stop singing his mountainy songs and I've made you grow like to myself. My very own child, see? When I'm gone, you'll be taking my place quite natural. And if only you was to bear him a daughter, and she'd be taking your place after. And her daughter and granddaughter, on and on. My grannie. My mother. Myself. Doing the same work for our men, always.

That's how it has been. How 'twill ever be. A chain o' women.
All alike. Every link. That life may hold unbroken. Life. Ah,
life's good, girl, good as a ripe apple to the taste, though the
side turned from the sun be bitter-sharp!' She was seized
with a storm of coughing that shook and twisted her, till it
seemed the creased skin must rear away from the bones.
When she was able to whisper again hoarsely, the compassionate listeners heard her repeating the one word, *'Life,
life, life,'* over and over again. 'I wish if I had mine ahead o'
me,' she struggled to gasp out. 'All of en. From beginning
to end.'

Her sons stared in distress. Then they shook their heads
and left her. 'Who could think as she'd be wishful now to
live?' In the kitchen they sat heartening themselves with ale,
for each was admitting in secret that this dying, in which he
desired not to believe for himself, must some day be expe-
rienced by him also. 'Fancy poor mother wanting to hold on,'
said Madoc; and then, hastily, 'Your ale is champion, boy.'
He took another gulp. 'If I'm drinking so much, I shall pay
my reckoning with the gout, indeed now.' And he drank yet
more until he was able to disregard the rasping mutter from
overhead and to impart his tidings of Dan. The robber was
turned landlord, having laid by his stolen goods and married
a woman of dowry. Some said she had been the artful keep-
miss of a rich old dotard: but it mattered little what her
history was, for they were settled in decent wedlock, in a
fine house purchased with her money, so that Dan treated
her respectful-like. Whether he had bribed or threatened the
magistrates none could tell; but sure it was he kept a good
table, went regular to church and relieved the poor; and as
no one dared to inform against him, his past crimes were
forgiven. 'Money,' said Madoc, with a complacent smile,
'money can buy the world and all.' And he began to boast
of his own wealth and of the deference it brought him.

As he listened, there awoke in Owain the disdain he had felt in youth for such opinions. He looked at his eldest brother's once handsome face, florid with lavish living, blunted by self-satisfaction, and his heart misgave him, lest he, too, should be falling into sloth of spirit. And as he searched himself, in a rare access of contrition, he heard a voice singing low and sad from overhead, so that behind his eyeballs tears were hot and a band seemed to constrict his chest.

> 'When loud in jest or anger
> The tale of man is told,
> Remember yet the stillness
> That held your breath of old.
> Once in hidden valley,
> On wide and airy height,
> Where quiet spake green waters
> Their many-leaved delight,
> By little lakes and lonely
> That shone in heaven's sight,
> The wind would tell my answers
> To dreams you dreamt by night.'

Then, because he was ashamed, he said to himself that the fault was Glythin's. Had she been less strange, he need not have feared the visions she had given, nor, in retreat from his fear, have ceased to be a poet.

''Tis queer,' said Madoc, 'Mother coming to take such a fancy of your strange wife.'

''Tisn't queer at all,' Owain answered tartly. 'A tidy, dutiful daughter-in-law has my Glythin been. And I've learned her to be as good a wife, too, as I could desire.'

'Not so prickly, man! I wasn't saying nothing against her. Only that she's *strange*.'

'She's strange no more, since I didn't wish it. Why, you heard poor mother tell how she's become like any other woman.'

Madoc did not argue but his look of disbelief provoked Owain. If the world could not see the change he had wrought in his mate, he must prove that she loved him too well to be other than he wished. So in front of Madoc, from henceforth, he ordered her about and fed his craving for mastery upon her mute submission.

*   *   *

The questions he had sent his farm hands to ask in neighbouring seaports brought Rhys and Gwilym home before winter. They were landed off a French merchantman and dressed as sailors, bringing a new swagger with them and many foreign oaths. Though they sobbed like children at their mother's bedside, they were soon telling Owain of adventures to which his pulses leapt. He would not have changed places with them – the vagabonds! But by tasting all manner of dissolute lives in his daydreams, he could lessen the dullness of his own quiet way of living.

'And what do you think,' said Gwilym, 'that brother o' ours, Howell – the one as ran away to sea an' poor Mother took for drowned – we was finding in a tavern at Aberyron. There he was sitting so fast you'd say as his backside were all of piece with the settle. Swilling down rum like a good 'un, he was. Drowned indeed! 'Tisn't in no *water* as *he'll* ever perish. "If you don't give over swallowing and come along o' us to pleasure the poor dying woman," we was saying, "we'll break every bone in your fat carcase, mun." Too big a belly he has to stir himself, see, even though the mother that suckled and reared him be at her last breath, damn his soul! He tried, indeed, in dread of our threats no doubt; but he couldn't be keeping up with the brisk pace we was setting. Leaving him in a ditch, we was, all wombly as a custard. But maybe he'll come rolling in here – the great soft barrel! – tomorrow or the day after.'

'Or maybe,' Rhys added with a wink, 'he'll drink out the month at every inn on the way. More particular if the innkeepers' wives be sportive.'

They laughed loud; then, repentant, looked up at the rafters over their heads. 'No, no, damn it! We mustn't be cracking no jokes with poor mother passing away;' and the tears started into their eyes. Scowling at Madoc, who was more decorously behaved but far less moved than themselves, they sighed before returning to their ale.

* * *

Owain's first feeling was one of contempt for the fat lazy fellow who sauntered into the house a few days later. Could not Howell have made haste? Did he value nothing but his own comfort? His flabby paunch and slack purple lips seemed to give the lie to all effort. But he proved to have the charm of easy nature, to be good company when Glythin was with the sufferer and the five men sat waiting, time-fretted, round the hearth. He had seen more of the world than his brothers in their soldiering; and, unlike theirs, his tales were never of killing nor of war's cruelties. For him, the life of a hundred ports had been one crazy-patterned play; and he could re-act its many clownish parts. Wadding tobacco into the bowl of his pipe, he cocked an impudent eye at Owain. 'I'm pitying you staid married men, afraid to enjoy yourselves, and ashamed to own as you're afraid, too.' Bland as a baby's were his blue eyes, with whites bloodshot by the end of every day; yet Owain felt diminished by their scrutiny and by the smile that stretched, wide and juicy, like a gaping cut in an over-ripe fruit, across the mottled face. Whenever he stared dejected at the clock, none but Howell could liven him with talk of outlandish cities where the women's hair was black and the robes they wore as the rainbow.

'I'd like to have journeyed the earth over,' he declared with envious regret, though he had never before thought of leaving his parish unless it were to make money at a neighbouring market.

Then Howell, chuckling in his throat, so that the flesh rippled in waves above his loose cravat, would tell of a pretty face seen through a half-shuttered window in some Spanish town.

'And you were after her, man?'

'To be sure. What are you taking me for – a fool to miss any pleasure life is offering? No, no, man, that were folly, indeed, seeing as we shall be a long time dead, and in the grave no fun, whatever.'

Of his craft, his laughing lies, success and humiliation, he told without shame, chuckling at how he had been chased once, naked, into the street by an outraged husband. Owain, who at first found such brazen confessions disgraceful, began to relish their humour. 'Go on,' he would urge with a smile, in spite of himself, 'what was happening to you then, you good-for-nothing lecher?'

But whenever Glythin's light footsteps from overhead made him start, he remembered with horror that his mother was dying. He knew, but could not believe it; and as he forced himself to creep up to her bedside, his heart hammered in hard little blows, as if a drum were beating within his ribs. 'Not yet! Not yet! Not yet!' Her staring eyeballs were frightful to see and her struggle for breath was a torture to hear; but he desired the continuance of her life with as great a passion as she fought for it, though he knew it were better for her now to die. Glythin was right, he was loath to acknowledge, to press no food upon her, but gently to moisten the cracked lips with water, and by her calm presence to help the release of a soul. She was without fear of death's approach, causing him to wish that he shared her wisdom and at the same time to resent her being so wise.

'Is the poor thing suffering much?' he whispered. And when Glythin nodded assent, 'Then 't'ould be a mercy if she went quick?'

'Yes. God's mercy. Soon 'twill be over now, I'm hoping.'

At that he was savage with her for not disguising the truth.

'You and your God!' he exclaimed, not knowing that he blamed them both because he lacked their answer to the riddle of pain.

Dan was the last of the widow's sons to come home; the least stricken by her battle for air, as the six of them stood watching her die. His hands were thrust into the pockets of his costly coat, and none might guess from the grim mask of his face upon what memories of violent death he brooded. Madoc wiped away a decorous tear with his silk handkerchief. Rhys and Gwilym sobbed aloud, using the back of a hand or a coat-sleeve at random. Howell muttered, ''Tis too painful for me to witness,' and lumbered out of the room. But Owain flung himself down and clutched the bedclothes, crying like a child, frightened of what is unknown, 'Mother! Mother! Bide you with me! Don't you be leaving me, Mother *fach*!'

Her glazing eyes stared past them all. She knew no one of them; but when Glythin stooped over her and murmured close to her ear, ''Tis all right, dear. You are going now – out o' the womb's hot narrow darkness, into the light and space,' she appeared once more to see and her vacant gaze changed to one of recognition. She tried to smile upwards into the calm face; and her hand, that was already cold in Owain's clasp, fluttered as though she would have it released to touch the one she loved. In desolation, he let it go, muttering, 'Hold you her, Glythin. Hold you her tight.' But in her gentle aloofness, his wife would not try to retain the withered hand of his mother. She let it fall, slack, the empty palm upwards, the loosened fingers outspread. 'Leave go. Leave go, little one,' she commanded in a clear voice. And smiling at her the old woman ceased to battle, with a laboured rasp, for life. They heard the last breath go out of her body in one long, weary sigh. Then, through the sudden silence, the sobs of the living broke loud.

'She is free,' said Glythin quietly, and going to the small window, she opened it wide. After that, she closed the dead woman's eyes, smoothing down the lids with her thumbs, as a sculptor might work upon clay, and folded the hands on her breast. 'Now go, all o' you,' she ordered, 'and send me the midwife as is knowing how to lay out a corpse. I will sit beside it for company, meantime, lest the released spirit, being unaccustomed, should linger, lonely, near the flesh for a while.'

They stared at her, bewildered, and went out.

*   *   *

It was not until evening that she came downstairs, without sign of having wept, and sank on to a stool to warm herself as if nothing grievous had happened.

''Tis cold,' she said, chafing her hands. 'Winter is coming on. I am tired. But this night I shall sleep well.'

The six men with haggard faces stood round her glowering. So kind did she look, to be of so unfeeling a nature, that they knew not what to make of it.

'Well,' said Owain in a dry tone, 'didn't we ought to be going up?' He was afraid of the silent room above, and hoped she would answer, 'No.'

But, 'Yes, if you wish,' she replied. 'Everything has been done, the midwife was telling me, according to custom.' She rose when the fire had unchilled her and stretched herself and yawned. 'How long 'tis taking, to be sure – longer even than a birth that's twisted!'

While she spoke thus composedly of death, the tearful maidservant came cringing up, dog-like, and murmured, as if ashamed to ask, 'Could you be sipping just a small little cup o' tea, Mistress *fach*?'

'No, no . . . Thank you kindly, none the less. Bring me my supper of milk and flummery. And oatcake, too, and butter and cheese, girl. I am hungry, now 'tis over.'

She ate with placid relish; and, in shocked surprise, the menfolk watched her. None of them had been able to touch a morsel but they had all drunk deep.

'Come on, boys,' exclaimed Owain, forcing himself at last to lead the way. ''Tis a scandal to bide in warmth and comfort here, seeing we did ought to prove our sense o' what's fitting.'

When he crept into his room at daybreak, he was worn with his vigil of grief and wishful to share with his wife the terror of death he had suffered. But she lay sleeping sound, her face so smoothed by peace that he could not credit it. In bitterness, therefore, he went down to the kitchen, seeking the company of such as understood his loss, being joined with him in a sense of its finality.

On the morrow, he commanded Glythin, 'Draw you fast the curtains.'

'But why, Master? The day is fine and sunlight is given us for a comforter.'

'Until after the funeral, the house must be kept dark.'

'Whatever for, *bach*?'

''Tis the custom. Do as I say.'

And he thought her a simpleton when she went on to ask, 'For whom are we to be in darkness, the living or the dead?'

'Do as I say,' he repeated, 'and give over your foolish questions.'

'My heart, I only sought to understand you;' and, as he kept silence with displeasure, she darkened every room, then went out from under his roof, taking her children with her.

The servant-girl set food before the brothers at such times as they were accustomed to eat. She had put on a black gown and showed decent respect for bereavement, her eyelids puffed up with crying for the old mistress who had been her plague. This contrast rendered Owain more sore than ever against Glythin, who did not return all day. 'Where is your flounce-about wife taking herself off to?' Dan asked; and he looked meaningly from one to another of his brethren as they sat in the curtained dusk, glum and stiff in their suits of mourning. When night fell, Glythin re-entered, dressed as usual. The fatigue of sick-nursing which had been about her eyes was swept away by mountain air, and their colour so come again that Owain felt this swift renewal of her youth to be an affront to his mother's memory. 'She do feel more free-like, since poor mother went. Why, in a manner o' speaking, so do *I*!' The truth shocked him; and while he was scowling at himself, she smiled at her boys, cautioning them to keep quiet within doors, since their father wished it; and kissing each in turn, she sent them to bed happy. Then, as she passed her husband's chair, she laid her hand upon his shoulder in a caress. He felt the compassion in her touch, but would not yield himself up to be consoled; for in his rebellious sorrow she had left him alone and this he resented. 'As if 'twere wrong or foolish to lament for my own mother,' he thought, 'and she, my wife, as did ought to share my trouble, were knowing better nor me!' And aloud, he said, 'Whyever have you brought them old branches in here?'

'Because they are pleasant to see. Our Nant was gathering them in the copse for you, Master. Look how bright are the mountain-ash berries. Like red and yellow jewels, they are.'

She put them into a jug; and Owain said to himself, 'From henceforth, she can treat as careless as she pleases the crockery by which poor mother set such store.'

Dan was watching them both with crafty eyes, ready to make mischief. 'One might think, Sister-in-law, as you were decking the place out gay for a harvest-home randy.'

'Throw your old trash away,' exclaimed Owain. ''Tisn't seemly to have no decoration for a burial.'

As she obeyed him, the green of her eyes and the faint pink that had stolen back into her cheeks faded, leaving her a pale and weary woman of middle age.

That night he took his turn again of watching beside the rigid corpse and was ashamed to acknowledge how glad he would be when it was gone from the house. When Madoc relieved him, he called downstairs in a whisper to his wife, 'Come on up to bed. You didn't ought to be spinning. Don't you know as you should behave as though 'twere Sunday? . . . Must I tell you everything?' he complained, when she came at his bidding; and as they lay down to sleep together, he turned his back upon her. Softly she touched his arm; but he pulled it away. The fierce loss of his flesh, he knew that she pitied and yearned to comfort; but since she did not partake of it, he was hostile.

Close to his pillow, she murmured, 'What is it, after all, this bodily dying?'

In sullen pain, he answered, 'It is the end.'

'I could be telling you otherwise. But you will not listen to me.'

'No. Leave me be! Leave me be! You are strange, uncommon strange. Small wonder the run o' folk don't want nothing to do with you!'

He heard her sigh but she did not reason with him; and for this, also, he was wroth with her, because he knew she could impart to him a secret concerning death, but that unless he sought her wisdom, she would keep it to herself.

* * *

On the day before the funeral, Madoc's Saxon wife arrived, so decorously deep in mourning that Owain forgot she had thwarted his mother's longing to enjoy her first hatch of grandchildren. After her came Dan's bride, wearing crape as heavy as a widow's and costly enough for a queen. Her face, the shape of which she could change in a twinkling, expressed more grief than she could well feel for the loss of one whom she had never known. Mistress Madoc looked through her hard as a stone, concerned, one might think, with the wall behind her back, as she cast down her bold eyes and made a show of weeping into a handkerchief more black-bordered than was needful. It was plain to see, even the men admitted, that in all she said or did she was acting the part of virtue; and Howell, pulling a comical face, whispered to Owain, 'That's the one to learn you tricks you'll never be taught by your own wife, man.' But Owain was grateful to her, wanton though she might be, for coming to the dolorous gathering so seemly clad, while Glythin put on no mourning attire until he ordered her to do so.

As he paced the fold on the morning of the funeral, he was tempted to count his stock and to plan the next barn to be built; since, year by year, as he had determined, he enclosed more of the mountain, and with his wealth added to his cares. But he thought it improper to dwell upon success while yet his mother's coffin was within his darkened house. And while he brooded on mortality, there fell upon his spirit that heaviness of the prophet who asked what reward a man should have of his labour, whose hours were numbered and who might not take with him into the night the treasured spoils of his brief day. As he reflected sorrowfully that she who had fostered his worldly ambition could never again rejoice in its fulfilment, he heard the stranger, to whom she had turned in death, singing in a near-by field.

> 'Home are sped the swallows
> With lisp of darting wings.

Alone, the lark soars sunward,
In heavenly space he sings.
Home to their lake at evening
The wild swans take their way,
But souls to God returning,
Life weaves a net to stay.

O cruel net, love-woven!
O web of man's despair!
Let pass the wings ascending
To move in freer air.
Birth in a mesh ensared them,
Desire, fear-warped, and pain.
The shears of Death release them
To have their life again.'

And listening, he was comforted, as if some merciful truth, which he had known in part long since, and for this while forgotten, were chiming like bells far away, yet within him, that he might be neither lonely nor afraid, as are the faithless in their blind solitude.

But Dan had followed him out of the house and when he linked arms with his brother in a show of goodfellowship, Owain felt the evil presence more close and pressing than the well of wisdom in his own heart; and he heard the harsh voice at his ear when Glythin's distant singing was died away.

'Was that your strange wife, now just, twittering blithe as a bird?'

'Why must you all be for ever calling her *strange*?'

Dan gave a shrug. 'My wife is finding her so. And Madoc's too. No harm meant.'

'Women!' retorted Owain, his moment of tranquillity departed. 'Jealous they are of her beauty.'

'Is Madoc jealous?' enquired Dan with derision. 'Or Howell,

that's hot after any comely female? Or Rhys or Gwilym, think you? Strange, the lot o' us are seeing her. And but for the neighbours thinking as we do, your grand voice and your harp-playing 'ould draw jollock company about your board. You're a wealthy man, now, brother. Yet what joy is she letting you have in hospitality? Accounted queer you are for having wed such a one. Yes,' he added with studied contempt, 'and for being so patient-meek under her rule so long.'

'What do I care for idle gossip?' demanded Owain, much vexed that people should suppose him ruled by his wife. ''Tisn't true neither. I am being master in my own house.' And seeing Dan's black brows raised in mockery, he went on in a stubborn tone, 'Her company's enough for me, what-ever, think and say as you please. She's been my consolation these dozen years.'

'Your consolation for the lonesome life you've led, poor boy?'

'Say no more. I'm liking my chosen way o' living fine.'

'Your way, or hers? Maybe as 'twasn't your choice.'

'*Now* what be you hinting at?' Owain flamed out at him.

'Ah, poor Owain, I'm afeard in my heart to make mis-chief – a thing as no man could accuse me of. A bold honest robber I've been, but never . . .'

'Out with it, man! Out with it!'

'Well then . . . take no offence, boy, mind, for I'm loving my kith and kin and am only minded to serve you.' He freed his arm and facing Owain, 'What if you'd been bewitched?' he whispered.

At that word Owain smarted as from the lash of a whip. 'Bewitched,' his poor mother had called him in the days of his courtship. 'Mother came to love her, though,' he blurted out.

'*Came to*?' Dan pounced upon the words with a grimace.

'Ah, yes, to be sure, she, too, fell under the spell, at the last. Poor woman! She was turning from you when she lay feeble and dying, her mind failing, off her guard, as the saying do go. Turned to the stranger, she did. We were one and all remarking upon it; as if some charm had stolen away her natural love for her favourite son.' He sighed, shaking his head; and his false compassion bit Owain to the quick; for he would have had his mother on her deathbed smile at himself. 'And how is this stranger you brought among us from the Lord do know where, repaying the fondness as our poor aged parent showed her?' Dan persisted. 'If she was having a human heart, could she be singing today as gay as any skylark?'

'Come,' growled Owain, turning on his heel, 'time we made ready to welcome the bearers;' and in a hard shout, he summoned Glythin indoors.

Throughout the halting procession of black-clad figures on its way downhill, during the sombre service and as the mourners climbed upwards again, gossiping in decorous murmurs, Dan's poison worked in Owain's mind. Around the open grave beside that pitiful small mound where her dead infant had been buried in her youth, he and his mother's five other sons had wept her loss. Even Dan, the hard-hearted, had covered his face when earth pattered on her coffin lid. Onlookers had sighed in condolence; the servant-girl had sobbed upon a tide of borrowed grief; and his children, seeing his sorrow, or perhaps because they missed their grandmother, had been in tears. But Glythin, favoured with that parting smile for which he had longed in vain, had stayed composed.

'She,' Owain's thoughts accused her, 'who cannot abide to see a dumb beast slaughtered and be too nesh to wring the neck of a chicken!' Ah, yes, at heart he knew the answer to her riddle! He, also, when he had courted her upon the mountain, had not shrunk from natural death as from a terrible thing. But now that others found her unfeeling, his own comprehension shrivelled away, as a plant, shallow-rooted, beneath a scorching sun.

Back in his kitchen, she looked to him for orders and he was irked by it, forgetting that he had trained her to be meek. Since his mother was no more present to take charge, she, as mistress of the house, ought to seat the guests in order of their rank; and it was but a gloomy pride that he took single-handed, in doing the funeral honours. However, he swore to himself, under his roof none should report a lack of respect for the dead. At his right hand, Dan's bride kept sighing as she ate mincingly and made play with her black-bordered handkerchief. She was a model of genteel dolefulness, while the rest of the staid gathering conversed in hushed under-tones and all his brothers showed a suitable melancholy, even Howell refraining from the slightest jest. In spite of their faults, Owain felt drawn towards them today.

But Glythin, at the head of his table, held her children close to her not seeking to hide affection which he condemned, for the while, as in poor taste. Their three bright heads and hers caught the light from the window; and though of middle age she looked in her innocence too young to preside as it was seemly that his wife should do. Round-eyed as owls, at first, the boys stared at their glum elders. It was only fitting, Owain considered, that his children should be too awed to touch their food. 'Nice and feeling,' the neighbours would call it; and his displeasure increased against their mother for bending over them with smiles and words of encourage-ment. Before long they were eating with healthy appetite and she was laughing aloud at the prattle of her youngest.

'*My* children know better than to behave so pert at a solemn occasion,' he heard Madoc's wife declare.

'No doubt; for they have a mother as can conduct herself

respectable,' Dan answered in a voice loud enough for all to hear.

Owain was mortified to think that a turnip-faced Saxon should teach his own wife manners. He had risen and gone, knife in hand, to the dresser close to her chair, that he might cut slices of bread. Behind him he heard the guests fall silent as his children's chatter grew more merry, and turning about, he saw shocked faces in a ring around Glythin.

'Keep quiet, can't you?' he thundered at the boys.

The smallest, a golden-haired rogue, dimpling with gaiety, quailed at the unlooked-for rebuke and cowered into his mother's lap, where he began to cry. She put her arms round him and looked up at her husband in wonder.

'What have they done amiss?' she asked. 'Is it wrong for them to be happy?'

''Tis your fault, not theirs,' he reprimanded her, 'teaching them on such a day as this to frolic.'

She smiled down upon the child who clung to her. 'There, there, *bach*! Father is not real angry, only sore at heart'; then, with grave dignity, she studied the faces turned on herself in disapproval. There was not one of them but had lost the candour of childhood; and she spoke her mind. 'No need have you elders to teach these little ones. For indeed they are come into the world more wise than you are grown in it, seeing that they still remember the nature of pure joy.' And smiling at the affronted company, she continued, 'But you, with your long faces, put on like masks, are learning children to dread that which the angels rejoice over – the going home of a soul.'

Owain turned damp with shame that neighbours and kindred should witness his disagreement with his wife; and with severity he ordered her to hold her tongue. ''Tisn't for you, whatever, to tell us Christians our business.'

'You, that we doubt have never been baptized,' jeered the blacksmith.

'Be quiet,' cried Owain, scowling at him; and to Glythin he said, more sternly than before. 'Behave yourself now. For we are come together to mourn the dead.'

She looked at him then in sorrow and pity; and in a voice still as her lake upon a windless day, she asked, 'Why not mourn for the living? Folk that have died are gone out of trouble.'

Because she had answered him thus before others, he was enraged against her; and not knowing what he did he cried out again, 'Be quiet,' and struck her with the flat of his knife.

She uttered no cry but turned so pale that her green eyes darkened in an ash-white face. Deep pools of water they seemed to him, holding the secrets of a man drowning; and in terror he gazed down into them.

'My soul! I did not mean to do this to you.'

'I know. I know. But it is done.' Without another word, she rose and like one in a trance, groped her way to the door.

The guests, open-mouthed, gaped after her, and Dan laughed with the single bark of a dog-fox.

'Stop you,' cried Owain in a panic, flinging away his knife. He heard the click of steel on stone, close to her feet as she swayed upon his threshold.

'That is *twice*,' she said very low. 'Oh, my heart! My poor rash heart! You, who mourn one departed in peace, having seen that larger room into which she was entering, now are your own troubles like to come upon you.' And she went out alone.

'Well,' exclaimed Madoc's wife, 'did you ever!'

'I was guessing it all along,' the blacksmith muttered. 'That one be no Christian mortal.'

Dan nodded; but no one else ventured a word until Owain had rushed past them from the house, calling, 'Glythin! Glythin! My lovely! Come back to me!' They heard his anguished entreaties ring through the fold and die away up the mountainside. Then they began to nudge one another, to wink and to whisper together.

'I ask your pardon, my friends,' said Madoc, clearing his throat, thrusting his thumbs into the armholes of his waistcoat and preparing a fine speech. But his wife plucked at his sleeve and he knew that in her hearing he would never be allowed to make one.

'Nothing can excuse such behaviour,' she declared. 'Nothing. Let us have no talk about it, pray.'

Bitter looks were exchanged.

'Come you,' Howell intervened, 'she's crazed, poor soul. Best pay no heed, mates, but finish the drink, is it?'

But everyone had been shocked; and, what was less agreeable, called to account for their hypocrisy. Black as a flight of rooks, and cawing in unison, they departed without delay.

*   *   *

Far up among the mountains, Owain found her; but not as she had been when first he sought her there. In the mourning he had forced her to wear, her solitary figure showed black beside the white cattle with which she had made him rich; and her shadow stretched ahead of her over autumn's browning sward. She was staring down upon it in sad reverie, her back to the setting sun. At her sides her hands hung empty and her head was bowed.

When he stood before her to beg forgiveness, she did not weep or upbraid him but replied with a gentleness that pierced him through with contrition, 'You acted after your nature, my love, as I after mine;' and, slowly twisting the two rings on her wedding finger, she sighed. 'It is our fate, on earth, not to be wholly one.'

'No, no,' he cried out, 'from henceforth . . .' But laying a warning touch upon his lips, she silenced the desperate boast. 'Come home with me, at least,' he entreated instead.

'Yes, dear heart, I will come; for you and I are bound together in bonds of love and fellowship. And I must stay with you, until you drive me away with yet a third blow of your iron.'

'That shall never be,' he swore, 'not though all the evil tongues in the world should strive to set us apart.'

'And what if you yourself desert me for one that has more o' your mortal nature?'

'You are, and shall ever be, my only love.'

'I was your first,' she said. 'Your last I shall be, also, whom you will look upon again when the waters of absolution wash over you in death.'

Their house was empty when he brought her back to his hearth. Beside the ashes of a dwindled fire, they clung together, their checks pressed each to each, and their tears mingled. Not with the passion of young lovers did they embrace, but sorrowfully, as fond married folk who dread a grievous parting.

'Hold me close,' she whispered; and holding her, he said in a tone chilled with fear, 'From this day on, how mindful I must be not to complete my doom!'

'Be true to that which you once went in quest of,' she answered him, 'and no ill can befall us.'

Winter

There is no way to sorrow more sure than that of fear. As the years slid past, Owain shunned the sight of his companion's gold, because so much of it was rubbed away, warning him that what yet remained might vanish; and to distrust his iron, also, with which he had struck her. Never again, in a mood of fondness, did he play with the rings on her finger; and from the nook behind the oven, where they had stood, his tools were banished to the barn. No longer busy scouring them with river sand and peat ash from his hearthstone, he durst not, either, whittle bowls or spoons of wood, since his knife-blade was now a menace. This indolence of a winter's evening caused the hours to lag and made him crave for some untasted pleasure, asking himself more often than before, 'What is it which I am missing?'

Nothing that he could think of did he lack. His children were comely, healthy and obedient. The number of his men and maidservants increased; and every night the firelight shone on the flitches of bacon which hung from his kitchen rafters, while a cheerful cricket, token of good luck, piped to the clock's safe ticking. So replete with comfort was his home that it put to shame his twinges of discontent. 'Poor Glythin shall never guess when I am thus unaccountable glum,' he promised his conscience; and that he might, with kind intent, deceive her, he often stiffened his mouth into an actor's smile. But as if in answer to his secret disquiet, she would of a sudden lay the harp upon his knees.

'Well, well. You 'ould have me sing, Missus, is it?'

'You did use to be happier singing.'

'A' right then. Fetch me some more ale, and tell me what the song shall be now?'

There was however, no eagerness within him. Having long neglected to make new songs of his own, he was weary of repeating other men's, and seldom raised his voice, except for the neighbours to hear in church every Sunday.

'Since you are mute,' urged Glythin, 'let me open the window, *bach*, that you may hear the rising gale, at least. Each tree is answering with a different note, after the fashion o' his own leaves and branches. And you, too, will give forth a song, though maybe a sad one, if you are listening to the wind's warning.'

But with an impatient shake of his head, he replied that winter drew near and the weather chilled his flesh. He did not care to hear the birches' shiver, the firs' thin sigh, nor the rustling of the ash. Their music of late autumn aroused in him regret. He therefore cut down those trees which stood nearest to his house; and, like his mother before him, kept doors and windows shut. Glythin's pallor grew more marked with this confinement; her step, by degrees, lost its spring of youth and her eyes the clear beauty which had enchanted him. But the plucked flower fades more slowly than the growing bloom unfurls; and he scarce noticed her changing, until after she was changed. Then, with a shrug, he argued that Time alone was at fault. If he remembered her grace when he wooed her where it had been hard to climb, his dissatisfaction turned inwards against himself; and he put away the remembrance, saying to himself, as a husband will, 'Love cannot but grow staled by years of marriage. No matter. We are fond enough as 'tis; and she is mine to have and to hold.' Moreover, he was well content with her in most things who, as she grew older, became ever more mindful of his comfort. Requiring little of her, save that she add to his wealth by her daily labours and soothe him into agreeable sleep of nights, he received as much as he sought.

'Go you on,' he jested one evening, when she put the harp within his reach and looked at him as one who would ask a favour, 'you're wishful for me to be a bard still, are you? But 'tis long since I heard you open your lips unbidden.' The glance she gave him was timid; and he said with irritation, '*Now*, whatever's on you – apt to go hurt at nothing! I can't be laying the lightest finger on you, but you bruise!'

'I was thinking, Master dear, how can I sing if you don't never wish to hear me?'

'To be sure you may take that for granted,' he smiled, at ease again, and settled in his father's great chair. 'Sing to me, *fach*, free and gay as a lark in air, the same as you did use to do . . . Well? Out with it!'

With a small smile, in which lurked sadness, she set down her knitting and sang to his command; but the song was one of his mother's that he himself had taught her; and under a roof her voice did not sound to advantage. It was sweet enough yet to give him a certain pleasure; and when she had done, he said, 'There's pretty!'

But in silence, motionless, she awaited his order to sing once more: and waited in vain.

*   *   *

Chief among his concerns was the rearing of his first-born to be an industrious farmer. As his mother had trained him, so he would train his son. The three lads were growing apace and had become horsemen of courage and sheperds of some skill. Owain smiled indulgently upon the younger two, if, playing truant, they plunged, white-limbed and lithe, into the dipping-pool, waded upstream, quick-eyed, to catch crayfish, or fashioned reed flutes on which to pipe a tune. It was only with Nant, his favourite, that he was stern. 'For he be the pick o' the basket, and the one to do me top credit,' he said to himself whenever he watched the child who most resembled Glythin. By the uncommon good looks of his eldest he was gratified, rejoicing to hear folk speak as though it were all his own doing. 'That boy o' mine be a queer sort,' he would boast, careful to speak with disparagement, lest he should be mocked for excess of paternal pride. 'However I coined to beget an elf like that one, I'm not knowing – such fanciful words do be in his mouth. Foolish! But pretty enough on times; indeed, yes. But there! He'll be growing more sense now just. I'm hoping so, whatever; and he did ought to, since I haven't never spared him the rough side o' my tongue.' He said this because, though he loved Nant, he was seldom quite at ease in his presence. This image of Glythin put him in mind, not of her past self only, but of a young poet who used to stride up the mountain in quest of neither wealth, comfort nor the esteem of neighbours.

'Look sharp, boy! Don't you idle there daydreaming,' he would shout from the fold. 'Have done with twanging my old harp-strings! Come you on out afield with me now quick, and I'll be learning you to harrow.'

Knowing that he would receive a blow if he tarried, the boy left off making the music that was his delight, and became diligent to practise all manner of work upon the farm. He was if he gave his mind to it, an apt pupil; and it flattered Owain to display his own deftness and his authority as a teacher. 'No, no,' he would exclaim, taking the hoe or billhook from the slim fingers and grasping the haft. 'There's terrible arkard you are holding it, boy! With nothing only some old harp or pipe are you handy. Here's the way to catch hold o' your tool, see?'

It was Nant he took with him to fair or market; Nant who must follow behind whenever he mixed among men. In the crowd, assured of respect because he was wealthy, of weight with his fists and known for a firm bargainer, he stood, a head taller than others, his feet planted wide apart, his shoulders thrown back, and valued sheep and cattle, horses and pigs, with alert and narrowed eyes. To whatever he told his stripling about the points of each beast, Nant dutifully gave heed.

'Now mind well what I'm saying.'

'Yes, Father.'

'Have you understood aright though? Why is the roan gelding yonder better worth a bid nor the bay?'

Nant repeated the lesson and Owain nodded approval. 'Tidy enough spoken, if memory o' what I do say 'ould carry you through life. Well, well, soon, I'm hoping, you'll be able to pick wisely for yourself, *bach*.' That his son might some day achieve so much independence did not, as yet, trouble his mind. The lad was wax in his hands; and that was as it should be.

Nant was grown as tall as himself before Owain felt the first stab of jealousy and was amazed to discover that this fruit of his loins might outrival him. Then, to his long-stifled dread of losing the mother through a third careless blow, was added an aching envy of their child's fresh youth.

They were at market together; and Nant, with his pleasant manner, had clinched a deal which Owain had failed to settle. 'Come on,' he said in a grim tone as soon as the business was ended, 'time as we two got home-along. And mind, the minute we're back, to see to that cow as is calving. No sprawling on the settle after supper, d'you hear me?'

'No, Father.'

'Well? What's on you, sluggard? Go you on quick and fetch my horse and your pony from the Green Dragon. Am I to wait at your heels like a dog while you're making sheep's eyes at the girls?'

A flush spread over Nant's handsome face, the skin of which was as fair as his mother's. He turned away in haste and Owain grinned to see how shy he was and easy to put out of countenance. But the petty triumph of mastery was short-lived; for at that moment his glance fell on two pretty maids, such as, in his own youth, when he was fancy-free, he could not have passed without a wish to court. They were both watching Nant; and seeing them whisper together, Owain was stirred by curiosity. He felt ashamed, but could not resist taking a pace up behind them that he might hear what they said. 'No harm,' he told himself, 'in my listening to my own boy being praised.' But when he began to eavesdrop, he suffered a shock, being used only to hear Nant spoken of as a child that did him credit.

'There's lucky you are to live near one so well-favoured,' the girl with chestnut hair tittered.

Owain, watching the brown one, who took his fancy the more, knew her for the daughter of his neighbour in the dingle, and was taken aback. She had been an urchin in torn pinafore, it seemed to him, scarce a month ago. Today, she was tall enough to be full-grown, yet of that womanly height on which a man likes to look down; and her bosom was as rounded as her waist was trim. The dark curls, which he had seen all over her head in disorder, peeped out, now, in neat ringlets from a cap laced with blue ribbons. On this was set her tall-crowned hat, whose brim of sable beaver enhanced the pink and cream of her complexion. Like many a black-lashed damsel, more threatened by time than the blonde, she had a slight dusky down upon her upper lip, and it was, as yet, no blemish. A shapely mouth, he recalled, she had always had; and between a pout and a smile, it was become of rare charm. 'Little teeth,' thought he, 'I'd like to see you nibble an apple – so dainty-white you are!' But it was her eyes that held him. Secret, beneath long lashes, in their moist shining depths was that awareness of his sex which, more than any pure beauty, arouses male desire. Those kindling hazel eyes, at once so soft and so bright, looked past the middle-aged farmer without interest or recognition.

'*Lucky*,' she whispered, repeating her friend's word with a sigh. 'Lucky indeed, is it? *That* one is having the cold heart of a stone, girl. Or else he's giving it away to his old harp, look you.'

'Singing, too, is he? Gifted as well as handsome? You don't say!'

'Singing? So I should think just! Singing all sense and virtue out of a maid, he is.' Her companion laughed and she hung her head for shame at her own admission; then tossed it in defiance. ''Tis easy for you to scoff, that have not listened to him, night and morn, on the far side o' the hedge. There never was a sweeter voice in man or bird or angel.'

When he heard this, Owain turned away so roughly that he half overset an old man at his elbow; and while he asked pardon, he hated the wrinkled face because it bespoke mortality. The chit was crazed! It was but yesterday that his lumper's voice had broken and he had made fun of the braying, now gruff, now shrill, which had taken place of the little boy's clear treble. No, no! Nant was nothing more than a hobbledehoy, and no heed must be paid to any such girlish nonsense. He forbade Nant to sing for many nights thereafter.

But when he next caught him unawares, singing in the stable's darkness, he stood behind him, very still and listened: and when the happy singer made an end, he pressed his lips together and gave a jerk of his head, finding it hard to swallow.

''Tis true,' he announced in a grudging tone, forcing himself to be just. 'Yes, indeed; you've as champion a man's voice now, boy, as ever *I* was having.' He did not add aloud, 'When I was at my best.'

To which tribute, Nant, unaware of pain and displeasure,

flushed hot with generous pride; and, stammering out his gratitude, slipped his arm through his father's.

* * *

Harvest time was come again. The steep fields which he had ploughed, toiling uphill behind Glythin's white oxen, day after day, so long as light lasted, rewarded with their ripened gold the ache and sweat of past labours.

"'Twas worth while,' he said; and before the sun could dry his plump ears of wheat and the glistening beards of his barley, he strode through the grey dew of daybreak to reckon up his riches. Leaning with crossed arms upon a gate, he thought, 'My sowing has brought forth an hundredfold. I wish if poor mother were here to see the crop garnered.' This season, he was a man fortunate beyond his hopes. Next year, he would be more wealthy than ever, and able, at last, to rest in enjoyment of plenty.

At breakfast he ate with relish all the good food his wife set before him. Then, having patted her shoulder, he marshalled his sons and his serving men and marched out at their head to reap. When he glanced behind him to give an order or to make a jest, he remembered his solitary toil and his mother's dread of poverty; and he was proud of the brave company he now commanded, with the sunlight flashing upon their crescent-shaped sickle blades. 'The weather be holding for me grand,' he declared and broke into a song.

But whenever he sang one which reapers had used down the ages, Nant, following after him, like his tall shadow, raised a voice more clear than his: and all the lad's happy songs were new ones of his own making. They were fuller of trills than the song of a linnet, and as passionless, blithe and sweet. If Owain felt envious, as he sometimes did, he could reassure himself by thinking, 'Come you! There be little enough o' feeling, nor of experience neither, in them childish ditties. Fine, indeed, is the lumper's singing voice; and ready I am to grant it. But not until he has felt deep, as I was feeling in my stormy youth, will he come to rival me as a bard. No, no! That day is far off – very far, as yet;' having said which, he amused himself by setting so hot a pace that he hoped to tire out his son, as he tired the whole line of reapers sweating in his rear. But though, at first, his great strength and maturity told in the race, he could not keep on hour by hour without fatigue. At midday, his muscles were aching, and if he flung himself down, as Nant did in the moist shadow of a hedge, he feared lest his limbs might stiffen. By evening, it was Nant's voice alone which heartened the older men; Nant who was laughing, still, and calling out, close on his heels, 'Get on with you, Father! Faster now! Faster! 'Twas you began the struggle, and I be gaining on you, see?'

When the last stook was carried and the gleaners had picked his fields bare, he led his band down the dingle to help his widowed neighbour; and ahead of her sons and labourers, he and Nant continued their jesting combat with song and sickle.

At noon on the first day, a girl came towards them with graceful movements, bringing meat and drink from the house; and when she was drawn near, Owain looked down into those shining hazel eyes which had disturbed him at market. But they were gazing up at Nant; and he – the fool! – was staring at her curved shadow that touched his feet.

It was Owain who took the proffered tankard from the bearer's hand and said to her with playful knowingness, 'You have been butter-making, Olwen?'

In surprise, she turned her eyes on him. 'But . . . well, I never,' she stammered, 'how was you knowing that, sir?'

'Because your fingers be white and soft as curds just.'

He made as if to touch them; but she drew away, swift startled as a fawn; and slowly Nant's shamefaced regard came up from the ground and settled upon her hands. There he stood staring – the great oaf! – with not a word to say, while Owain paid her compliments and was answered by blushing silence and the shifting of her weight from one foot to the other.

'There's pretty, small little slippers you have, girl!'

She tried at once to hide them beneath her skirt; but it reached only to her ankles; and down slid Nant's gaze again till it was fixed just below the hem. At last, with a grimace, Owain wiped the froth from his mouth and ordered his son back to work.

'What manner o' use be your grand voice now?' he could not refrain from asking, as Nant stared in a stupor after the girl's retreating form. 'Why, mun, you dursn't utter a sound, no more nor our born-mute, Thomas!'

The young man did not defend himself but, red in the face and scowling, worked with such a vengeance for hours thereafter that the hired men grumbled for mercy.

Next day, the widow came out afield to offer choice food and to thank Owain for his aid. She was the stout scarecrow of her daughter, with a bristle of hair upon her creased upper lip, beaded sticky with sweat; and she fanned herself with her apron and panted, 'Indeed, neighbour, you're uncommon kind, working so wonderful hard; while as for your eldest son – well, well, 'tis a swift on the wing he be, surely to goodness! Olwen, here, and I have been watching him; and the flash o' his blade through the barley, 'twas fair dazzling our eyes; yes, indeed, 'tis the truth I'm telling you. I wish if *I'd* such a boy o' my own. Worth two he is.'

The girl looked up at Nant from under her curved lashes and smiled demurely. A dimple came and went in her left cheek; and, this time, he smiled back at her. They were both flushed; but neither of them spoke, though their elders went on talking and all the reapers, when they had drunk in turn, joined in the conversation.

On the morrow, as she gave him to drink from a pitcher and the two of them stood a little apart, as if by chance, Nant took a gulp and said, 'There's a mort o' rabbits in the corn.'

She looked at him and away again as though she were afraid. 'Is there?' she murmured.

'Thirty-six I was counting.'

'No, indeed?'

He gave her back the vessel; and so careful were they to avoid their hands' meeting, that between them it came near being dropped. 'Clumsy I am!' he muttered. And after a pause, in which it seemed that they desired to end their constraint by parting, but were held together, victims of a spell, she repeated, 'Thirty-six rabbits. Dear, dear!' Then, in a little while she added, stealing a glance at him, 'Fancy that now!'

'Do your mother bake rabbit pie?' he enquired, frowning over her head at the quivering, hazed horizon.

'On times she do.'

'Are you liking it?'

'Yes . . . Good enough . . . Yes, thank you.'

'In that case, I'll be snaring you plenty o' rabbits when they do come prime, under the hunter's moon.'

'Oh, thank you kindly,' she said, scarce above a whisper; and the colour of a wild rosebud tinted her neck, overspreading her face and forehead right up to her dark curls. 'I thought as you took heed o' nothing nor nobody, only your singing?'

'I'm changed,' he told her with a sombre stare. Then, hurriedly commonplace once more, he asked, 'Shall I call by passing to see when your mother could do with them rabbits?'

Their eyes met; and taking fright anew, she snubbed him

in a prim tone as she turned to go. 'No need for you to
trouble. My brothers are catching all the old rabbits we do
want.'

'As you please,' Nant addressed her straight back in
anger, and snatching up his sickle, he slashed away at the
barley.

Owain, who had watched this scene from the corner of
his eye, while he made pretext of binding sheaves, told
himself, for his own comfort, that the young were more
foolish than owls in daylight.

At the widow's harvest-home gathering, he noted with
satisfaction how Nant and Olwen shunned each other: he
singing at random, turned away from her guarded scrutiny;
she, whenever he glanced in her direction, responding with
over-bold gaiety, for so modest a maid, to the sallies of other
admirers. Both were bright-eyed and fever-flushed, laughing
and talkative; yet neither looked happy; and at the supper's
ending, their two plates stayed piled with food. At parting,
he was profuse in thanks to his hostess and her sons, his
civil words stumbling forth in a bashful rush; but he did
not bid Olwen goodnight. 'She's had enough o' him. Small
wonder,' thought his father, until he looked back from the
threshold to see that her eyes were flooded with tears, though
a company smile struggled to keep itself firm on her lips.
Then, once again, he was stabbed with jealousy; not that he
hankered after Nant's sweetheart, but because these two had
their courtship ahead of them.

Under the stars, Glythin touched her son's stiffened arm
and passed her hand down it in a soothing caress. 'Go you
back, *bach*, and find me my shawl, will you, dear? I was
leaving it in Olwen's keeping.'

Without a word, he went. The lamplight from the doorway
shone forth and vanished so fast, it was evident he had
rushed in headlong.

'Was you doing that on purpose, Missus?' Owain asked.

'They will hurt themselves needless-like, those two,' Glythin answered.

'If our lumper thinks to start courting at his age, I shall put a stop to his folly. Sharp, too.'

'Oh, Master! Have you forgotten?'

'Go you on! Our case was different.'

'How may you tell the difference, who are not within his breast?'

'Different altogether,' Owain repeated with obstinacy. 'I hadn't no father alive; nor no home so prosperous as he's having.'

'Or . . . d'you mean, you'd have submitted to act more wordly-wise nor you did in courting me?'

'No, no,' he said, taking her arm, 'I've never regretted my choice – or but rare and seldom, indeed. And then, again your gifts have been making me rich. But what is that foolish boy knowing?'

'His own heart,' she replied; and added with a sigh, 'soon he will know it, whatever. Yes, Master; for good or ill, the choice be his, not ours.'

They were half-way home before Nant overtook them, walking very fast with light steps, and whistling a lively air.

'Here's your shawl, Mother *fach*. And lucky 'twas, look you, as you'd left it behind.'

'Why, dear?' she asked, but Owain knew from her voice that she was smiling in the dark.

'Oh, 'twas winning me a bidding to sing at our neighbours' again. Tonight . . . indeed and indeed,' he hesitated, anxious for reassurance, 'I wasn't doing myself credit, was I now?'

'No, *bach*. You were out o' temper.'

'Well, I'm not out o' temper no longer, see?' He laughed and kissed her, hugged his father's arm, and sped on ahead of his parents with strides that leapt uphill to the dance-measure of his whistling. Over them, as they followed soberly, the night wind sighed.

'Where have you been so disgraceful late?' Owain demanded, strict as a schoolmaster, before the next moon had waned.

Nant, sheepishly entering the kitchen, long after the maids and his brothers were gone to rest had no ready answer. 'Out-about, same as other young men,' he muttered, turning his back to prolong making fast the door.

'I'll not have it, d'you hear, boy? No matter what randy trickses the careless-reared may get up to, I'll have *my* sons behave respectable.'

'One 'ould think I was still in petticoats,' grumbled Nant; and below the sun-bleached locks which clustered at his nape, his parents could see his strong, tanned neck, brick-red.

'Speak civil to your betters, can't you!' cried Owain, ready to release the anger pent within him for weeks.

Glythin stayed her spinning. 'Master dear, when the song has been sung, not the bard himself can recall words gone from him. Neither, when the child is begotten and has left the womb, can father or mother retain him. Let our son go the way of his own choice. We may hinder, vex and thwart him; but we cannot stop his loving.'

'You're over soft, Missus,' said Owain. 'I am master, still, under this roof.' And when Nant turned to face him, he repeated, 'Where have you been, boy? No telling lies now.'

Man to man, they looked straight at each other.

'To ask her mother's leave to keep company with Olwen.'

'I never heard foolisher nonsense!'

'I'm a child no longer, Father.'

'You'll bide at home o' nights.'

'But we are to be wed.'

Owain measured him from head to foot in hostility. 'Go you up to bed this minute, or I'll take the strap to you yet! And don't never again let me hear you talk so dull.'

Made brave by love, Nant stretched out big sinewy hands and defied his father with a smile. 'Look you! There's good enough proof o' my power to keep myself. *And her*,' he brought forth with a gasp. 'And–' his flush deepened – '*Our children*, hers and mine. There's dull you are talking yourself now, that went courting in your day.'

'Don't you dare stand there answering me back!'

The young man's lips ceased to smile and tightened in resolution. 'If you're seeking to hinder our wedlock, I'll be gone from here tonight.'

Owain made as if to strike him but Glythin came between them. 'To pleasure me, *bach*, go you to bed, dear, without no more talk for the while. Your father and I will take counsel when both o' your tempers be cooled.'

And seeing her look of entreaty, Nant obeyed.

*   *   *

Once Owain was persuaded that he could display command by holding out for an ample dowry, he enjoyed his bargain with the widow. Nant sulked or pleaded: Olwen wept or pouted, in turns induced to haughtiness by her kindred, or rendered fearful by her own desire, lest she should lose her suitor. At times, virgin modesty betrayed her into furthering her mother's resistance; at others, Nant's fits of jealousy enabled his father to ask a higher price. They brought their quarrels and their tender fears to Glythin. There was running up and down the dingle, hotfoot, and fluttered consultation at all hours, while the younger boys grinned behind their brother's back but durst not tease him, so short was his temper grown. To Owain, the lovers did not open their anxious eager hearts; for the more he discussed the business of a marriage portion, the less belief would he show in the force of their passion.

'Why must you vex our poor boy by making light o' his feelings?' Glythin asked one evening as she and her husband strolled homeward after paying a visit to their neighbour.

They had been ushered into the musty parlour and offered, not tankards of ale, but a thimbleful each of elderberry wine. 'There's genteel!' Owain had scoffed in a whisper, giving Glythin a nudge, while to their hostess he praised the colour of her liquor. Because she harped upon the market value of her daughter's beauty, he had retorted with a grin, 'There's another side to the case, Ma'am. A haggling mother be apt to out-tire so young a suitor.' His nettled jest had driven the sweethearts, wincing, from the room; and he was a trifle ashamed, but laughed now at his wife, answering her question with one of his own.

'Why must you take so serious the common heat o' young blood?'

'Listen,' she cautioned him; and slipping her hand into the crook of his arm, she brought him to a halt.

'Listen to what, Missus? You're gone fanciful.'

'Over there,' she whispered.

In the dusk, not a breath of wind stirred the crispening air. Above their heads the massive branches of an oak tree spread in black immobility; but as they strained to see, a leaf or two that would have been golden bright but for night's oncoming, floated slow to earth: and there was sadness in the tarnished gold of leaves already fallen about their feet. When Owain moved in impatience, they gave forth a dry rustling.

'That's what you heard,' he muttered. 'Nought but my tread on dead leaves.'

'No, no. I was hearing our child's voice,' Glythin breathed close to his shoulder.

And giving ear with attention, he caught the low murmuring of a man and a maid. He could not tell what words they were exchanging, who stood on either side of their parents' boundary fence with their hands interlocked. But he knew their talk to be tender and brave and hopeful; and to him, of a sudden, the lovers seemed much to be pitied, while yet their promised joy stabbed him with envy. Their faces were veiled by the darkness deepening about him; but he had no need of sight to know that they gazed into each other's eyes and found there what they were seeking – all the loveliness of earth, all the magic wonder of dreams, incarnate in one dear being. Then, because this gallant miracle of faith or folly, perennially fresh as the renewal of spring, was enacted in his presence, he smelled the sweetness of rising sap, heard the thrushes' first song of the year, tasted the drop of honey in flowers he had once sucked dry, and saw again a rainbow long since faded.

'Is ever the full-blown blossom as shapely fair as the bud?' Glythin's whispered question responded to his thoughts.

For her consolation, he was minded to answer that beauty comes to completion with maturity.

'No,' she said, before he had time to speak. 'Do not tell me aught but what you are truly thinking.'

'That you and I are getting on,' he sighed. 'That's what was in my heart, *fach*.'

And though, as they went their way softly, not to disturb the lovers, she spoke, that she might cheer him, in praise of sunset and autumn, he could not but dwell with regret upon the daybreak in April which would never come again.

When they were entered into their house, from which all the young folk were gone in quest of their own adventures, he laid his hand on her wrist as she took up the tinder-box to kindle the lamp.

'Stay! I've a song has just now come into my head. In the twilight I'll be singing it you.'

'Is this the tune?' she asked, and hummed one that was plaintive, set in the minor key, but neither apt for hymn nor dirge, being, he fancied, the echo of a love-song he had heard her carolling years gone by; yet not the blithe song itself.

'Ah, then, 'twas from *you* that I had it? Or something like it, whatever? Indeed now, I thought the sad melody was my own.'

She did not answer but said, 'We'll be singing it together, shall we?'

In the deserted, darkening room, where there was none to listen but themselves, their voices mingled without accompaniment save the ticking of the clock. And these were the words they sang:

> 'Winged youth with plaything arrow
> For lad and maid, thy dart,
> With lively pain, half-pleasure,
> Stabs quick the eager heart.
> Crowned with their hopes they see thee
> And guess not what thou art.
>
> Scarred from thy naked battle,
> Undaunted through all shame,
> To fading eyes, a cripple,
> Bearing a warrior's name:
> Grown old, shall I distinguish
> Or swear thou art the same?'

'Was it you or I made up such sorry rhymes?' Owain would have asked; but, as she turned away from him, he guessed by the raising of her hand to her face that tears were sprung to her eyes. He did not wish to shame her and was himself afraid of the heavy silence fallen between them; so, when at last she struck a light and set straight the kitchen before she followed him to bed, he was careful not to look her way.

*   *   *

That year, before winter set in, autumn blew wild and wet. Throughout the long evenings beside his hearth, Owain listened, but gave small heed to the talk of his younger sons and to Glythin's quiet laughter. With a pretty maid on either side of her, she sat spinning in the firelight; and the low hum of the wheel made such a lullaby as he demanded of his wife, an assurance of calm and comfort, so steady that he almost ceased to hear it. She was a beautiful woman, he saw when he looked at her, trying to discover surprise in beauty too long known; but fine lines of loving-kindness were written around her eyes and her once golden hair was faded. The silver threads upon her temples were fair after their fashion, as the bright gold had been; but they threatened the oncome of age. Her figure had grown mature and in the house her movements were staid. His glance slid away from her to first one girl and then the other. She was more comely than either, for they were but common clay. Yet how pink were their rounded cheeks, how red and full their lips, their glances how saucy as they chattered! He liked to tease them about suitors and to watch them blush. There was no harm in such sport, surely, for he was a decent man and knew where a joke ought to stop.

In the midst of mirth, the door opened. He heard the wind's challenge, the trees' tossing, and felt the gale sweep in upon him. The sluggish blood in his veins was whipped alive by these autumn storms. Compared with them, spring blew mere breezes; and he said to himself, 'I could sing more lustily now, nor ever in my youth, if only I were wishful to sing at all.' When Nant came close, he chose not to look up; for he knew the lad was from his sweetheart, that his face was rapt and his eyes strange with dreams. Olwen had little of loveliness but that which passes away at prime, as her likeness to her mother proved without pity; yet so great was Nant's worship, that, thinking on her, he looked like one kneeling before the Holy Grail. And the sweet blind folly of this made Owain more covetous than ever of his son's youth.

'Sing to us, Nant,' Glythin urged, smiling fondly at him; and though he was turned miser of his secrets, grudging to share them even with his mother, to please her he took up his father's harp and sang the songs he made in praise of his betrothed. At first he faltered and was abashed; but soon he forgot himself, as Owain had done before him, in love and in music. Then, strong in early manhood, his voice, like his father's long ago, throbbed with rapture. The woman's wheels were silenced and in each heart his ecstasy was echoed. Owain, then, could no longer refrain from watching his son. To see him forget his listeners, to hear him pour forth his soul, as free from thought of onlookers as a lark in air, caused envy to ache, as an old wound will do, though it be healed. 'Would that you were forgotten, oh, my youth! And a new generation out o' sight,' Owain lamented in secret. 'For I was never fulfilling my early promise as a bard; and, therefore, unsatisfied, I cannot abide to grow old.' And when Nant made an end of singing and a cricket's chirp broke the stillness, he repeated to himself, 'The grasshopper shall be a burden, and desire shall fail.' Not yet! Not yet awhile.

Howell was with them on his yearly visit. Age and drink had made him soft. He told fewer bawdy tales; but talked with yearning of joys gone by and the love of women long dead. As Owain glanced at him, he saw the purple lips hang loose in a grimace and tears in the blood-shot eyes.

'Ah, the bitter-sweet o' first love,' Howell muttered, staring at Nant, and his fat carcase heaved. 'Only once be it shining, a rainbow in our sky, never to fulfil its promise.' When none gainsaid him, though Nant looked wise in lover's confidence, he smiled ruefully. 'But mind you, lesser loves will gleam in passing. Don't you deny them while you be in the way; for the dark days come too soon, and night without love is cold.'

'What do you most regret, man?' Owain asked this brother of his, who had lived in cheerful self-indulgence, lacking decency and shame.

Without demur, he answered, 'The chances o' pleasure as I let slip.'

That was an impenitent saying; and Owain judged Glythin right when she objected, 'But for every manner o' gain we must be paying, surely? And some have found it worth selling all they had – those lesser riches you do speak of, Brother-in-law – for a single pearl o' great price.'

'You and I have ever been o' that opinion, same as all tidy married folk, Missus,' said Owain.

But Howell cocked an eye at him. 'Are you speaking true?' it seemed to say. ''Ould you not like to have been me, boy, as well as your staid tidy self?'

*   *   *

On the morrow, as he rode to market, he recalled Howell's words and look; and he was restless. Next week, even his younger sons would be treating the girls of their choice at the November Fair. As the travelling showmen were already on the road, he was not surprised, at a bend of the valley, to come upon the yellow caravan of gipsies. Once, he had sought adventure in crossing a dark palm with silver. Now, a man of means, he agreed with the magistrates that such lawless folk should be clapped in the stocks. While they were about, he must look well to his poultry. Still, there was romance in the foreign faces gathered about a wayside fire; and the smell of a savoury stew made his nostrils distend. He would have liked to share their meal, less from hunger than in curiosity to taste a new food. The crooked hag who crouched over the cauldron, with wisps of grey hair and of smoke swirled about her shoulders, was evil and ugly. He could not tell from her wrinkled face nor the cunning slits of her eyes how he knew that she had been a lure to men. But sure of it he was; and when she called after him, offering, in sugared speech, to read his fortune, he heard her wanton past echo in her deep voice, and paused, not ill-pleased by her lavish praise of his figure, his fine clothes and mettlesome horse.

Having smiled, he said to her, 'No, no, Grannie. I'm too old for such green, boyish folly. My fortune be laid up now, safe enough to need no telling.'

'Too old, pretty gentleman? A splendid gentleman like you?' She cackled with sly laughter. 'There's fortune in love, as well as in wealth, ahead of you, the wise can tell at a glance. Why, many's the hot sweetheart you could win yet – if you chose, my dear, if you chose!'

Was that true, he asked himself? He hoped so: but how could a man be sure of his power to please women, who, keeping faith with his wife, never put it to the test?

And this doubt was gall to his conceit, so that he answered, 'Try your old nonsense on the flighty,' and rode on.

But as he passed the caravan, a face looked out at him and for a moment he was held by eyes as dark as midnight lit with stars. She was young, the savage beauty who smiled at him with a flash of teeth whiter than sugar. Her look of invitation followed him as he jerked his horse into a trot. The black plenty of her hair, tied loose in a scarlet ribbon, the red glass rings in the lobes of her small ears, and the curve of her tawny throat: he dwelt upon these things with a stinging pleasure.

When his business was done in town, he thought of her again as he jogged the lonely miles homeward; for a man had to think of something new, for a change, who had struck the normal good bargain and would eat the usual good meal at his journey's end. What sport she would offer to an unmarried man! A younger man. Ah, if he did not love his wife, he would be young enough yet for a sinful flutter! Or would the saucy trollop scorn him, preferring a lank youth like Nant, as Olwen had done? He found himself craving to know whether the gipsy would welcome him for her suitor; but never could so unseemly a question be answered. With eyes averted, he passed the caravan. Best not risk a sight which had stirred longings that must be held in check. They had troubled him more than once of late; and he blamed Howell's lewd talk for it. Unsettling, his stories were, to any husband, however faithful.

Turning into the lane that led uphill, he tightened his reins of a sudden and sat listening. Never had he heard a woman's voice so passionate and so begetting of passion. What if the singer should be the girl he had seen that morning? '*If*,' he said to himself. 'But there be no *if* about it. Sure I am 'tis she.' For this voice matched the dark face at the window and the smile which had bidden him enter. The rain had ceased but the mountains towered purple against a grey scurry of clouds. An angry wind moaned in the branches hurled the last russet leaves, cold as toads, against his face; and, rising and falling upon the blast, he heard a song that stung him like a whiplash. The melody had a harsh, discordant cadence; the words were in an uncouth language; and both excited him. If this were gipsy music, why had he not heard it before; why, for so many years, forgotten that he was a bard? All who sang the blood afire were his kindred, no matter what their custom or colour. He must have word with this kindling singer, cost him what it might.

When her wild song ceased, he stood up in his stirrups and looked over the hedge. She was crouched on the ground, setting a snare; and he watched with lively pleasure her lithe movements as she sprang up at sight of him and twisted away, one bare arm flung above her face, as though she feared a blow. Furtive and fierce, from beneath its graceful curve, like an animal at bay, she challenged him with those great eyes, so dark and bright. He looked her over, slowly relishing her defiance and timidity. Her waist was slender enough for his two hands to encircle but her breasts were full-rounded, a pillow for his head. In fancy he laid it there, telling himself that no harm came of a man's idle daydreams.

'Stay where you are, my pretty. Don't you be running away,' he called aloud.

With a supple gesture, she hid the snare beneath a naked foot. 'I was only singing in the field, kind gentleman,' she cooed. 'Not doing any mischief, as your Christian God's my witness.'

'I saw what you were doing,' he told her with a laugh.

She grew brazen at that and smiled into his eyes, the pupils of her own contracting to black pin-points. 'Is this some other Georgio's field, sweet gentleman? If so . . .' With a shrug, she stepped aside and exposed her snare of stick and string. She had no shame and he liked her the better for it.

'Don't you never lie,' he laughed, 'unless 'twill serve your turn?'

She put her head on one side and looked at him through fluttering lashes. 'To *you* I'll tell the truth . . . *Is* it your field, generous gentleman?'

'Yes, yes. 'Tis my land you're poaching on, you hussy! But you're welcome to a rabbit for that fiery hot song o' yours.'

'Shall I sing you another, my tall, blue-eyed, beautiful Georgio – my noble prince on horseback, dressed so grand?'

'As many as you please. And pay me all the honeyed compliments you will. I'm relishing your buttered tongue, you rogue!'

'Then cross my palm with silver – only for luck – there's a kind gentleman,' she wheedled.

'Go you on! Why should I pay you for poaching? There's a brazen piece you are!

'But I can see in your handsome face 'tis your nature to be open-handed,' she answered. And with a swing of her rounded hips, coming slowly up to the hedge, she thrust her hand through it and looked coaxing.

'There's dainty small your little brown hand is,' exclaimed Owain; and he leant out of the saddle to fondle it. 'I never saw one with fingers so tapered, for all 'tis weathered dark.'

'Your silver will suit it, you'll see.' And when she had hold of his coin, she made fine play with her glance as she was thanking him. 'God bless you, generous gentleman! If only I were your sweetheart, how white I'd keep my skin! I am not brown all over,' she told him with an edged laugh. 'And now shall I sing you a song of love, Your Honour?'

'Are not all your songs of love, that you sing in that deep, witching voice? If not, the voice itself is making them so. I knew it for yours afore ever I saw you in the field.'

'You are clever, as well as handsome. Tell me how you knew?'

'Because 'tis twin to the smile o' greeting I had from your window, passing by this morning.'

She laughed in her throat. 'You should have stayed to visit me, my dear, my handsome one.'

'Would you have sung to me?'

'If that's what you had asked for.' And she began to chant very low and soft, looking into his eyes and swaying her body in time to the slow seductive tune.

'And if I had begged for a kiss, as well?' He had meant to be playful; but suddenly he commanded her with harshness, 'Come here at once and kiss me!'

The veins in his temples were throbbing and his mouth was parched. Still he intended to do no wrong, but only to take a swift kiss across the hedge. But such scant pleasure was not enough for her. She chose to goad his lust with an artful show of reluctance, dragging her little bare feet through the grass and hanging down her head, while she stole, a step at a time, towards him.

'Come,' he said, resisting a strong temptation to leap down and vault over the gate. Whyever should he not do so, he began to ask himself. Howell would never have held back, but would crow over the scruples of a married man, could he see him at this instant. His hand gripped the mane; his foot was already slipped free of the stirrup, when from higher up the track he caught the clear notes of Nant's whistling, sweet and pure as a thrush's. And all at once he was ashamed. Without another word to the gipsy, he struck his horse a blow that made it rear and in a moment was galloping fast for home.

*   *   *

'I 'on't come to the pleasure fair with you young folks,' he told his sons that night.

'Whyever not, Father? You are one to enjoy it, even at your age.'

'Let my age be,' he answered, short of temper; and, controlling himself, he added, 'Your mother isn't caring for noise and jostle. And indeed I did ought to know better myself at the time o' life you're reminding me of so often.'

'Come you,' said the youngest, in boyish patronage. 'You're young enough at heart yet, I shouldn't wonder.'

'Younger nor any o' you, maybe,' Owain told him with a grim smile. 'If you was able to look into my heart . . . Still, I'll bide at home with the Missus here. 'Tis my duty.'

'And for me to have your company is pleasure,' she answered with a grateful look, slipping her hand into his as they sat together in the shelter of their inglenook. Idly he played with her fingers and noted how the work she had done in his house for twenty years had coarsened them. Nor were they as supple as they had been. To his dismay, he saw, distinct as though it were the well-known, the kind one, which he held, the small brown hand of the gipsy, with backward-curving, cruel, pretty fingers.

'No more gadding about for me,' he declared with such vehemence that Glythin looked at him with a question in her eyes; and they were grey as a clouded sky. 'No more listening to Romany song and flattery,' was his unspoken thought.

Nevertheless, Howell induced him to go to the fair. The ageing fat man, too lazy to bestir himself in field or fold, looked forward with childish greed to an evening's outing.

'We two old brothers 'ull be company for each other,' he urged. 'The lads 'ull be off hot-foot after the girls; and what 'ull I be consoling myself with then, mun? Nothing only cask and bottle.'

Owain reminded him testily of the fifteen years between them in age. 'We old brothers, indeed! 'Tis only along o' my having married so young, as you're seeing me middle-aged. I'm not long turned forty, when a man is in his prime.'

'Forty and four,' chuckled Howell. 'Don't you forget the four, now. Every step is leaving its mark on a man when he's climbed to the watershed. 'Twas up all the way to that point; but 'tis downhill ever after.'

'Go you on!'

''Tis the truth I'm telling you, Brother. That's why you are not liking it.'

*   *   *

As they strolled past booths and peep-shows, the rank smell of damp canvas recalled to Owain the boy who had craved to miss no sensation, good or ill, that he might become a famous bard to whom all secrets were known. Now, as then, he blinked at the hot flares and gazed up at the stars, remote in night's vast sky. Smoky orange and pure silver: he was stirred by them both. But tonight the resin-tanged lights of the pleasure fair were the more to be desired. He was elated by the clash of music, one tune vying against another, by the laughter of a holiday crowd, by the happy screams of girls in swing-boats.

'There's no fun,' thought he, 'without some spice o' fear and danger in it.'

Howell took him by the arm and began to chuckle. 'Not wishing me to mention as you were a day over forty! Ah, you poor-spirited stay-at-home! You be mortal unwilling to part with your youth. And why, man? Because you've missed to enjoy it.'

'I've enjoyed it in my own way, well enough, Brother.'

'In *one* o' the ways laid open to you, say. Not in all, mun. Not in all.'

'No man can walk every road at once,' Owain answered with regret.

'But each in turn, he can . . . Look, there's a pert little piece been flaunting herself afore you this half-hour. And all you durst do is keep your back on her, like a coward in flight from naked combat. Go on, man! Put your arm around her. Give her a squeeze. I never saw an unstayed waist so fetching. Kiss her, you fool! Such ripe red lips for the offering; and 't'on't be for long now, a pretty wench is giving you the chanst!'

'I'm not wishful to take it.' But as he said this, Owain knew that he lied. He had feared to come into this place of foolish levity, lest he should meet the gipsy whom he had lusted after; and sure enough, she was in pursuit of him, a menace and a joy. Jostling in the enclosure between the giddy whirling roundabouts, was an army of younger men. The harsh light flickered upon their ruddy faces and lithe limbs. Those that had not brought their sweethearts, clasping them tight for safety, were bright-eyed in quest of one; and quick, hot, shallow love was in the air. She, with her bold allure, a crimson shawl sheathing her figure, her neck and arms exposed to draw all male glances to her, could have taken her pick of venturesome youth, for whom the modest girls in bunched petticoats, sleeved to the wrist, were too tame. Yet, unasked, she followed *him*. From the corner of his eye, he saw her toss her head at this fine lad and thrust that one aside. Hands were laid on her body to detain it; but she threw them off and would look at none but himself. He did not pause to ask whether his wealth were in any way concerned, but let his flattered vanity betray him at last into answering her smile with a wink. No sooner had he done so, than he regretted it, for she came close and whispered, 'You begged me for a kiss the other day, sweet handsome gentleman.'

'Gone is the day that's over,' he replied with an uneasy laugh.

'And can't its promise never be renewed, dear Georgio?'

'How could I be kissing you, you baggage, with watchful neighbours and my grown sons about?'

'Have you forgotten my yellow caravan? There it stands empty, waiting.' As she pointed, her hand brushed his cheek and he felt it flame. 'Many and eager are the young men who have entreated to follow me in there tonight.' He drew back; but she put her warm lips to his ear and her breath set it a-tingle. 'We should be safe from prying yonder, my lovely princeling . . . Well? What's hindering you? I can promise you such keen pleasure as you've never tasted – gipsy love, sweet in itself, and a rare new treat for you.' He shook his head, but stayed to hear what brazen offer she would make him next. 'Come,' she crooned, 'I'll pleasure you for nothing, because you please me so, though gold and silver and trinkets I could gain from a dozen that offered to empty their purses in my lap.'

'No, no,' he said in belated haste to escape. 'T'ouldn't be right.'

'Why did you come here, dear foolish Georgio, if you thought it wrong to enjoy yourself for once?'

'I wish as I hadn't come now. Let go my arm, you hussy!'

But her caressing fingers slid down it to the bare wrist. 'I'll sing to you,' she urged. 'Does that not 'tice you, who are loving music?'

''Tis 'ticing me, yes. 'Tis a sore enticement and hard to withstand.' Then he remembered his wife and frowned as he wrenched his wrist free from her rival's artful stroking. 'Get along with you! Sing your unchristian songs and hawk your indecent wares to others.'

He had hoped she would leave him in anger; but she laughed in his face and the sugar-white of her teeth delighted him. Nevertheless, he tried to move away, only to find himself held by his brother.

While he was ogling the girls, Howell's bloodshot eyes had been bland. Now they were hard as stones and his loose mouth gone tight with contempt.

'Are you calling yourself a man?' he jeered. 'Maybe you're afeard, at your age, to fail? The decline o' forty and four is holding you back from manly pleasure, is it?'

Owain gave him so rough a push that he reeled sideways. 'A'right,' he said in a rage-thickened voice to the gipsy, 'take me to your stolen nest, you little cuckoo! *I'll* be showing you if I've aught to dread from my years, see?'

Behind him, as he went with her, he heard his brother's lewd laughter; and ashamed to own that he was become as Howell had been, a common lecher, he sought to decorate lust. A bard, he told himself, sees the animal beauty in passion. The girl's deep voice rekindled his slumbering dreams; and had not her supple limbs grace to quicken his eyes to earth's wonders? To hear, to see, to feel, these were his chief duties.

What was a sin in others, therefore, for him was needful and right. So he argued, he having let slip the knowledge that in a single love, if it be deep enough, every lesser one is revealed.

Beneath the swaying fringe of crimson shawl, he watched the trollop's ankles as she climbed the ladder. Her skin was brown but smooth-glossed, pleasing to handle rather than to see. There was mud on her naked soles, but what did he care? She was the child of the pleasure fair that would vanish with all its gaudy caravans and piebald lean horses tomorrow, leaving the churned field to nature's swift recovery. Often, he had seen Glythin's white feet dance light through dew-fresh grass. Washed in pure water was her body, scentless-clean and of maiden modesty, still, in its shy ways. He had been proud to own a wife so dainty; but this was a new adventure; and no man sings the same songs all his days. Moreover, it was long since he had sung her cool ones on the hill-tops; and his mother's old fireside melodies were grown stale with repetition.

Into a very small space he followed his light-o'-love; and though he stared at her greedily, he was aware of many things at once. Women's bright-coloured clothes were tossed on the shelf that was her bed. Like the gay rugs and cushions which littered an unswept floor, they gave out a pungent odour. This was compounded of some sweet perfume, blent with fumes of gipsy cooking, of staled sweat and tobacco. To it was added the oil-reek of a lamp. 'A man could be drunk through his nostrils, only, here,' he thought; and when she poured out a draught of powerful liquor and held it to his lips, he tasted and knew well enough, despite his mounting excitement, why she had given it him to drink.

'A love potion?' he heard himself ask and listened to the rasp of his own laughter. 'There's little need o' that, I can tell you . . . Come here.'

But she slipped out of reach, fluttering her lashes at him, and began to draw the pins from her hair till it tumbled in long snake locks to tail about her thighs. Above the rim of the tankard, he watched her swaying movements while he gulped. She drew a shutter over the tiny window. She slid a bolt across the yellow door. He saw the lines of scarlet along the panels, and the red glass-earrings, like drops of blood, in the darkness of her hair, and the gleam of her shoulders when she unwound her shawl and stood before him stripped. He heard his heart thudding. He relished the sharp intake of his breath and hers: panting they were, and mingled. In a moment he had gripped her body and was looking down into her eyes, so close to his that they were blurred, wide open, moist and shining. As he crushed her limbs against his own, those fierce eyes shut in languor and her head fell back. His teeth closed upon the throbbing flesh of her neck. Fire seemed to consume his bones; and he was too shaken in the flame of his own burning to utter a word of endearment. Nor did he feel any love. Almost with hatred, in a rage of desire, he took her; and when she lay limp beneath his slackened weight, he again heard himself laugh. It was a proud sound, untender as the crow of cock in the bleak hour before daybreak.

*   *   *

In the small hours of the morning, when spirits take flight from the body, he crept with candle, hand-shaded, into his own clean room. Glythin sat graven as marble within the recess of their bed. The white coverlet showed shapes of knee and feet extended straight and pressed together as though she were stiff with cold. Her face in the wavering light looked so haggard that he was startled.

'Whyever are you not asleep?' he asked her.

'Oh, my heart, my poor sick heart, I had an ill dream of you!'

She held out her arms to him. They were white, still, as the cotton-reed that flowered in June beside her lake; but they were not the arms of youth. He stared at them, remembering others, brown and hot, which had clutched him, and little sharp nails, he could feel, that dug into his flesh. Gently, if he went to her, his wife's arms would fold round him in love. He turned his back on her. 'Mine cannot be the kiss of Judas,' he thought; and aloud he said in a rough tone, because he hated himself, 'Go you to sleep again. Foolish you are, giving way to dreary old fancies; and I am over weary to get arguing.'

Every night, thereafter, he lay long awake, seeing in the dark a naked body writhe; hearing in the silence quick breath and a woman's short cry, neither laugh nor sob. Nightly he was aware that Glythin, close beside him but untouched, uncomforted, kept vigil. She did not stir. Sometimes, he fancied, she wept. If so, she made no sound. But always he felt her presence, uncomplaining, sad; and his pity for her pricked him with shame, goading him on to make excuse for himself. The mother of grown children, surely she no longer desired his embrace? Almost, he persuaded his conscience, it would be unseemly for her to do so. Only her pride, perhaps, suffered? Ah, yes, she was proud! She would not stoop to ask him what was wrong. Had she loved him with ardour, she would have upbraided him wifely; and he might have found ease in confession. At moments, he longed to confess; yet, afraid to do so unurged, he argued that her cold reserve was at fault. Did she guess the truth, or, being no common mortal, did she know it for sure? Asking himself such questions, he grew daily more taut in her company and stinted her of those caresses which for years had sweetened their toil and talk. That she missed these sorely, he could see;

but if he forced himself to kiss her, he thought, ''Tis the kiss o' betrayal. Deceit has driven all pleasure out of it.'

So it came to be not lust for the gipsy alone that spurred him to visit fairs far and wide, riding further afield than he had ever done. To be gone from the home in which he had been at peace was now a relief; and any excuse for absence would serve. His younger sons begged to come with him, but he bade them stay and work; and Howell, like a gelded cat at the fireside, blinked slyly at him and treated his trouble as a joke. Whenever they were alone, he wheezed out a worldling's advice.

'T'ont last long – the wanton's favour; no more nor your own spurt o' youth. The candle is giving a fine last flare afore 'tis douted. Make you the most o' it boy. Soon 'twill be over; and small harm done, look you. A fond wife and a patient is bearing no ill-will. Well enough she is knowing the case to be a common one. Why, I have seen a score o' such, I tell you. And who be you to set up yourself above other sinful men?' Then he would chuckle and add with a wink, 'See if you don't start singing again more tuneful nor ever before, same as the birds that be game to venture a second hatch!'

Owain, wishing to believe him, came to do so, while supplied with such handy arguments. 'When the season o' fairs is passed,' he reasoned with himself, 'the gipsy will be gone. Then, having relished this brief sin, which 'twere a pity for me to have missed, I shall again desire my own good wife as I was doing formerly.' Never need she know the cause of his present coldness – unless she already knew? Covertly watching her in this suspicion, he became ever more constricted, and with the passing of weeks a blight fell even upon his affection, because he could no longer be frank, so that his manner towards her turned surly. Often he spoke without civility, blaming her in a harsh tone for trifling matters, not her fault; and when she replied with forbearance, it made him sore. Had she answered him back, they might have quarrelled and the blame not have been all on his side. He came near hating her at times for that goodness which he had once prized.

'You led me astray with your wicked talk,' he growled at his brother. ''Twas you made me fancy adultery was only pleasure; unlike marriage, imposing no bonds whatever. You lied, God rot your soul!' And he slammed out of the house. In the fold he was rough with the cattle, their helpless patience provoking him to cruelty, who had been accounted a merciful man. 'The cheat,' he often murmured, thinking of Howell's lies; and he would strike some dumb beast that hindered him, and swear at the servants whom he had used to praise. Howell had urged him to be free; and behold, he was chained by an increasing hunger of body for the gipsy, Miriam, and by the irk of duty to his wife. While the new flame burned ever more fiercely, lit by that which it fed upon, old memories of a love more gracious haunted him, like ghosts which no door can shut out. The double set of fetters dragged him this way and that, causing his eyes to grow hollow and his temper, week by week, more sour.

*   *   *

Christmas came; and in the blaze from his hearth, he watched with envy the faces of young folk, and heard their singing.

The two pretty serving maids were arch with a suitor apiece. His younger sons made merry in a herd of boys and girls, not yet paired off, but a-quiver to one another as leaves in the breeze that foreruns a storm; while Nant sat in a corner thrumming the harp. From beneath his golden lashes he gazed at his betrothed. It seemed he could never tire of winning her swift shy smile, his rare reward. Howell, round as a barrel in their midst, lolled, tankard in fist, jesting at everyone's expense and at his own. When he had drunk enough to make him sentimental, he wiped his watering eyes and declared he would give his soul for a night of youth and tenderness.

'Such callow lad's love as be content to stare,' he said, and then began to quake with laughter that shook his great belly. 'Only fancy! I mind onst stealing a maiden's small little shoe and hiding en under my pillow to kiss by stealth o' nights. Ah, but then, I remember different – mortal different – fashions o' spending the dark hours! Why, when I shipped to Lisbon . . . !'

'Hush, Uncle, for shame,' Nant cautioned him, lest Olwen should be put to the blush.

Glythin moved quietly among her children's guests, serving them all with a kind word and a smile. At the end of each song she clapped her hands and at every joke she contrived to laugh. But when her face stilled, it was pale-drawn with grief; and seeing her listless, shadowed eyes and her lips' pensive droop, Owain was impatient again for Miriam's bold laughter and roguish flashing glance. He took his harp from Nant and sang the ballads he had learned in boyhood, pouring the lustful throb of gipsy rhythm into the purer music of his race.

'That's a new way you have, Father, o' singing *Watching the Wheat*,' Nant objected. 'Singing it you are as if it did ought to go to drum-beats, not to harp-strings.'

''Tis how I always sang it: no different from others, boy.'

'No, no. You are making it sound . . . Well, I don't know indeed? Not like wheat in a cool breeze, wet and new-green; but as if the heat and clash of a fair was in the tune.'

'Go on! You're over-fanciful, same as your mother.' And in defiance, Owain asked his wife, 'Am I not singing that old favourite o' yours, the same as I did when we were first wed?' Stooping over the fire to roast nuts, she professed not to hear. 'Come,' he said, frowning, and asked the false question again.

She rose and looked mournfully into his eyes. 'No,' she answered in a low tone and turned away.

* * *

Because he was not happy, Owain determined the more to disport himself. Nant's wedding was due in March; and throughout January, frost-bound and bitter east-winded, he spoke much of the festivity. When he could find no cloak for spending day or night with Miriam, he was caged at home and began to loathe the four walls of his kitchen. 'I've passed enough dull hours in my dutiful time,' thought he. 'And more will follow when my lively vagabond is taking to the road in spring. So at least one day this drear winter will I make worth remembering.'

In Olwen's house, since the haggle over her dowry had been ended to everyone's satisfaction, he was welcome; and thither, to escape Glythin's presence, he went often to plan the marriage feast. On an evening in February, depressed by the lead-grey sky, he stared out of his neighbour's kitchen window. She, in her black dress, sat over against him, placidly knitting. Behind her, the wall was lime-washed, spotless white as the hardscrubbed table, while dresser, chairs and stools were of oak so darkened with age, their hue was that of the peat sods stacked beside the fire. Colour was what he craved for. A crimson shawl swathed around a girl's body glowed within his eyelids when he closed them.

'How 'ould it be,' he said, before caution could stay desire, 'to give your wedding guests a treat out o' the common?'

'A capital notion, indeed,' assented Olwen's mother, 'if I was only knowing how to contrive some rare thing.' Then, having studied his face, she screwed up her faded lips, that mimicked the shape of her daughter's, and smiled knowingly. 'Out with it, Neighbour! You're like a small little lumper before the jam-closet door, afeard to speak your request.'

'I was only thinking . . . an idle fancy, maybe . . . suppose you was to have the gipsies to dance and sing?'

She threw up her hands in dismay, letting drop the knitting needles into her stout lap. 'That low lot in a tidy Christian dwelling!'

'I'd be answering for their proper conduct. And paying them for you myself, I'd be.'

'Well, well, whatever's come over you who 'ould bargain for the skin off o' your grannie's corpse!' He sat in sulky silence, wishing he had not spoken, and she went on to enquire, 'However could you make sure, man, as they 'ouldn't be stealing nothing?'

'Why, I'm buying horses off them, look you. They dursn't cross *me*, Neighbour. What's more, if you should happen to miss any trifle, I'd be making good the loss.' She looked so amazed that he hastened to say, 'Such music as they 'ould give us be worth a fraction o' risk.'

'You're knowing a deal about them. *I* never heard no gipsy music in my life. But they've been after my hens, the villains!'

'You'd like their singing grand; and 't'ould cause your girl's wedding to be the talk of a generation.'

'Like as not. But 'ould it seem respectable?'

'If they only came in late, after dinner and grace were ove . . .' And he continued to urge her consent until, reluctant, she gave it.

*   *   *

Next day he put on his best clothes in which to visit Miriam and rode whistling into the market town. Having stabled his horse at an inn where he hoped that none knew him, he went in stealth after dark to an alley in which a row of dirty hovels leaned like drunkards against one another. He was ashamed as he tapped on a broken window-pane stuffed with rags.

For a man of his standing, it was humiliation to flatten himself
under eaves of rotting thatch, lest any passer-by should see
his face. And yet, whenever he did this, the sport of a boyish
prank relieved the squalid adventure, bringing back a small
part of his youth before Glythin was known to him. How
sweet the stolen apples had tasted that were seasoned with
dread of a beating! Howell had taught him to laugh at
himself, as Howell laughed at all men. 'There's comical I am,
a rich farmer and highly respected, stuck fast to this grimy
old wall like a lick o' paint,' he reflected, making belief with
a grin that there was no sting in such self-mockery. The hag,
whom he had first seen in autumn crouched over the gipsies'
camp fire, opened the door in answer to his signal. He knew
her well by now, with her traces of ravished beauty and her
hunger for the gains of a whore-mistress.

'God bless you for coming, kind gentleman,' she whined.
'In a dying fever of love the poor doting creature has been.
Heaven's my witness, dear Georgio, she's wasting away for
you. As I live, I've to pour out wealth in 'ticing her to eat
dainties. She wouldn't touch a morsel, else. She'd fade away.
And what it's all costing the poor old Romany Grannie . . .'

'Yes, yes,' he said with impatience. 'I've been hearing all
that tale before now. Is it more of my money you're wanting?'

'Only a small little coin or two,' she wheedled. 'You'd
never grudge Grannie the keep of one that dotes on you so?
Give me silver, sweet generous gentleman, a trifle to drink
your health and this night's happiness to the two of you.'
As soon as ever he put his hand in his pocket, she dropped
the pretence that Miriam was ailing and began slyly to cackle.
'You'll find her worth gold, not silver, since you've kept her
waiting for nights. Pay me well, rich Georgio, and I'll keep
from the house till dawn; by your Bible book I'll swear it.'
She held out, palms upwards, the skinny hands with tawny
clutching fingers and blackened nails which he hated,

because, in their gestures of greed or malevolence, was an ugly likeness to those of his pretty doxy. And in contempt that, like a trapped animal, bit back hurtfully at himself, he threw her a coin.

'There! Now be gone; and mind to keep away.'

'Only *one* piece of silver? And you so wealthy and open-handed!'

'Here's another then. Get on out o' my way.'

As she caught the crown piece and cringed in thanks, he stood aside to let her pass. She had the sour smell of age and dirt, added to that hot pungency of Miriam's which spurred desire. He dreaded to be near the foul witch, for in her decay she foretold the unlovely future of her granddaughter. Moreover, her leer and her whispered promises of bought pleasure made him wince. But when he was entered into the disordered room, reeking with odours both sweet and stale, and Miriam darted panting into his arms, he forgot everything but the warmth of her limbs twined around his own.

'Oh, you are come! You are come! Let me feel you. Kiss me again. Now again. Again. Hold me tight. I thought I'd die for sure, waiting so long. Have you missed me? Have you lain awake these barren nights?' He told her 'Yes,' but that did not satisfy her. 'Have you betrayed me?' she demanded. 'Have you lain with that cold wife of yours? Ah, you look guilty! You have! And I'm faithful to you, though I burn. Tell me you've not given her such kisses as you give me? 'Twas I taught you to kiss. I could kill her for sharing the least of you. 'Tis to *me* you belong.'

She was mad with jealousy of Glythin if he had been absent from her for a single day and in a frenzy of curiosity to know all he had said and done. He forbade her to speak of his home. For the love he bore Glythin and the flame which this burning girl lit in his blood were at war. Yet her hatred of his wife fed his vanity, and he could not look in a mirror when he shaved without smiling to think with what violence he was desired by a beauty young enough to be his daughter.

This night, as on many others, when passion had spent itself and they were tired and hungry, she rose to stretch and yawn delicately as a cat. From a cupboard she brought food and spirits, and sitting on his knee, fed him with morsels and, laughing, sipped from his glass. 'No, not that side, sweet Georgio,' she crooned. 'My lips must touch the same place as yours, look.' Then, once again, she began to wheedle him into talking of his marriage. 'Tell me, gorgeous lover, that pale one I saw walking mute to church, *she* never made you happy as I do? Don't turn away your head or I shall cry. Say "No", say "Never".'

'No,' he muttered. 'But let us not think o' her.'

'Not even when she was young? *Did* she? No? Swear it, to make me happy. And now she's a faded, an ageing woman, years, *years* older than yourself. Why,' she coaxed, nestling closer to him, 'you're not a day older than I, my strong tireless lover, my lusty sweetheart! Only tell me, to make me glad, as *she* never gave you any o' my joys?'

'I had liefer not speak o' her to you.'

'You are cruel to your poor Miriam. Don't you know I love you to madness? Did *she* ever do so? Oh, no! She married you for a home and children. 'Tis them she loves best, not you. *I* ask for nothing. She is taking all. *I* only crave to give.'

Such impudence made him laugh. 'Your grannie's a giver, too, I suppose, pocketing my silver?'

'Oh, you don't understand nothing,' cried Miriam. 'What if my poor folk take a little o' your wealth – don't I share sweeter things with you? Nothing that's mine but you may take, my greedy dear! And the world, I'd steal in your service. Murder, I would, for you. And hang for it, willing. Would *she* do as much? A comfortable life *she's* had by making you marry her. While *I* . . .'

'Have done. Leave my wife be, can't you?'

She leapt off his knee and standing before him with flashing eyes, stamped her foot. 'You torment me, praising her, the dry withered leaf! The dead thing bound to you by law! You'd laugh if you drove me to plunge this knife in my heart.' She seized one from the table, with a gesture so wild that he was alarmed at what she might do and wrenched it from her. They struggled together in anger, and when she had yielded, she flung herself at his feet and sobbed for pardon. 'Forgive me! Your own poor wretched Miriam! Love me again. See, I'm tamed to your will. Beat me, my great strong Georgio! I'm your slave. Nothing durst I ask. Not so much as to know as I give you pleasure.' She knelt before him, abject, wiping away her tears with the hair tossed over her bare, heaving shoulders. Her abandonment stirred him to pity; and caressing her hot flesh, he told her that none had ever given him such delight of the body as she aroused and assuaged. She started coaxing again, while she rubbed her wet cheek against his knee. 'Your cold wife wasn't never pleasuring you to the full? Tell me that much? I'll vow not to ask you no more. Come, say it, do! *She* never made you happy as *I* can?'

'I do love my wife. And I am grateful to her. I'm loving you, also, after a different fashion. I cannot be talking of her with you.'

She renewed her sobbing. 'Then 'tisn't true you love me. No, not after any fashion whatever. I wish I were dead. When you are gone from me to her, this very dawn I'll take my life, d'you hear?'

To comfort her, at last, he told her Glythin's secret. 'She is of the Fair Tribe. Ah, yes,' he sighed, 'I am needing you, not only for that you do renew my youth o' body, but because you be wholly mortal. While she . . .'

Miriam sat back upon her heels and gazed up into his face.

'Then what folk hint of her is true?' she asked in an awed whisper.

'Oh-aye. True enough.'

Her eyes widened in terror. 'Has the pale one power to cast a spell?'

Owain smiled. 'Have no fear for yourself. She be more harmless innocent nor any Christian ever I met. Yet many fear her, seeing she is strange. What men cannot understand, t'ould seem, they are hating. I, too, on times, am afeard o' the unprofitable dreams she was bringing me in my youth.' He stared at the dirty walls enclosing him and remembered the mountain-tops, the early morning freshness of sky and pool. 'Fearful, too, since then, have I grown o' losing her altogether.'

'How might that be?'

He did not note the eagerness that underlay Miriam's question, but answered as though showing to himself a hidden sore, 'If I should strike her but once more with iron, she must depart from me for ever.'

When he said this, the fear went out of Miriam's eyes. They narrowed, and black as the treacherous pools in a turbary, stared past him, unfathomable. 'If you should strike her with iron?' she murmured.

'Yes. T'ould be the end.'

'She would be driven back to her own place?'

He nodded gloomily. 'The dread o' bringing this doom upon myself has long made me ill-at-ease when she and I be together. 'Tis not her fault, poor soul.'

'If you should strike her with iron,' the gipsy whispered again.

'Come, my pretty. Let us say no more o' this weary matter. Talk to me o' the music you will make at my son's wedding.'

'Yes,' she cried, springing up and clapping her hands together. 'That shall be a day of frolic – of rejoicing. For me,' she added and laughed. Then, wriggling she began to dance before him in her hair-clothed nakedness and to sing a song whose words he did not follow.

'You are full o' gaiety, my cuckoo. That is how I am liking to see you.'

'Yes, my own princely lover. Mine! *Mine*! I've cause to be glad.' And spinning round so that her hair whipped his face, blinding him, she laughed again yet more wildly, as though he had made her crazy with joy. 'Mine, and no other's!'

*   *   *

One dark month stole out and another followed. Time crept. March did not bluster in, scented with rising sap; for winter still held earth in a cruel vice. Neither ploughshare nor spade broke the iron soil. Black-frosted budless trees rose grim as gibbets against a sky from which no sun shone, no rain fell. When the weather changed, it was from a black frost to a silver; and in the dead of night, ice-weighted branches cracked loud as pistol-shots. Starved birds moped at the house door with feathers fluffed out, and Glythin fed them. She stood motionless upon the threshold, her hands outstretched, while finches and robins fluttered about her wrists. Blackbirds and thrushes pecked the crumbs at her feet.

'Can't you be shutting the door,' exclaimed Owain. ''Tis mortal bitter.'

'Yes. Quiet, too, as the grave. Listening today, you'd say all breath o' life had ceased. Yet not being perished quite, these poor creatures do suffer.' Giving the birds a compassionate glance, she came back to the fire and chafed her blue-cold fingers.

'One might think as you made your living by them,' Owain grumbled. ''Tis the stock *I'm* fretted over.'

He feared for his cattle as fodder grew scarce; and on the bald mountains, his sheep, too, were like to die. It seemed as though no blade of herbage would ever sprout nor any leaf unfurl; and in vain he longed to hear, to see or to smell some promise of renewal. 'Spring's late,' said the labourers, content to lounge in the stables' acrid warmth. 'Spring 'ull be still-born,' muttered Owain. 'This age o' winter can be delivered o' nothing only a corpse.'

One day he had been looking to his ewes that might fail in strength to bring forth lambs alive. He strode in gloom down the dingle that was wont to be filled with the sound of running water. Now there was not so much as a drip. The brook was a glacier; and stooping over it, boughs of alders held each a black bone within a limb of ice. Ferns on the crest of either bank had withered away to nothing; but those which, being sheltered, had escaped the first onslaught of frost, were set as if under glass, their fronds a pattern such as he saw daily upon his windowpane. His foot struck a dead rook and it, like the ground, was stone-hard. He scowled at it, thinking that a buzz of carrion flies and the odour of decay, from which fresh life is fed, would be more welcome than this fossil state. Then he became aware of a presence; but was not sure whether human being or spectre were near him.

Glythin was crouched in a dark cloak beside a waterfall, now frozen and silent. The icicles were not more rigid than she. She neither saw nor heard him; in her, as in the stream, life was suspended. Her hands were locked so fast that he saw their knuckles, skeleton sharp and white as snow. Her head was bowed and she stared into the void with eyes as green as shadows cast in ice. Within them it seemed that her tears had frozen. If he kissed her, would they flow again or was her heart frozen also? If he stabbed her with his shepherd's knife, would blood spurt from the wound, or the flesh gape open, powerless to bleed? Even her hair was colourless. 'She is dead,' he thought, 'I dare not touch her. 'Tis useless to cry her name.' And choking with dread, he turned away, not knowing what he had seen or whether for sure he had seen it.

When, in the dusk, she came quietly into the house and went about her work, he fancied it was a ghost that stirred the air in passing close to him.

Next day, a thaw set in. Wind came moaning out of the west and sleet shrouded the sombre hills. Cold rain fell in the valleys, causing water to trickle over the ice and man and beast to slip and fall. Owain forgot his terror of Glythin's death. He was a master of men and must set to work those whom he paid. 'Ploughing 'ull be hard,' they complained. 'The frost has been biting deep.' But he ordered his team of oxen to be yoked and slithered ahead of them over the unyielding ground that was thinly slimed with mire. 'No time to lose. My son's marriage 'ull be 'ticing me off profit, to pleasure, afore the week is out.'

The days passed and so busy was he that he forsook his visits to Miriam. Scarce until the eve of Nant's wedding did he dwell on his long-planned treat. After that, in a few weeks, his light-o'-love would be gone her vagabond's way. Soon enough then for him to return to wedlock and abide thenceforth in safety. Passion spent, he would no more remember it than the earth remembers winter when spring returns. But passion should be satisfied to the full before he let it go.

'Tomorrow will be a jollock time on us,' he told Glythin, as he yawned and lay down to sleep.

'Pray with me that our child may be happy, my heart: more lasting in his happiness, because more wise, than you and I.'

'Do you be praying for the both of us. I have laboured hard and be over-tired for saying prayers.'

As his eyelids closed, he knew that she was kneeling in the dark upon the far side of their bed and striving to pray alone, as he had bidden her do.

*   *   *

At dawn he awoke to see his breath cloud the air and vanish. So brief seemed his little warmth that he felt diminished, in need of consolation, and stretched out his hand for her. He had dreamed that she wept in silence, cast away from him, inconsolable; and both for pity's sake and comfort he longed to be united with her once again. But the place where she had lain was empty, and fear stabbed him wide awake. He sat up, his body taut, to hear the whispered crackle of a woman's hair being brushed. Peering through the twilight, he saw her figure, darkly dressed, and a pallor spread over her shoulders. It seemed as if that fair hair of hers had turned grey in the night.

'Glythin?'

'Yes, my heart?'

'Are you safe, girl?'

She drew in her breath, stood still, and did not answer.

'Why are you risen so soon?'

''Tis our son's wedding day.'

'So 'tis. I had forgotten it.'

'And our own?'

'No,' he said: and as he dashed cold water into his eyes and put on his best clothes that he wore to visit Miriam, he remembered a May morning three and twenty years ago and the glad confidence in which he had sworn to make his wife happy all her hours. Now, through his betrayal, she suffered and he was wretched. 'Life is to blame,' said he. 'I am power-less, being but flesh and blood. Howell be for ever telling me as I could not help myself. Yet I wish this had not changed poor Glythin so. She was comely so long as I desired her, but now is gone faded as a pressed flower.'

When he went down to the kitchen, she was standing at Nant's chair, giving him breakfast. Eager and innocent, aglow in firelight, the youth's face looked up. 'I was like him, once,' thought Owain, and stood beside Nant's mother. 'Are you so wonderful full o' joy, my son?'

Shyly smiling, Nant nodded and ducked his head.

'Yes, Father. Wonderful. It cannot be spoken.'

'Then see as you're making Olwen so. Always in your keeping is the life o' her whom you wed.' As Owain muttered this exhortation he felt no irony in it; but he dared not look into his own wife's eyes.

Together, in the doorway, they embraced their boy and watched him vault on to his pony. He waved a gay salutation as he rode away to meet the troop of young men who would race to fetch his bride. Softened by their bond of parenthood, Owain took hold of Glythin's hand and found it trembling. Her fingers interlaced with his as they had used to do when she led him up the mountain; and in a spasm of loyalty, he asked himself, why, name o' goodness, had he bidden the gipsy wanton to their son's marriage feast? What a rash and ungentle thing that was to have done! But it was too late, now, to undo. Maybe it would not matter? Still, he must be careful lest his poor wife suspected treachery. It irked him to think that, through his own folly, he must guard word and glance this evening when he had longed to be free and merry; and, in resentment against her curb upon his actions, he demanded: 'Does Glythin own me, then?' Such a question did her injustice; and he was vexed with himself as well as with her whose love for him, once a blessing, was become a burden. His hand held hers the faster, yet the rebel in him desired to be rid of her. Not for long, said he to himself, only for a while, only until lust was appeased.

While these thoughts tugged, right and left, in his mind she had laid her head on his breast. He felt the weight of her body heavy against his own, and clasping it to him he wished, in confusion and unrest, that they two had been alone in the world. Then they might have been happy to the end. As he released her he looked down into her face. Seen in this chill light, it was grey and worn. Was it he who had made her old before her time?

'We're not done with winter yet,' he said between chattering teeth, and went indoors, calling to her over his shoulder, 'Wherever have you been putting my pipe and pouch?' As was her habit now, she followed and waited upon him in silence. And when his eyes fell on his disused harp, put by in its corner, he scowled and turned away.

*   *   *

The bustle of festivity had begun. Maidservants ran downstairs with scarlet cloaks over their arms and blue ribbons in their best caps. While they re-laid the table, they chattered like starlings. After them clattered the younger boys, demanding breakfast in haste, before they galloped to join their brother. Thomas lumbered in and grinned his dazed response to cheerful greetings. He stared at the mistress, seeming to wonder why she was dressed for Sunday in mid-week.

'No sense in taking the mute with us,' Owain announced. 'He's not understanding nothing, only his daily work. I'll set him to slaughter the calf we'll be eating while our relatives be here.'

For Madoc and Dan with their wives were come to stay, and it was their host's pride to stint them of nothing. So he beckoned Thomas to the byre and by signs told him what to do. A brindled black and white calf with mild eyes gazed at the men who planned to cut its throat. Feeling its rough tongue suck at his fingers, Owain thought: ''Tis well to be having it killed and the blood washed away afore Glythin do come home.' The sweet breath of kine recalled scents of a dawn in May and the very young, pure white calf which he had carried down from the heights. In a mood of tenderness, he had vowed: 'This one, I 'on't never kill.' How lovely Glythin had been, the maiden in her green robe, before she became a working farmer's wife!

On his return to the house he found Howell winding a gaudy cravat round his neck. The flesh of his flabby body was shaken with mirth; for Dan's wife jested with him. She had the sly look of one who has just whispered a joke not to be spoken aloud; but when Madoc's Saxon sailed in, the minx became demure. Owain, however, caught her ogling him from beneath her lashes. She found his mature good looks to her taste, well he knew; and would have invited him to sin, had she not set herself to act the part of virtue. He smiled in disdain but was flattered to note how much she desired him. 'And I am loved by a younger beauty, more hot than she,' he told himself with relish. Glythin ought to forgive him, seeing that he was not a man untempted, but one whom wantons would not leave alone. At his sister-in-law's side, he rode downhill towards his neighbour's farm. The compliment she paid him with a gaze of veiled lechery was salt to his thirst for the gipsy, making him sportive with her, while thinking of another.

''Tis you did ought to be the bridegroom, Brother-in-law. Too young and handsome you're looking to be so soon made a grandfather.'

She had borne Dan no children and Owain detected an envious jibe in her pleasantry. Next year, would they call him 'Grand-dad'? The threat of such a title made him wince. Laughing, to prove that he did not care, he boasted, 'Tonight I'll be out-dancing all the young fellows, you'll see.'

'And who will you choose for your partner? Your wife, that used to be so fair?'

Used to be! He hated the spiteful trollop. It should not be about *her* that he put his arm, but around Miriam's slender, unstayed waist. Would that be prudent, though? The flame of her body robbed him of self-control. He ought not, he warned himself, to touch her in Glythin's sight. Perilous enough to watch her from afar: to hear her voice that went to his head like drink!

Brooding on Miriam, he came to his neighbour's fold, where the din of a mock battle accorded well with his mood. Nant and his bachelors were struggling with the bride's brothers who barred the door. Owain leapt off his horse and with boyish gusto joined in the rough fun. He rejoiced in his strength, greater than that of any slim youth whom he thrust aside. His laughter and tallyhoing rang loud through the house as Nant sought for his hidden bride. But in the midst of riot a pitiful contrast struck him. There had been no such sport at his own wedding and none to defend Glythin. Having forsaken another world to abide with him, she had orphaned herself. 'And 'twas to save my life she came from her place of peace to dwell among men who misjudged her,' he reflected. In the noisy crowd he looked for her; but she was nowhere to be seen. The fickle wind of his mood veered again and he said to himself, ''Tis her duty to follow *me*: not mine to be for ever seeking her out.' And in his annoyance at the trouble she gave him, he forgot to wish for her companionship. Let her go her own way and he his! When he found her at the church door he was further angered to see her face sorrowful among so many that were glad.

Throughout the solemn service, he felt her grief at his elbow, as if it had been a burial, not a marriage, they witnessed side by side. The vows of lifelong fidelity, which he heard his son utter, sounded in ghostly echo of his own voice long ago. He could not endure his selfreproach and wrenched his mind from the haunting past, forcing it to justify his present. What, after all, had he done that was so much amiss? No worse than many another man who was respected: for he had not been found out. He loved his ageing wife, after a fashion; clothed, fed, and treated her not ill. It might be even that he would turn to her once more with quickened desire when the gipsy was gone out of his life. He made her suffer, meanwhile, only because she pried into his secret thoughts.

It was her fault, not his, that she had the comfortless gift of a seer, and she ought to keep to herself knowledge to which she had no right. Today, she disclosed it to the neighbours in her mournful eyes. Her doing so made him smart; and he accused her of betraying him.

'Come,' he whispered in anger, as they followed the bridal pair into the porch. 'Everyone is entering into their gladness. Why must you alone be glum?'

'As he put the ring on her finger, I had an ill foreboding.'

'What folly to be cast down, like a woman that's carrying, fancying this and that!'

'I *did* carry him once and I am knowing his nature. They will not be happy.'

'Whyever not? They are young,' said he, eyeing them with envy.

'Too young in wisdom, which has no age on earth but do come from elsewhere, to some folk early, to others not at all.'

'What more should Nant desire? She be uncommon comely.'

'Her beauty will soon fade.'

'Go you on! She's healthy.'

'She will wither as mown grass in its season of flowering.'

'Have done with your raven's croaking! And what if you are right? Beauty and health are not all. She is bringing him a tidy dowry and I'm setting them up in a farm.'

'Riches will not bring my son joy, no more than they have brought you peace, my heart.'

'Be quiet,' he exclaimed so roughly that on the ride back she uttered never a word.

Over the ice in the rutted track a gloss of water slid. The horses slipped and must be held up with a steadying hand. 'Careful, man! You be riding for a fall,' cried one or two as Owain set a reckless pace. But in defiance he spurred past them, whistling a tune in turns passion-fierce and madly gay. Curiosity made the aged blacksmith keep up with him to his peril.

'That throbby snatch you were whistling now just, whatever was it, man?'

'Gipsy music.'

'Oho! And a gipsy learned it you?'

'I'm free to listen, I suppose?'

'As free as folk be to wag their heads at you.'

Owain glared at him. 'What are you hinting at, mun?'

The smith winked and there was malice in his chuckle.
''T'as been the talk o' the district, your bidding them low
Romanies to sing at this night's rejoicing.'

'I'm known to favour all kinds o' melody.'

'Oh-aye. And you're said to have been slinking, like a dog-
fox at dusk, to the street where a black-eyed hussy has lodged
winter-long.'

'Where I do go is no man's business.'

'Nor you wife's, neither?'

'No, damn you! Not hers. I am master.' To teach both her
and the busybodies a lesson, he would enjoy himself without
stint this evening.

But joy, he found, is not to be caught by resolution. Though
he talked brave, toasting this one and that across the table,
he heard what he was saying as if another spoke, and listened
to his own laughter without share in its mirth. A part of his
mind looked down upon himself, at kindred and wedding
guests, wondering what was the nature of each, a stranger,
in a world wherein all were alone.

'The truth of a moment,' he mused, 'that be hid by word or
deed, but which 'ull peep out from those slits in our mask,
the eyes, maybe as I can fathom, perceiving the innocence
o' first love beneath Howell's lechery, and in myself the singer
o' dreams, whom the prosperous farmer has well-nigh over-
laid. But though every secret of a man at one time be revealed,
can God hisself tell the core of a being apt to alter as worm
to g b-in-case, and grub to moth? For whiles we do crawl;

and then, lo, we spread brave wings and soar! Is there indeed any truth to be found, save that mankind be constant only to change, as the tides to their ebb and rise, the soul renewed no less often nor the body?' And asking himself this question, he stared at his unknown neighbours.

At first his gaze settled upon an infant that slept with head thrust into its mother's bosom. The soft skull, on which hair would grow, was downy as a day-old chick and the plump face showed faint hint of features to come.

'Once,' said Owain to the listener within him, 'warmth and the flow o' milk into my toothless mouth did satisfy *my* needs, also; once, to suck my thumb 'ould render me content. Ah, but I have clean forgot that which I have been – a blind stirring within the red womb, a nurseling at the white breast.' Into his own past he strove to recede, only to find it foreign as the tale of some wayfarer met upon a road.

The first thing he remembered was fear of the dark; but this had not come until he was grown aware of safety and danger, having been taught the giant words Good and Evil. After that, ugly shapes lurked in the shadows, causing him to entreat protection from the speared angel who fled the room with his mother's candle.

Now, turning his regard from the babe in arms, he looked at a small boy with jaws at work upon a slice of cake and he tried to recall the sticky relish of sugared crumb along his own upper lip before it grew firm and stubbled. The round eyes surveyed with resolution the food piled on the table level with the chin. They showed no interest in the talk of elders, exchanged overhead. 'I, too,' reflected Owain, 'have listened unheedful to the voices o' those tall ones. I have savoured goodies, sweet to my palate, and they have been my most quick taste.'

His memories unfurled, like petals of a flower, opening out from a tight bud. He saw himself as he was forty years back, on tiptoe at a harper's knee, staring upward into a bearded face. The grimaces which the hairy man made were affrighting. From his rippled throat poured sounds that turned a child gay or grave, he had no notion why. This only he knew: gone was his wish for supper, hungry though he had been. If mother sought to drag him away to bed, he must struggle against her, sobbing. For he had found a new thing, a better even than food. It was mystery; and out of it sprang delight. The puzzling verses were all in praise of Love, until that hour supposed to be a naughtiness or folly. He had heard young men and women titter in courtship, when they fancied he was not eavesdropping from behind the settle; while old folk, with a gold ring upon the third finger of the left hand, spoke of courting as an antic to be smiled at with indulgence, should it lead to wedlock rather than to 'shame'. Flighty, lovers were dubbed in any case; and at first it amazed him that a bard should make their foolishness appear so noble, their joys and sorrows of such magnitude. Then, he knew, beyond doubt, that it was so; and he was proud of his dis-covery. Driven to copy whatsoever a big man did on the morrow he made uncertain noises and plucked the strings of an imagined harp. 'Mother,' he piped, 'listen, Mother. I'll be singing you a love-song.' In confidence he looked to her for reward. But she laughed, pushing him aside, and went to her oven, declaring that he was 'a queer one'. He had not forgotten his rage of humiliation. Yet now it was matter for jest, being so far away. Because of it, he had carried wonder, hidden, as he hid in his pockets pebbles of rare shape, twin-kernelled nuts and other marvels of whose worth she knew nothing. 'Pity on her! Look what she's missing,' he had taught himself to think, with enough contempt to salve his own hurt pride.

Soon, when he roamed the dingle below their home and the limit of his world became the valley of the great river, he had met perilous adventure, climbing trees and fighting other boys. Next, he learned to kill bird and beast; and when the dread was gone from touching a limp carcase, to enjoy a hunter's mastery over life and death. As his strength grew, he was forced to bear toil on the farm, until bodily effort took his mind from the shy magic of chanting, over and over again, words which he began to find he was able to rhyme together. 'Not one boy, but a dozen I was,' he mused. 'And which o' the bunch were most truly *me*? In windless weather, I have seen raindrops fall upon a sheet o' water, each drop causing a ring, and every ring overlapping. All were in motion the while, spreading outwards, so that no weaver o' fine silk could unravel so cunning a pattern. Even so is the mind o' man.

'At twelve I cared chiefest, for my victuals and for mischievous pranks. Later, a hymn tune at a funeral took me by the throat and twisted me religious.' That wave had passed, also, he could not say how or why; but restless sorrow remained. For, though his joy in singing tunes increased with practice, he guessed that to repeat tunes and verses composed by others would never satisfy him. As he hung about the forge, committing to heart such songs as the blacksmith could teach, or ran after a strolling harpist that he might mimic his tricks, this bygone Owain was goaded to surpass his masters. That which other lads learned in careless fashion for the pleasure of melody, to him was the means to an end desired with anguish. 'Some day,' he had vowed, 'there shall leap to my lips a song as shall be my own.' And then, he believed, he might boast, 'I am wholly happy.'

But at sixteen he was mopish. His lean wrists thrust out beyond his coat sleeves and his mother grumbled that in a summer's passing a new suit was shrunk too small for him to wear. 'You're costing me more nor you're worth, you careless idle lumper,' she railed. 'Your arkard loose-jointed limbs be terrible coltish-clumsy.' Sometimes he loved, and sometimes almost hated her; but never could he be deaf to her endearments or scolding. At work in fits of fierce vigour, he broke tools, flung them aside and gazed in a trance at the mountains. It was upon their summits he longed to be, hearkening to the music which the wind piped among sedges. At that stage, he, who had craved for companions as a child, shunned company. Yet he thirsted in his loneliness for one who should understand him. To the neighbours he had nothing to say, flushing a blotched red if girls glanced his way, to make him timid with their invitation or to flick him raw with their disdain. Never, before such pert teases, would he risk the songs that formed themselves, vague and unfinished, to his thrumming of a harp. Sacred, these were, and secret, not for the common ears of Betto, Polly or Megan. Somewhere, scarce on this earth, it seemed to the hobbledehoy, there awaited him a harmony that he must seek. When he found it – what then? His soul would fall in love. At dawn and twilight on the far hillsides, he began to seek the fugitive. In awe and with pain, he brought forth at last a man's voice and the verses of a poet.

'Poor mother,' he admitted, remembering how he returned when hunger drew him to her larder, guilty of negligence and sullen at approach of chiding. 'Was I indeed that loutish, hang-dog dreamer? Small wonder as I did use to vex her so! But she was proud a'right when other folks praised my less fanciful ditties – leastways, if there were enough folk in a bunch together. "Why be the judgment o' ten-score fools more just nor that o' one?" I 'ould taunt her. Yet what other yardstick had she by which to measure the rare thing I was after? And I, too, was relishing my conquests. What a man can do easy and well, he is liking to win credit for. 'Tis the hard to attain, the most precious, as is keeping him shy and humble. That has been my undoing, I shouldn't wonder. Too many quick gifts I have had.' He smiled in complacence to think with what skill he had plied the blacksmith's craft when he set his hand to smelt iron. 'And an able farmer have I not proved to be, since I turned my mind to that trade? Where is my like in the district? And yet, as I'm looking back . . . Well, well! Who is having the fill o' his heart's desire?' The timidity of his teens overcome, he had danced more fleet than any of his rivals and had numbered prettier partners awaiting a wink. No girl at a shearing supper rebuffed him when he trod upon her foot under the table. No indeed! The hussies used to sidle along a bench to provoke that coveted honour. Hot, brief and light his encounters had been, loud and sure his singing, until one day the craving for solitude drove him again uphill to the silent lake, where he gazed for a great while at his own reflection and saw it turn into that form of which for years he had dreamed.

'Ah,' he sighed, 'was it when I wooed my Fair One that I were most myself?' And he was complacent no longer but asked in regret, 'Did I, maybe, stifle the life she awoke in me when I led her down to my dwelling to make o' her my daily helpmeet and servant? Should it have been upon those heights, where she learned me to sing strange songs, feared by my mother and a puzzle to the crowd, as I did ought to have bided, her lover and her pupil?'

He durst not look at Glythin, for he knew that in her he would see only the middle-aged housewife whose coarsened hands served him with food, whose listless eyes reflected, as in a mirror, the loss of joy that dulled his desire for her. Yet it would be grievous to lose her quite. 'Terrible empty my life 'ould be were she gone. But I 'on't never strike her with iron no more; so why should I let this foreboding daunt me?'

To escape from it, he began to stare at an ancient labourer. With shaking fingers, bony as bird's claw, he fumbled meat

into his toothless mouth. Like those of a baby, his slobbered
lips sucked in greed; and what was said around him, he did
not comprehend. 'The mind of a full-grown man is gone
from him with his failed sinews. 'Tis as if he were dwindled
backward to'ards infancy afore the womb is enclosing him
again,' brooded Owain. 'And a cold mother 'twill be, in
whose body he shall find shelter. Yet when I were a small
little weakling, he stood up a powerful fellow, able to set
me down, even as I, in this present, might overthrow and do
pity him. If I, who am reckoned handsome and lusty by
Miriam, should chance to live as long as that one, a generation that knew not the bard o' promise nor the husbandman
o' weight, will see me puling and feeble and will know me
only for the poor dotard I am become.' Was this the sorry
answer to the question he had asked: what was the truth
concerning man? Bound to a wheel which never ceased to
revolve, the flesh was carried full-circle from birth to death.
'Then let us eat, drink and be merry,' his sore heart beat in
defiance of oncoming doom, 'for tomorrow we die.' Flinging
back his head, he drained the tankard in his clenched fist
and shouted for more ale.

'Fill up again, girl. Fill up all round. Come, friends, drink
you another toast to the bridal pair, to their children and
their children's children. As we do wane, so these 'ull wax.
"Life," my poor mother was saying when she lay abed, like
a fish on the bank, agasp not to perish. "Life. Life. Life."
Dwall, it had the joke on her, giving the valiant fool the slip!
But how she did fight to keep it, her tormentor, to the last!'
He laughed at this, so that his fellow guests were taken
aback. 'Don't you be gauping at me for telling you the truth,'
he defied. 'Look at the weaned child yonder, filling his skin
out with food. Look at the trembly old simpleton with gums
chewing steady as Time. What do they care for me and my
wild fancies? And will the young bride this night see upon

the bleached bed curtains the shadow o' the midwife as do lay out many a corpse? Not she indeed! For who hears any tick o' the clock save that which do strike, this instant, the listener's ear? Only the poet, I tell you. And if you were knowing the nature o' his hearing, 'tisn't envying him you'd be.' In a lowered voice, he added, 'Courtship and dreams do go by. Belly and mouth alone be constant from cradle to grave. Go you on, babe in arms, suck your fill. Chew away, dotard, gone childish in the head. You be right, the both o' you, to pay me no heed. For a bard's mournful visions they are going down the wind with the songs he did strive to fashion in his April gleam o' gladness – these songs, no matter how noble, as never contented him quite.'

'For shame,' broke in the bride's mother, 'to talk so rank in front o' the girls.'

Morosely, he stared past her at the tired face of his wife. 'I tell you,' he muttered, 'beauty 'ull go the way o' the bright shining water as did turn the mill wheel once, but cannot come again. Lost at sea are the fine hopes and ardent prayers. Lost at last are all loves whatsoever.'

'Come you,' interposed Howell, seeing the company shift as if pins were stuck, for an ill jest, in their chairs. 'This be no time, Brother, for quoting the Preacher, "Vanity, vanity; all is vanity under the sun." Let it be so. I'm not one to gainsay a bitter true thing. But must you stir us to *think*, when we've a chanst to swill? There's a dull old way to go on! Who's asking to hear admonition from your high pulpit, mun? And, o' all seasons, at a wedding jollification?'

'You be wise,' answered Owain, forcing a laugh. 'Drink up then, mates. Drink; and we'll be dancing, is it? Dancing mad, we'll be now just, so soon as we've ceased to be sober and to see life for the cheat it be. Make merry, one and all. I've a treat in store for you. The gipsies be coming that snap their slim fingers at preachers, and 'ull dance their blithe jig down into hell.'

'Hush,' the hostess warned him but his voice rose harsh above hers. 'Deep under, they'll go dancing, over the burning cobbles.'

He did not care if she bade him hush, if Nant and his bride hung their heads and gripped each other's hands in their confusion, nor that he was thought unmannerly for taking command in a house not his own. This was the day on which he had sworn to enjoy himself, and he would not be thwarted. Having slipped into a doleful reverie, he said to himself that it was Glythin's fault. She ought not to have come with him, a remembrancer of vows he had broken and of loss he had sooner forget.

Such was his brazen mood when he heard drawing close the tinkle of a tambourine, and springing up, ran to the threshold to seize Miriam by the forearm.

'See, here's one to dance the blood a-boil.' He made her known to the gathering with a parade of ownership. 'Set chairs against the wall. Make room for her whose feet have black magic in them. Watching, we shall cast off our mopish yearning for the past. Listening, be freed from our mortal dread o' hereafter.'

In the centre of the room he stood, holding her tight. The ball of his thumb, pressed upon the pulse within her wrist, began to tingle. She, who had never failed to give him that fiery elation which comes from the first draught of spirits, today was heady as a love potion. He shook as he had done once when overtaken by summer lightning upon a naked hill-top. Fire in the air, fire, liquid as water, running along the drenched earth, had threatened to consume his flesh; but so keen an excitment had he felt, that he had not feared his peril until it was over. Nor did he scent peril now. There, in obedience to his order, the young men were dragging chair and settle, table and stool across the floor. It gave him pleasure to hear the harsh grate of wood upon stone. The elders had taken their seats, packed in a half-moon, and the maidens, standing back, herded together. Everyone stared at him and at Miriam, linked in their midst, the men with envy, the women in such misgiving of their own charms as whetted the edge of their dislike for the foreigner. For was not this light-fingered Romany the flower and the foe of her sex? He tasted the bitter-sweet of flattery underlying blame, and gloried in the tension, akin to that before thunder, which made the kitchen sultry with pent feeling. If he should touch a harp, he was sure the strings must snap. 'And others, too, be aware of it – braced up and a-quiver,' he was pleased to note. Studying the hostile girls, he smiled to see the blue eyes and the grey, the hazel green and those amber ones which matched the peat-stained pools of a mountain brook, shine with jealousy. Small wonder, since, when the floor was cleared for Miriam, the youths and young farmers who were not wed came crowding round. Those behind craned forward. The near-to, wishful but afraid to touch her, gave no quarter and grinned in foolish fashion.

'Stand back civil, can't you?' he cried out. 'Make way and let her dance.'

Two gipsy lads, with faces smooth as polished walnut, and an elderly man whose wrinkles were graved by cunning, had followed her in. They watched the scene as if they nursed the sly contempt of slaves for stupid masters.

'Strike up, you,' Owain shouted at them. 'What shall it be?' Miriam murmured. Her lips close to his ear, breathed a caress. They seemed to say that for himself alone would she do her tricks.

'That one,' he commanded, 'as is starting faint as drum-beats from over the hill.'

'This?' She hummed a stave and let him see the tips of her teeth in a smile.

'Yes, yes. Growing faster and louder till 'tis my own heart pounding.'

'Mine too.' She turned her head to look him full in the face; and he heard the bride's mother whisper, 'Bold wicked baggage! Clapped in the stocks she did ought to be. I'll not countenance such goings-on 'neath my respectable roof.' Then, with a frown, he let Miriam go. He must not be so incautious. But she laughed at him in her deep throaty way and stepped, swaying, into the open space to jangle her tambourine and show the whites of her eyes. 'Same as those o' a vicious mare,' someone at his elbow tittered. He clenched his right hand, tempted to strike out at random so much did he hate all scoffers. To her, however, they seemed of no concern. In her teasing speech she was chattering with the musicians who squatted on the ground with their outlandish instruments. The young men leered up at her, treated to a joke from which he was excluded, and one of them was shaken with soundless mirth. Owain scowled at the three crafty faces, over which derision slid as if it had been oil. Were they making mock of him? 'Where's Glythin?' he was prompted to demand. 'Wherever has she gone *now*?' Pushing through the throng, he took his place at her side. There! All could see how united a couple they were. None should pity his wife, for that would offer insult to himself. Neither had they just cause to blame him, a bard for whom one manner of music could not suffice. The narrow, dull-eared lot! He could afford to despise them but concerning his wife, try as he might, he could not set his conscience at rest.

Her back being to the window, the dulled light of wintry afternoon fell on her bowed head and stooping shoulders. He had been startled, before now, to fancy her hair turned grey, her cheeks gone haggard; and as he looked down upon the hands in her lap, he was more shocked than hitherto so wrinkled was the skin between her locked fingers. 'Surely to goodness, 'tis nothing only the fade o' day do make her seem pallid and lined?' he reassured himself. 'True, she is aged o' late faster nor I could wish. But the east-bitten twilight from without be accountable for that corpse-cold hue as was giving me a turn. I'll not look at her no more, till after the candles be lit.' He put his hand on her arm but fixed his gaze upon Miriam who had begun to dance in the red glow of the hearth.

A scarlet kerchief was about her throat. Ruby glass beads winked in the lobes of her small, pointed ears, while red and orange ribbons, like tongues of flame, darted from the tambourine as she whirled it high above her head. She was shod in slippers of crimson leather that twinkled the more gaily because her dress was black. Spinning and leaping, she flung herself to and fro to keep pace with the mounting madness of music. A low throb at first, it rose to a clash, pierced by weird cries beaten down, time and again, by drum-taps and stamping. Faster and faster she span past him, until scarlet, yellow and black were merged in a dizzy pattern, and her skirt, taut over her hips but full at the knees, flew up and outwards. At the hub of its wheel a foam of white appeared, and her lithe bronze limbs, from ankle to thigh, were exposed. A background to his drunkard's joy, he could feel the shocked quiver of the crowd, see staring eyes and the tightening in common of every man's sinews. In unison, all leant forward to miss no lightning step, no abandoned gesture. 'Damn you,' he swore under his breath, enraged, that so many should share his delight, yet ready to crow aloud, 'She is mine!' When the clashing ceased on a last fierce yell and she sank limp against the dresser and was still, he could not endure the hush. Before the stunned watchers dared break the spell, he sprang into the space which she had left empty and began to shout.

'No, no! Don't you dare, none o' you, to make an end with your clapping. I'll be singing the song that is matching with her tune. Strike up again, musicians. Keep going our own hot melody. Again from the start, d'you hear? The blood shall not cool, the heart slow down, until I will them to.'

What were the words he sang as the throbbing was renewed and rose to its savage climax, he did not know. For they were in her unchristian tongue and she had taught them to him one night when he held her naked on his knee. But their sense he understood well, because they were paired to her dance and to the music which whetted his own lust. When the gipsies uttered once more the sharp cry of mating, he, too, fell back for dead, into a silence which none made bold to break. Within the lids of his closed eyes, red wheels span and stars sprayed in a dazzle. He heard a clock strike before he was calm enough to look about him.

'Well, neighbours, well? You can give the both o' us your clapping now.'

Before applause had ceased, he turned cold, seeing, distinct among blurred faces, the pale one of his wife, and her eyes, like water glazed with ice, stare blank into his own. 'Make up the fire,' he said, astounded to find that he shivered. Though he tried to move away, he could not stir from Miriam's side. She held him trapped, leaning close, in the ease of triumph. Her supple hands rested upon her hips and her figure remained curved backwards. The weight of it was upon one foot. With the other she beat an echo to the tune she had made him sing. 'You sang it in my praise. Did you know?' she whispered; and he saw her pass the tip of her tongue across her lips. 'Sweet,' she said, and looked at him, never flinching, with a smile to melt granite. The pupils of her black eyes were big as if she had dropped into them the juice of deadly nightshade; but the lashes were half lowered. Liquid, shining and narrowed those bold eyes told such a tale that they who studied her nudged one another to see her thus flaunt her hunger.

'Come on, all,' exclaimed Howell, having glanced from

the trollop to the wife and pitied the one whom he little understood. 'Enough o' this. Let's be playing a game.'

Then Miriam started wide awake out of her daydream and flashed arch smiles at the company. 'Yes, yes! Everyone here. Young and old. Wedded and single. Blindman's bluff. Blindman's buff.' She pulled the scarf from about her neck to flourish it so swiftly about her head that it made a circle of scarlet in the air. Owain felt the wind of it fan his cheek. His moment of misgiving over, he echoed her order. 'Blindman's buff. Blindman's buff.' And, catching the fever of her gaiety, folk jumped up and voices in chorus proposed, 'Hide the thimble. Hunt the slipper.' Owain shouted them down, 'No, no! Give her her way. She has earned it.' In the midst of the tumult, she ran to Howell, claiming her right of choice.

'Here, one o' you handsome Georgios, come quick! Give me a kerchief. Tie it about his eyes.'

'Take you your own blood-red scarf,' a married man mocked her. 'You could be hoodwinking any Christian alive, almost, with that gaudy silk o' yours, young 'oman.'

'I'll keep it for my own use, and not to bind you with, impudent!' She grabbed the little shawl from the bosom of a girl who shrank from her in outraged modesty, and blindfolding Howell, spun him around three times before sending him with a push to stagger across the room.

'Mercy on us,' he cried, with a gust of wheezy laughter. His flesh shook like curd as he blundered about, to grope with outstretched hands and blunt fingers spread apart. '*Oow!* Oow! Drat the hussy! I'm gone too old for her crazy frolic. Here, for pity's sake, let me catch holt o' one o' you youngsters and have done!'

But boys and girls skipped out of his reach, prodding and pinching him as they darted away, until he howled in mimic wrath and everyone, save Glythin, was laughing loud. She stood alone as if too dazed to note what was going on; and

Miriam found it easy to push Howell towards her. He lurched against the figure pressed to the window-pane, and clutched it in his arms.

'Oho! I've hooked one o' you artful slippery fish! A kiss is the forfeit for being catched, my pretty! A smacking great hearty kiss, see?' He tore the bandage from his eyes, to stare into the unsmiling face of his sister-in-law. '*Ddwch*,' he muttered, letting her go. 'Better blindfold one o' the flounce-abouts. 'Twill be more sportive like.'

'Yes, yes,' Owain agreed. He had seen how void was her gaze, and it put him out of countenance. 'One 'ould think she didn't know me,' was his accusing thought.

But Miriam cried, 'No!' Before he could hinder it, she sprang forward and bound the shawl tight over Glythin's brow. Her fingers gave the knot a trapper's tug. 'There! She's safe in the snare. She can see nothing. Twist her about, the blind woman! One, two, three!' As she gripped her rival by the nape of the neck, her nails dug into the white flesh; but it seemed that the helpless body felt no hurt. As though it were numbed, Glythin suffered it to be sent spinning round, to be driven here and there, without raising a hand to ward off its tormentors. So little sport did she afford them, that the din of the young diminished and the elders looked askance at the gipsy who whirled between husband and wife, with a mocking cry of, 'Blind woman! Blind woman! Overtake me if you can!' She had been twisting her scarlet scarf as she sped among the players, egging them on to slap Glythin into motion. 'Look,' she exclaimed, 'I'll show you Georgios a way to make game of her! Was there ever one so lifeless? Here, take your kerchiefs and knot them, thus, see? Now flick her with them as you pass. *She'll* never guess who strikes her.'

The lads and maids, flushed from their fun with Howell, gave no thought to the matter but jumped about, lashing the plaything at their mercy.

'Go on, go on,' urged their leader. 'You must goad her to act her part,' and she thrust her own scarf into Owain's hands. 'Strike her with it.' When he shook his head, she whispered in his ear, 'Why frown, my prince of Georgios? Won't she let you join in a joke, even? Are you so henpecked, you meek husband? Fie!'

He was nettled by this, yet ill-at-ease as he swung his doxy's token, not meaning to touch Glythin with it. What harm could he do the poor staid woman by making light of revelry?

'Come, Missus, don't you be acting the kill-joy,' he muttered. 'Sham as if you didn't mind, see, and they'll be giving over.' Because she gave him no answer, his vexation soured. 'Can't you make merry with us?' he demanded. 'Can't you? . . . Name o' goodness! Is it losing your speech you are?' And in anger he struck at her with the scarlet silk.

'Mind what you be doing, Father,' he heard Nant warn him, too late.

The knot tied by the wanton left a welt on Glythin's cheek. She uttered that clear cry, like a wild bird's in captivity, which he remembered from long ago; and her hands, groping up to her face, unbound her eyes. Still as an image of snow, she stood; and she looked strangely at him.

'Was I hurting you?' he asked, so sick with dread that he felt his mouth parch and emptiness in his stomach.

'Look,' she said in a low tone, and pointed at the rag he had let drop.

He picked it up; and while his fingers were a-fumble at the knot, he heard a voice that came in a gasp – not his own voice, surely? – enquire, 'What is this? Something hard be hidden within it. I did not know. *By the land*, I did not know!'

Miriam darted forward. 'Give it to me! 'Tis mine!' She snatched at the silk and when he held firm, fought to wrench it from him. 'Let go, you fool! Let go!'

'Something is here deceitful. Let go yourself. D'you hear me?'

As they strove together in enmity, there fell on to the floor between Glythin's feet and his, a piece of iron. 'That is thrice,' she said, and he knew, though he dared not look, that she held up her right hand with three fingers raised.

'No,' he cried, '*no*,' turning upon her, enraged as a beast that bites its own limb in a trap. ''Tis sinful o' you to punish me for what I was never plotting. Ignorant I was, I tell you, ignorant as the unborn, o' the wicked whore's treachery. How could I guess what lay hid in her raiment? *I* am not to blame. Indeed and indeed, I do swear it. You cannot hold me accountable. 'T'ould be spite in you to do so.'

While he upbraided his wife with the clamour of panic, swift decay overtook her. She, whom he had forced to take the place of his mother, like her, at the last, was stricken with sickly old age. The hair turned ashwhite, battle and sparse upon her head. Deep ploughed with wrinkles, her flesh shrank over the bone. The lips were skim-milk coloured, sucked in by toothless gums; and, above the faded eyes, lids which had lost their lashes crumpled like hoods of parchment. A small flat-chested crone, shaken with palsy, confronted him, blinking and mowing in weak shapes with her mouth.

'No, *no*,' he kept on crying. 'Tell me as 'tis not true? Or, if it be, as you can undo what I did to you?' She answered him only with mumbled words whose meaning was lost in his terror. 'Mother, Mother! What's on you? Ah, God, o' mercy! Look, neighbours, what's happened to her!'

But when he reeled backward and turned about to implore their aid, he perceived that they were staring amazed, not at her but at himself. It was as if they supposed he had lost his senses. Could it be that in Glythin they did not see the change, which he saw with such horror? 'Are you stone blind, the pack o' you? Can't you *see* as she be transfigured?' It was a child who answered him with innocent delight. 'I can! I'm seeing her lovely. Like a Lent-lily she is, on a tall stalk, swayed by the wind: in a green mantle; and her gold hair, long and loose, be tinged with pale green, too.'

'There's nonsense,' exclaimed many voices; but Owain, staring at the boy in a cramp of envy, knew that he spoke what was, for him, the truth.

Miriam was laughing, laughter steady and low as a cat's purr. 'Stay that noise,' he shouted.

'Come, honey-seed,' she was quick to change her tone. ''Twas you that were blinded by your own youthful make-believe. Loyal you are, but it can't be kept up for ever. Now you can see her plain for what she is. Come, like a sane man, turn to me, my sugar.'

She sidled up to him but he flung her away and rushed to the old crone for whom he trembled in a storm of com-passion. '*Mother*! No, no, 'tis *wife* I do mean! Sweetheart, as you were once. You that did use to set me singing, wherefore is your magic dwindled?'

''Twas never there, you doting fool,' cried Miriam, stamping her foot. 'You saw what you looked for only.'

'No need to tell me that. 'Tis bitter true. But I can bring back her beauty by cherishing it again . . . Glythin, let me hold you safe, *fach*.' The ancient hag twisted aside beyond his reach. 'Stay with me,' he pleaded. 'Shrivelled so pitiful tiny though you be, my song shall have the strength to restore you.'

It was vain. Feeble as she was, she fled from him, out of the room, out of their neighbour's house, across the fold and up the lane. He ran after her, to slip and fall upon the melted ice; and each time he arose, shaken and swearing, his knees trembled with excess of fear and cold. 'This cannot happen to *me*,' he told himself. 'For sure it is not happening! 'Tis an ill dream, one I have suffered from infancy: to strive after that I be driven to overtake, to know I am cursed should I fail to reach it; yet to be bound as in swaddling-clothes or a shroud, feeling the ache o' chained strength, the gnaw o' thwarted life in my clogged limbs. Ah, yes! 'Tis a common nightmare. 'Twill pass with my waking, and Glythin's head, in safety, be found upon my pillow.'

He shut his eyes tight and opened them wide. Still the bent figure in black hobbled ahead of him; and the lowering landscape was that of a sick man's fever. The steep track by which he staggered and slid uphill was dark with frozen mire. Trees and hedgerows on either hand stood leafless as charred sticks. The fields of sallowed grass, dead stubble and sodden tillage, with muddy pools in every ditch, were of a jaundiced hue. Overhead the sky was dreary. There lurked within its pall of cloud that tinge of sulphurous yellow which presages a snowstorm. 'Heavy are the heavens,' he thought. 'A weight they are upon earth.' And he tried to cry aloud, 'I will lift up mine eyes unto the hills from whence cometh my help': but their green freshness of an April morning would not be recalled, and, when he looked at them for consolation, they were sullen crouching giants, upon whose slaty sides thin ribs of snowdrift appeared as a skeleton's bones. Like a child, he buried his face in the crook of his arm, but was torn by a man's dry sobbing.

Soon, following after and gaining upon him, he heard hastening footsteps and voices which urged him to stay. He would neither answer nor slacken his pace, however, until his sons closed upon him.

'Father, Father! Stop you and listen to reason.'

'Leave me be.' But he was forced to look into Nant's eyes and to pity him because he was sad and frightened on this, his wedding day. 'I did ought to have done better by you,' he muttered. 'The gifts she brought and the children she bore me, a wiser man 'ould have guarded.'

'Father,' said Nant, tugging at his sleeve, 'don't you take on so needless. Vexing mother you were, so that she has gone home-along.'

'Home she has gone, my son. But not, I fear, to ours.'

'Where else has she to go?'

'The silent place where I found her.'

'Call after her then to stay.'

'She cannot, boy, she cannot. I have left it overlate. Can a man, having bound a bandage over his eyes, beg the light to pardon him and shine in?'

'I'm not understanding you, Father.'

'Safer so. You have sung love-songs in your season, and will give over when you beget children o' your body. But the one I wooed, I was pledged to serve lifelong. A doom and a blessing be laid upon the bard. His ardour must not cool, nor his homage tire. Stern is his rule as a saint's, unsure to the last o' salvation.'

'But, Father, *bach*,' his younger sons began to argue with him.

'Turn you back from me,' was the only reply he would make. 'Envying simple folks I am now, that did use to fancy myself their better. Best is he who has faith to endure true to hisself. Now I am left as you see me – a rich man, terrible poor . . . Go. And my blessing go with you.'

Though he had little hope to find her there, he went back alone to his own house. The fold-gate was open, swinging with rusty creak upon its hinge. Going to the house-door, he entered and searched through every room. All were empty. His footsteps awoke an echo. The fire was out; the whitened hearthstone cold. 'Winter,' he said aloud. 'Such iron winter as I dursn't look ahead, in autumn, to foresee.' Startled by his own voice he shuddered and pressed in his lips. What was the use of talk? She would never again make answer. There was nothing of her left to keep him company, but the carded wool on the distaff, awaiting her hand to spin, the curds she had set in the bowl from which she would no more sup. 'In their bedroom he opened the closet where her clothes hung. Beside his jack-boots stood a slipper, worn down at heel and shaped to the little foot that had trodden its house-wife errands in his service. Before the mirror, which showed him his lone face, lay a comb; and one hair was in it, like a thread of honey. He turned from these sights in desolation. 'I cannot dwell in this house as was our home,' he thought. 'The clock has stopped since noon.' He went, as a sleep-walker might, to pull up the weights, but stayed when the chain was chill under his fingers. 'No, no! I couldn't abide the ticking away o' time.'

Then, put aside in a corner, he saw the small harp which he used to carry. 'Same as a lover's locket, forever round your neck,' his mother used to scoff. He took it up with reverence, and tears dripped warm on his hands as he slung it about his breast. 'Poor harp! You have suffered a sore neglect. But 'tis I now who am silent.'

When he came forth wearing it, a small shadow wavered ahead of him, mounting the track down which he had led his betrothed. 'Is that my love?' he called, straining his sight until he made sure of a figure kin to his mother's ghost. Sharp was his disappointment as he asked, 'Is that all I shall see henceforth?' None the less, he called after her, begging her to stay. But she went on; and it so grieved him to watch her tired feet lag that he flung himself on his knees. 'I will not drive you further with hasty pusuit,' he promised. 'Look you, how patient I'll wait, how humble for your return! Glythin! Glythin! *Gly*-thin!' In the vast stillness, his entreaty died away. 'Grant me my sight again to see you as you were.'

With back turned to him and face hidden, she halted to listen. But she remained an old, shrunken woman, clothed in widow's weeds. To clutch at her, he knew, was useless. He could only stretch out clasped hands from a distance. ''Tis like the early morning. . . Are you remembering my gifts?'

The grey head nodded.

'Can I find you no more in that fashion?'

She gave no sign of assent. He spoke again; but received neither glance nor reply.

'Yet at the eleventh hour, even, were I to offer you all as I have held back?'

A shiver stirred her bent body.

'Be that a sign o' hope? . . . Oh, *ddwch*! You'll tell me nothing; and indeed I've no right to complain. For I've been deserving no answer. 'Tis *I* must cure my late blindness, if by striving it can be cured?'

At length with an effort of faith, so hard that he tautened and shook, he began to imagine her beauty as it might be renewed. And when he could find the lost words, he broke into a song he had made in her praise while he was young and her suitor. To ungathered wild flowers and to foam, he likened her, to the flight of birds and of wind-driven clouds, a shaft of moonlight, a rainbow curved by leaping fish, the gauze of a May-fly that lives for a single day: to all things brief and lovely, not to be grasped, to all that the bard most desired and the carnal man had wasted.

Before he had made an end, he saw her standing above him. Though her lips were parted and smiling in her eyes shone the hope of youth, it was not at him that she looked but away towards the mountain-top. In its withdrawal from him, her beauty was a torment sharper than its fading had been. 'I never was seeing you lovelier,' he cried out, and wept. She was dressed in the frail gay green which spring brings forth, fresh and tender, with each generation of leaves. The hair, loose about shoulders pale-skinned as hawthorn petals, was the soft gold he had played with. Had she been closer to him, he would have stooped to kiss her unshod feet, that scarce seemed to touch earth, or have reached up for her hand, unpledged by wedding ring. Nothing in her, beloved and sought in boyhood, had suffered change. Only the dim of winter's dusk stole colour from her charms as he yearned after them anew. 'She is no ghost; yet is looking faint as the haunting moon rainbow,' he mourned. 'For night be falling and I am grown old. 'Tis my own sight do rule what I see. To those gone blind there is nothing visible in the million wonders o' creation.'

As he sorrowed over this thought, she turned to the east and the west, the north and the south, and called her cattle home. 'Windflower! Snowflake! Dewdrop! Come, bring your milk-white calves! Blossom, and Curd and Lily! My sweet-scented Clover, *fach*! Come, Oxeyed Prince, come lead me back my herd!'

Owain could not stir from his knees; and being stricken by this parting summons so that he lacked heart to watch her, he looked to right and left and saw pale shapes moving towards her. Up out of the fields which he had tilled and over the hill pastures, unhurried but unswerving, came her kine. And still she called to more of them, to each by the name she had given; until there appeared the bull whose great-grandsire she had brought with her, the cows increased to a hundred, the heifers, calves and bullocks. Even the yoke of oxen obeyed with which Thomas the mute had been plough-ing. Fast as his splayed limbs would carry him, he lumbered after the plough, but the traces fell asunder and the team passed beyond him. The silence of oncoming night was broken only by the sigh of a rising wind and the cattle's breathing when they were drawn close and gathered in a circle.

The last for Glythin to call was the calf who had been slaughtered. 'Brindle, *bach*,' she cried, 'get you down from the hook, quite whole. Come home with me too, little one, whose throat men have slit with their steel.'

After the others, all alone, he came, very willing, but feeble, because he had been so young when hanged up bleeding to death, that his big-jointed legs could not hold firm his slip of a body, but swayed it hither and thither. His ears, that should have perked upright, drooped limp as damp paper funnels. As he tottered across a snowdrift, denting it with a waver of hoofprints Owain saw the knife-wound yawn wide beneath his dewlap. Behind him lay a chain of crimson drops, as it might be a ruby necklace looped in the snow.

'Herein is a symbol o' life's enchantment and cruelty,' Owain brooded upon the strange scene. The hills were charred black, whitened with bones of snow. The blood dripped red, but darkened as it froze. The patient beasts stood in a ring about the mistress who had never hurt them: and she was more dear to him in her beauty about to vanish than ever she had been when his to have and to hold. He hung his head and from uphill heard her speak to the calf. 'Poor hurted thing, you cannot mend, I see, being brindled as you are. But water 'ull wash you clean.'

When Owain arose, she lifted up the wounded creature, and as if her strength were great, with light step carried him in her arms. The encircling herd parted and fell into line behind her as she went swiftly forward towards the mountain-top. Through water-courses, where the sound of flowing was heard from beneath the ice, up jagged black rocks and over soft white drifts which soon merged together in darkness, the cattle followed her in pale procession, their heads raised, their nostrils aquiver, scenting fresh pasture. Owain, with bowed shoulders, toiled at the rear. The wind rushed down upon him from the mouth of the first steep gully and whipped a curtain of sleet between himself and the world. In shrouded night, far colder and more blinding than the mist which had veiled his bridal, he groped his way, higher and higher, into air hard to breathe; and after hours of

struggle, breasted the rise that should overlook the lake.
But no trace of the lake was to be seen as he peered through
whirling snowflakes towards the vanished shore. It might
have been upon the edge of hell's abyss that he stood a-
tremble and ached. The gale flung javelins at him, filling his
eyes with tears. Though he drove them away with clenched
fists, like a child, it was only within his lids that whorls of
coloured light span. Without was nothing, anywhere, on
which to fix his gaze. His hearing was sharpened, however,
so that he longed for a deaf man's peace, to escape from the
saddest clash of music to which he had ever listened. The
thaw having broken the deep lid that winter-long had lain
upon the silent pool, the water was free again and lashed into
waves by the storm. But the work of the terrible frost was
not yet undone. Huge blocks of ice, driven against the stones
along the strand, were piled upon one another to groan and
crack in conflict. He could not see, but he envisaged pale-
green fangs tearing, and water monsters heaved up on end
among a fume of spray and splinters. 'Her dirge they be
shrieking and wailing, because I have lost her,' he moaned.
'And I have lost the voice with which so much as to make
lamentation. Silent, without breath, I am; but if only I could
sing out my woe, 't'ould be something to break the heart.
Then I 'ould find, in death, the mercy o' peace everlasting.'
His tears rained faster now, and hot enough to melt his sleet-
bound lashes. 'Blind grief,' he gasped, 'how certain sure you
do tread in the track o' blind passion! The two shall drown
together, which cannot be severed, no more nor sin and
sorrow.'

When all his tears were spent, a worse fate than grief befell
him. Chill to the heart as a corpse, he stared aghast at the
demons which men cannot see who never beheld an angel.
All that is evil and ugly beset him in most foul shape. 'This
is her last and terrible gift to me,' he thought, quaking, 'the

double-edged vision which they escape who, having lacked wings of faith, never soared heavenward, nor fell, as I am fallen, lower than the beasts.'

And then he prayed, heart-broken. 'My love! My love! Let this not be thy final lesson to me.' He opened his scalded eyes and thought that he saw a white face among the snowflakes. Close to his own it was; and above the grinding of ice, the whistle of tempest and splash of driven waters, he heard a voice sing frosty-clear, as if cold lips touched his cheek. The tumult subsided. The elements ceased to war. Like a nurseling lifted back into his cradle, he was stayed from crying out by the music of a lullaby.

'Farewell. It is a lonely soul
Looks on the calm pool's depth from whence it came;
Leaving its hurtful and beloved home,
The body's dear companionship and shame.

For this long while, thy pulse was mine –
Long by the moments counted in earth's style –
Beating to death within thy blood-hot cell,
Poor prisoned heart – my tomb for this short while.

Lie still. When I am gone
Upon a voyage, where no rising sun,
Nor setting, casts brief shadow, thou shalt rest;
Our loneliness forgot, where all is one.'

The Bard Keeps His Secret

'His sons was never finding him,' the old harpist told the children who jostled at his knee.

'Neither him or her?'

'Neither one nor t'other.'

'Then she *was* o' the Fair Tribe? And she *had* cast a spell upon him? Such marvels *do* be true, then?'

'I'll not swear to nothing as can't never be proved.'

'Oh, go you on, do,' they screamed like gulls a-flap about a fisherman. 'You are knowing! You are knowing, aren't you?'

But he shook his head. 'There now, give over. Whoever'd start telling parables to greedy-gutted lumpers, if he foresaw how 't'ould end? Best keep mum and credit what your soberer elders do say. 'Twas nothing only idle talk and soon shamed out o' the gossips – all that about the magic dowry she was bringing him. Only a crazed fellow, they'll have you believe, he were: one that, having quarrelled with his way-ward wife, drowned hisself after her – the simpleton!'

'But what are *you* believing?' asked the gravest of the children, the boy with eyes round as dew-ponds, who yearned to know the bard's secret.

He smiled and gave his head and shoulders a shake, as a dog does, returned from a swim. 'Well, well, 'tis my stock-in-trade, see, to fancy a mort o' marvels.'

At this the children grew quiet again, knowing that if they could be patient, he might say more. What he let slip when he forgot his listeners was worth the pains of waiting, even though it could not be understood. And sure enough, over their craned heads, he began to talk, as it were to himself alone.

Iron and Gold

A black night it had been; and, out shepherding afoot, he had lost his way. Afraid he was, having neither horse nor dog to keep him company, and in his mind the dread of the lake he was warned by his elders to shun. In the tranced hush before daybreak, he saw the gleam of water at his feet and started back, ready to turn and run for his life. But how quiet a mirror it was when he looked down upon it, giving back the first light of a sky washed clean of clouds, empty and pale and pure, the stars being faded and the sun not yet risen! As he stood watching it brighten, he forgot the distraught sinner whom folks declared had ended a vain life here, and remembered only that he had once sung, innocent-free as a bird. What, now, did the body matter, which he had laid aside, as men nightly shed the clothing by which they mark their rank? It would have been changed beyond knowledge, had he lived to grow old. But his songs would live unaltered in the hearts of those who received them.

'And then,' said the ageing bard, beset by his fresh-faced hearers, 'what d'you think I was seeing, sudden, with my own eyes, in the first pink o' the east, as did set the water blushing, rosy as a bride?'

'What, Badger? Tell us!'

'What, Grandad? What?'

'A small little harp, afloat, 'ticing me, yet far out o' my reach. Safe as a boat at anchor, 'twas looking – the precious strange thing. Indeed I 'ould have been half ashamed to seize en, so tranquil calm did it seem, beyond the fret o' earth – the mischance o' my playing it ill.'

'But wasn't you wanting a harp? Didn't you tell us once as you lacked one when a lad?'

'Yes, yes. And in spite o' my awe, I was waiting and hoping for this one, many an hour.'

'And did you grasp it at last?'

'No, never the one I saw – the harp more finewrought nor

this, as I made myself later. The lovely harp was sinking afore the breeze o' morning brought en ashore.'

'Was it the crazed man's, drowned with him maybe? There's a pity!'

'I can't say as it was belonging to any mortal, ever. And as to *him* – well, he was singing champion, so long as he kept his faith . . . There now, that be all as is called to mind, his wickedness being forgiven and his follies forgot.'

'You are remembering his verses, whatever.'

'They, also, 'ull be forgotten, no doubt, when I do die . . . But come you,' he added. 'Others 'ull find their like, and better, I shouldn't wonder. For music in the air there'll always be, for those as do listen. Yes, indeed. So long as the four winds blow and any man be left alive with ears to hear and the heart of a child to wonder . . . Hist! There's your mother calling, boys. Run along, sharp, to your supper, or my foolish old legend 'ull be getting the blame.'

'Apple pie,' they chorused; and were gone in a scamper.

But one child would not run after the rest. He stood and pursed his lips to ask yet another question.

'No, no, boy,' he was answered, before he could speak. 'There be secrets you'll find out for yourself, or never at all. Look long at the sky above, and at the water below and keep your heart a mirror for whatever you're loving best.' And the bard added, 'Not *half* your heart, mind, but the whole. For that's what our trade be demanding.'

'Ours?' said the little boy; and as he turned away his eyes shone with fear, pride and humility.

Appendix

'The Lady of Llyn y Fan Fach'
from John Williams (Ab Ithol), ed.,
The Physicians of Myddfai (1861)

When the eventful struggle made by the Princes of South Wales to preserve the independence of their country was drawing to its close in the twelfth century, there lived at Blaensawdde near Llanddeusant, Carmarthenshire, a widowed woman, the relict of a farmer who had fallen in those disastrous troubles.

The widow had an only son to bring up but Providence smiled upon her, and despite her forlorn condition, her live stock had so increased in course of time, that she could not well depasture them upon her farm, so she sent a portion of her cattle to graze on the adjoining Black Mountain, and their most favourite place was near the small lake called Llyn y Fan Fach, on the north-western side of the Carmarthenshire Fans.

The son grew up to manhood, and was generally sent by his mother to look after the cattle on the mountain. One day, in his peregrinations along the margin of the lake, to his great astonishment, he beheld, sitting on the unruffled surface of the water, a lady; one of the most beautiful creatures that mortal eyes ever beheld, her hair flowed gracefully in ringlets over her shoulders, the tresses of which she arranged with a comb, whilst the glassy surface of her watery couch served for the purpose of a mirror, reflecting back her own image. Suddenly she beheld the young man standing on the brink of the lake, with his eyes riveted on her, and unconsciously offering to herself the provision of barley bread and cheese with which he had been provided when he left his home.

Bewildered by a feeling of love and admiration for the object before him, he continued to hold out his hand towards the lady, who imperceptibly glided near to him, but gently refused the offer of his provisions. He attempted to touch her, but she eluded his grasp, saying –

| Cras dy fara; | Hard baked is thy bread! |
| Nid hawdd fy nala. | 'Tis not easy to catch me; |

and immediately dived under the water and disappeared, leaving the love-stricken youth to return home, a prey to disappointment and regret that he had been unable to make further acquaintance with one, in comparison with whom the whole of the fair maidens of Llanddeusant and Myddfai whom he had seen were as nothing.

On his return home the young man communicated to his mother the extraordinary vision he had beheld. She advised him to take some unbaked dough or 'toes' the next time in his pocket, as there must have been some spell connected with the hard-backed bread, or 'Bara cras', which prevented his catching the lady.

Next morning, before the sun had gilded with its rays the peaks of the fans, the young man was at the lake, not for the purpose of looking after his mother's cattle, but seeking for the same enchanting vision he had witnessed the day before; but all in vain did he anxiously strain his eyeballs and glance over the surface of the lake, as only the ripples occasioned by a stiff breeze met his view, and a cloud hung heavily on the summit of the Fan, which imparted an additional gloom to his already distracted mind.

Hours passed on, the wind was hushed, and the clouds which had enveloped the mountain had vanished into thin

air before the powerful beams of the sun, when the youth
was startled by seeing some of his mother's cattle on the
precipitous side of the acclivity, nearly on the opposite side
of the lake. His duty impelled him to attempt to rescue them
from their perilous position, for which purpose he was hastening away, when, to his inexpressible delight, the object
of his search again appeared to him as before, and seemed
much more beautiful than when he first beheld her. His hand
was again held out to her, full of unbaked bread, which he
offered with an urgent proffer of his heart also, and vows of
eternal attachment. All of which were refused by her, saying –

| Llaith dy fara! | Unbaked is thy bread! |
| Ti ni fynna'. | I will not have thee. |

But the smiles that played upon her features as the lady
vanished beneath the waters raised within the young man
a hope that forbade him to despair by her refusal of him, and
the recollection of which cheered him on his way home. His
aged parent was made acquainted with his ill-success, and
she suggested that his bread should next time be but slightly
baked, as most likely to please the mysterious being of whom
he had become enamoured.

Impelled by an irresistible feeling, the youth left his
mother's house early next morning, and with rapid steps
he passed over the mountain. He was soon near the margin
of the lake, and with all the impatience of an ardent lover
did he wait with a feverish anxiety for the reappearance of
the mysterious lady.

The sheep and goats browsed on the precipitous sides of
the fan; the cattle strayed amongst the rocks and large stones,
some of which were occasionally loosened from their beds
and suddenly rolled down into the lake; rain and sunshine
alike came and passed away; but all were unheeded by the
youth, so wrapped up was he in looking for the appearance
of the lady.

The freshness of the early morning had disappeared before the sultry rays of the noon-day sun, which in its turn was fast verging towards the west as the evening was dying away and making room for the shades of the night, and hope had wellnigh abated of beholding once more the Lady of the Lake. The young man cast a sad and last farewell look over the waters, and, to his astonishment, beheld several cows walking along its surface. The sight of these animals caused hope to revive that they would be followed by another object far more pleasing; nor was he disappointed, for the maiden reappeared, and to his enraptured sight , even lovelier than ever. She approached the land, and he rushed to meet her in the water. A smile encouraged him to seize her hand; neither did she refuse the moderately baked bread he offered her; and after some persuasion she consented to become his bride, on condition that they should only live together until she had received from him three blows without a cause,

Tri ergyd diachos.   Three causeless blows.

And if he ever should happen to strike her three such blows she would leave him for ever. To such conditions he readily consented, and would have consented to any other stipulation, had it been proposed, as he was only intent on then securing such a lovely creature for his wife.

Thus the Lady of the Lake engaged to become the young man's wife, and having loosed her hand for a moment she darted away and dived into the lake. His chagrin and grief were such that he determined to cast himself headlong into the deepest water, so as to end his life in the element that had contained in its unfathomed depths the only one for whom he cared to live on earth. As he was on the point of committing this rash act, there emerged out of the lake two most beautiful ladies, accompanied by a hoary-headed man of noble mien and extraordinary stature, but having otherwise all the force and strength of youth. This man addressed the almost bewildered youth in accents calculated to soothe his troubled mind, saying that as he proposed to marry one of his daughters, he consented to the union, provided the young man could distinguish which of the two ladies before him was the object of his affections. This was no easy task, as the maidens were such perfect counterparts of each other that it seemed quite impossible for him to choose his bride, and if perchance he fixed upon the wrong one all would be for ever lost.

Whilst the young man narrowly scanned the two ladies, he could not perceive the least difference betwixt the two, and was almost giving up the task in despair, when one of them thrust her foot a slight degree forward. The motion, simple as it was, did not escape the observation of the youth, and he discovered a trifling variation in the mode with which their sandals were tied. This at once put an end to the dilemma, for he, who had on previous occasions been so taken up with the general appearance of the Lady of the Lake, had also noticed the beauty of her feet and ankles, and on now recognizing the peculiarity of her shoe-tie he boldly took hold of her hand.

'Thou hast chosen rightly,' said her father; 'be to her a kind and faithful husband, and I will give her, as a dowry, as many sheep, cattle, goats, and horses as she can count of each without heaving or drawing in her breath. But remember, that if you prove unkind to her at any time, and strike her three times without a cause, she shall return to me, and shall bring her stock back with her.'

Such was the verbal marriage settlement, to which the young man gladly assented, and his bride was desired to count the number of sheep she was to have. She immediately adopted the mode of counting by fives, thus: – One, two, three, four, five – One, two, three, four, five; as many times as possible in rapid succession, till her breath was exhausted.

The same process of reckoning had to determine the number of goats, cattle, and horses respectively; and in an instant the full number of each came out of the lake when called upon by the father.

The young couple were then married, by what ceremony was not stated, and afterwards went to reside at a farm called Esgair Llaethdy, somewhat more than a mile from the village of Myddfai, where they lived in prosperity and happiness for several years, and became the parents of three sons, who were beautiful children.

Once upon a time there was a christening to take place in the neighbourhood, to which the parents were specially invited. When the day arrived the wife appeared very reluctant to attend the christening, alleging that the distance was too great for her to walk. Her husband told her to fetch one of the horses which were grazing in an adjoining field. 'I will,' said she, 'if you will bring me my gloves which I left in our house.' He went to the house and returned with the gloves, and finding that she had not gone for the horse jocularly slapped her shoulder with one of them, saying, 'go! go! (dos, dos), when she reminded him of the understanding upon which she consented to marry him: – That he was not to strike her without a cause; and warned him to be more cautious for the future.

On another occasion, when they were together at a wedding, in the midst of the mirth and hilarity of the assembled guests, who had gathered together from all the surrounding country, she burst into tears and sobbed most piteously. Her husband touched her on her shoulder and inquired the cause of her weeping: she said, 'Now people are entering into trouble, and your troubles are likely to commence, as you have the second time stricken me without cause.'

Years passed on, and their children had grown up, and were particularly clever young men. In the midst of so many worldly blessings at home the husband almost forgot that there remained only one causeless blow to be given to destroy the whole of his prosperity. Still he was watchful lest any trivial occurrence should take place which his wife must regard as a breach of their marriage contract. She told him, as her affection for him was unabated, to be careful that he would not, through some inadvertence, give the last and only blow, which, by an unalterable destiny, over which she had no control, would separate them for ever.

It, however, so happened that one day they were together at a funeral, where in the midst of the mourning and grief at the house of the deceased, she appeared in the highest and gayest spirits, and indulged in immoderate fits of laughter, which so shocked her husband that he touched her, saying, 'Hush! hush! don't laugh.' She said that she laughed 'because people when they die go out of trouble,' and, rising up, she went out of the house, saying, 'The last blow has been struck, our marriage contract is broken, and at an end! Farewell!' Then she started off towards Esgair Llaethdy, where she called her cattle and other stock together, each by name. The cattle she called thus:

Mu wlfrech, Moelfrech,	Brindled cow, white speckled
Mu olfrech, Gwynfrech,	Spotted cow, bold freckled,
Pedair cae tonn-frech,	The four field sward-mottled,
Yr hen wynebwen,	The old white-faced,
A'r las Geingen,	And the grey Geingen
Gyda'r Tarw Gwyn	With the white Bull
O lys y Brenin;	From the court of the King;
A'r llo du bach	And the little black calf
Sydd ar y bach	Suspended on the hook,
Dere dithau, yn iach adre!	Come thou also, quite well home!

They all immediately obeyed the summons of their mistress. The 'little black calf,' although it had been slaughtered, became alive again, and walked off with the rest of the stock at the command of the lady. This happened in the spring of the year, and there were four oxen ploughing in one of the fields; to these she cried:-

Pedwar eidion glas	The four grey oxen,
Sydd ar y maes,	That are on the field,
Deuwch chwithau	Come you also
Yn iach, adre!	Quite well home!

Away the whole of the live stock went with the Lady across Myddfai Mountain, towards the lake from whence they came, a distance of above six miles, where they disappeared beneath its waters, leaving no trace behind except a well-marked furrow, which was made by the plough the oxen drew after them into the lake, and which remains to this day as a testimony to the truth of this story.

What became of the affrighted ploughman – whether he was left on the field when the oxen set off, or whether he followed them to the lake, has not been handed down to tradition; neither has the fate of the disconsolate and half-ruined husband been kept in remembrance. But of the sons it is stated that they often wandered about the lake and its vicinity, hoping that their mother might be permitted to visit the face of the earth once more, as they had been apprised of her mysterious origin, her first appearance to their father, and the untoward circumstances which so unhappily deprived them of her maternal care.

In one of their rambles, at a place near Dôl Howel, at the Mountain Gate, still called 'Llidiart y Meddygon', The Physicians' Gate, the mother appeared suddenly, and accosted her eldest son, whose name was Rhiwallon, and told him that his mission on earth was to be a benefactor to mankind by relieving them from pain and misery, through healing all manner of their diseases; for which purpose she furnished him with a bag full of medical prescriptions and instructions for the preservation of health. That by strict attention thereto he and his family would become for many generations the most skilful physicians in the country. Then, promising to meet him when her counsel was most needed, she vanished. But on several occasions she met her sons near the banks of the lake, and once she even accompanied them on their return home as a far as a place still called 'Pant-y-Meddygon', The Dingle of the Physicians, where she pointed out to them the various plants and herbs which grew in the dingle, and revealed to them their medicinal qualities or virtues; and the knowledge she imparted to them, together with their unrivalled skill, soon caused them to attain such celebrity that none ever possessed before them. And in order that their knowledge should not be lost, they wisely committed the same to writing, for the benefit of mankind throughout all ages.

And so ends the story of the Physicians of Myddfai, which has been handed down from one generation to another, thus:

Yr hen ŵr llwyd o'r gornel	The grey old man in the corner
Gan ei dad a glywodd chwedl,	Of his father heard a story,
A chan ei dad fe glywodd yntau,	Which from his father he had heard,
Ac ar ei ôl mi gofiais innau.	And after him I have remembered.